"Funny and captivating . . . in the style of the Sookie Stackhouse series [with] an intrepid and expressive ~~~~~ Look out, fans of the paranor~~~~ heroine in town . . . Tate Hal~~~~

"I love how Garnet handled ~~~~~ with grit, humor, and attitud~~~~ ~~~~~~ some serious butt! . . . Hallaway keeps you glued to the pages."
—*Romance Junkies*

"[Hallaway's] concise writing style, vivid descriptions, and innovative plot all blend together to provide the reader with a great new look into the love life of witches, vampires, and the undead."
—*Armchair Interviews*

Titles by Tate Hallaway

DEAD IF I DO
ROMANCING THE DEAD
DEAD SEXY
TALL, DARK & DEAD

Dead If I Do

TATE HALLAWAY

BERKLEY BOOKS, NEW YORK

THE BERKLEY PUBLISHING GROUP
Published by the Penguin Group
Penguin Group (USA) Inc.
375 Hudson Street, New York, New York 10014, USA
Penguin Group (Canada), 90 Eglinton Avenue East, Suite 700, Toronto, Ontario M4P 2Y3, Canada
(a division of Pearson Penguin Canada Inc.)
Penguin Books Ltd., 80 Strand, London WC2R 0RL, England
Penguin Group Ireland, 25 St. Stephen's Green, Dublin 2, Ireland (a division of Penguin Books Ltd.)
Penguin Group (Australia), 250 Camberwell Road, Camberwell, Victoria 3124, Australia
(a division of Pearson Australia Group Pty. Ltd.)
Penguin Books India Pvt. Ltd., 11 Community Centre, Panchsheel Park, New Delhi—110 017, India
Penguin Group (NZ), 67 Apollo Drive, Rosedale, North Shore 0632, New Zealand
(a division of Pearson New Zealand Ltd.)
Penguin Books (South Africa) (Pty.) Ltd., 24 Sturdee Avenue, Rosebank, Johannesburg 2196,
South Africa

Penguin Books Ltd., Registered Offices: 80 Strand, London WC2R 0RL, England

This book is an original publication of The Berkley Publishing Group.

This is a work of fiction. Names, characters, places, and incidents either are the product of the author's imagination or are used fictitiously, and any resemblance to actual persons, living or dead, business establishments, events, or locales is entirely coincidental. The publisher does not have any control over and does not assume any responsibility for author or third-party websites or their content.

PRINTING HISTORY
Berkley trade paperback edition / May 2009

Library of Congress Cataloging-in-Publication Data

Hallaway, Tate.
   Dead if I do / Tate Hallaway. — Berkley trade pbk. ed.
      p. cm.
   ISBN 978-0-425-22753-4
   1. Vampires—Fiction.   2. Goddesses—Fiction.   3. Weddings—Fiction.   4. Chick lit.   I. Title.

   PS3608.A54825D42 2009
   813'.6—dc22
                                                                    2008051710

PRINTED IN THE UNITED STATES OF AMERICA

10   9   8   7   6   5   4   3   2   1

For Shawn

Acknowledgments

It would be easy to forget, after so many under my belt, the people who make each book possible. Thanks must go to my editor, Anne Sowards, and her loyal assistant, Cameron Dufty. Also much, much continued gratitude to my tireless agent, Martha Millard, without whom none of this would be possible.

My writers' group, Wyrdsmiths, deserves praise (and credit for all the truly clever bits): Eleanor Arnason, Bill Henry, Doug Hulick, Naomi Kritzer, Kelly McCullough, and Sean M. Murphy. Extra special thanks goes to Naomi, Sean, and my partner, Shawn Rounds, for reading the first draft at the midnight hour and making this book that much better. Also in need of a shout-out are the very fine folks at Amoré Coffee who keep me caffeinated and in quiz questions: Cathy, Paul, Cole, Glen, Zollie, Michele, and the rest!

First Aspect: Conjunction

Introducing your fiancé to your parents for the first time is always tough, but when you add that he's a vampire . . . ?

Plus, add into that awkwardness that my parents and I have been benignly estranged since I turned eighteen, and I haven't shared as much as a postcard in all that time, well . . .

Let's just say: oy.

The four of us sat in a darkened booth at Porta Bella's, a place voted by the local newspaper as one of the best romantic restaurants in Madison, Wisconsin. Sebastian and I occupied one of the tiny, pewlike wooden benches and my folks the other. Darkly colored tapestries hung on the walls. A candle flickered in a cut-glass container at the center of the wooden table. Pine garlands accented with glass icicles draped the wood beams of the ceiling.

The atmosphere at our table was as chilly as it was outside. Though the waitress had brought crusty bread and garlic-flavored oil, it remained untouched. We all hid our faces behind the red leather menus. Occasionally, my mother would peep out from behind hers to stare at the garlic and glance at Sebastian like she expected him to burst into flames.

Honestly, I hadn't meant for everything to come spilling out like that during the introductions.

All last night I'd thought about clever ways to naturally insinuate the topic of my lover's vampirism into everyday discussions about the price of chicken feed and egg production, but instead, just as soon as we met at the restaurant, I'd blurted, "This is Sebastian Von Traum, my fiancé. He's a vampire."

My mother had simply said, "Isn't that interesting," in that Minnesotan way that implied I'd made a major faux pas. I blame the state's Norwegian heritage that Minnesotans tend to be so polite that they won't say what they mean.

Even so, silence had followed. No one had spoken a word for the last ten minutes and counting.

"So . . ." I started, but no one looked up from their menus.

I sighed and searched my parents for a safe avenue to start a discussion—any discussion—about. My folks are farmers, but they're also pot-smoking hippies. Even though it had gone gray and thin, my dad still wore his hair long and straight; it hung in a tight braid down to the small of his back. A ball cap advertising some organic seed company kept his bangs from falling in his sun-brightened and weathered face. His plain cotton shirt revealed forearms that might have belonged to a younger man but for the dusting of fine white hairs. Where a watch usually would be he wore several woven friendship bracelets.

Mom wore a hand-dyed dress and a necklace she made herself with leather strips and beads imported from Africa. Her hair was cut short and utilitarian, but her shoes were Italian leather. She sported almost no makeup, just a little light brown mascara that highlighted pale blue eyes—the color mine used to be before the dark Goddess Lilith possessed me . . . another something I hadn't quite gotten around to talking to my folks about.

Though she hadn't said anything about my eyes, my mother *had* noticed my hair. She'd fussed and clucked about the pixie cut when I'd met them at their hotel last night. Finally she'd shaken her head and said, "The black dye just makes you look so severe, dear." Dad pointed out he'd hardly recognized me, and he'd thought I was "some hooligan coming to cause mischief." I probably should have told them I was intentionally in disguise, what with the Vatican witch hunters potentially still out there trying to kill me, but instead, all my teenage rebellion came flowing back, and I'd basically told them all the cool kids were doing it.

You can imagine the conversation that followed.

I had really hoped today would be different.

"How about them Packers?" I ventured, trying to make a joke. To ask about the local football team, in this case, the Green Bay Packers, was a well-seasoned conversation gambit, on a par with "How's it going?" and "What's up?" I knew my folks weren't into sports, but they should get the funny and acknowledge my attempt to get conversation rolling again.

But my dad just grunted, and my mother rolled her eyes. Sebastian, at least, gave me a little smile. See, now, we could talk about how awesome Sebastian was, if my folks weren't all hung up on the vampire thing.

I mean, what parents in their right minds wouldn't want their only daughter married to a man this well-heeled and nicely put together? Sebastian's shoulder-length black hair was pinned back at the nape of his neck. He was perfectly clean-shaven, which was actually kind of unusual for him, but he'd gone all out for tonight. You'd think he'd be every parent's dream in his gray silk shirt and black dress pants.

I should never have mentioned the vampirism.

Sebastian, I could tell, brooded a bit. Because he could walk around in the daylight, Sebastian completely passed as human. He hated it when I felt the urge to out his supernatural origins. In fact, we hadn't actually gotten around to agreeing that we *would* tell my folks. He'd said he thought the whole thing was on a need-to-know basis and, frankly, it was no one's business but our own.

Right now I could totally see his point.

"The linguine's good," I offered into the stillness.

Without looking over the menu, Sebastian added, "Yes, I recommend any of their pastas. They make them fresh on the premises."

It was a noncommittal show of support from Sebastian. I could tell he was still mad at me, but he was willing to put up a united front to the parents for my sake.

"I'm getting the goat cheese–filled ravioli," I said, a note of cheer creeping into my voice. Maybe if I kept talking about mundane things, everyone would pretend to forget what I'd said earlier, and we could all have a do-over.

My father's menu hit the table with a snap. "So, Sebastian, is it?" My father's voice was full of judgment. His shoulders squared against the hard back of the bench, and he crossed his arms in front of his chest. "What is it you do for a living, then?"

The *then* implying "since you're some kind of freak." I could hear it in my father's tone.

I chewed the edge of my fingernail, my eyes darting to Sebastian anxiously.

Folding his menu, Sebastian very carefully and deliberately tucked it under the bread plate. He laced his fingers on the tabletop in front of him and leaned forward slightly, like a CEO brokering the big deal. "I'm a car mechanic."

My dad nodded, considering. "That's a pretty good living."

Mom was less sure. "Did you go to college, dear? Education is very important in our family."

Which was a nice little dig at me, of course. I'd gotten a degree in English, but I was in the middle of a long, extended, all-but-thesis master's when the Vatican paramilitaries assassinated my coven and sent me into hiding. I'd always figured my folks disapproved of my career in bookselling, even though I now owned Mercury Crossing, the premier occult bookstore and herb emporium of Madison.

"Sebastian has a Ph.D. and teaches an extension class at the UW in herbalism," I offered, hoping my folks would choose to bond with him over the growing of things.

"If you can teach, why work on cars?" My mother again.

Despite the fact that she and Dad were farmers, she was a snob when it came to collar colors. She preferred white.

"Magic," Sebastian said with a nod and a smile. "Alchemy."

I loved him for that answer, but I could see the confusion in my parents' eyes. He'd told me the same thing when we first met, and I'd understood instantly that he was talking about elemental magic: fire, air, water, earth. My mom looked to me for a translation. My dad gave a little snort that seemed to say, "Yep, crazy as a loon."

"No, seriously," I started. "Carburetors bring in air, see, and spark plugs, fire. Gas and steel are earth—" Thank the Goddess the waitress interrupted my attempt to "clarify" Sebastian's comment.

My father opened his mouth and, afraid he was going to ask for more time so that he could grill Sebastian about his answer, I yelled out my choice, "Goat cheese–filled ravioli for me!"

"Honestly, Garnet. No need to shout, she's only right here," my mother admonished.

"Sorry," I muttered, my cheeks brightening to crimson. Could I feel any more like a four-year-old?

Somehow we managed to talk about the weather be-fore the food arrived. For my parents, this hardly constituted small talk. The fall had been dry again, so all the Finlayson farmers were hoping for a heavy snowpack now that the winter had started. Even though my folks only raise chickens, the ins and outs of the climate are serious considerations.

Until I lived in Wisconsin, I never realized how Minnesotans use the term *weather*. "That was some weather that blew in last night," my dad said. "How many inches did you get?"

Enough that my arms still ached from using the snowblower the full length of Sebastian's driveway, but I'd done my homework. I'd had the news on at breakfast just so I could answer this question authoritatively. "Six inches in some places, they said."

My mother made a comment about the previous season's drought, and Sebastian mentioned how much snowier he remembered winters being generally. We were all getting along nicely for the moment. I should have realized that meant we were doomed.

I noticed the smell first. A combination of rotten meat and sickly sweet flowers, the scent tickled the edges of my nose. I had to hold back a sneeze. Looking around for an open kitchen door or exposed garbage can, I saw nothing. I chalked it up to some odoriferous anomaly and was returning my attention to the riveting discussion of snow, when a figure lurched toward us.

A low hiss caused everyone at the table to look up.

"I curse you," said a woman in a harsh whisper. Still dressed for outside, she had on a knee-length down coat, and snow clung in clumps to her windswept long black hair. She could have been beautiful in a haughty, aristocratic way, except for her too-thin face—plus the dead-bluish lips and wild eyes, which stared possessively at Sebastian.

I might have mistaken her for some random, deranged druggie, but that Lilith growled low in the back of my throat.

I knew instantly this woman was some kind of creature of magic and a dangerous one at that. Given the smell and the trouble we've had in the past, my first thought was, *Zombie!*

"Teréza!" Sebastian said at the same moment.

"Teréza?" I looked at Sebastian for confirmation. Teréza was his . . . what? Betrothed? Fiancée? Only she was supposed to be, well, not quite dead, but definitely not up and moving around.

Well, *this* was certainly awkward.

"Who is this?" my mother asked, clearly miffed that I hadn't instantly offered introductions.

"Uh . . ." I was really hoping for help from Sebastian here, but he was still gaping, openmouthed, at Teréza. "Well, this is Teréza. She's Sebastian's . . . uh. Sebastian and she . . . uh . . . Teréza is Sebastian's late—really late—uh, almost wife?"

How was I supposed to explain Teréza anyway? Back in eighteen-something she'd been dying of consumption, and Sebastian had tried to turn her into a vampire. Since his vampirism came from alchemy and not from a Sire of the blood, he failed—kind of. She didn't die. But she didn't exactly live either.

"She's mostly dead," I added. "That is, until recently, she was . . ."

I was stumbling over my words so much that I was actually kind of grateful when Teréza lunged at Sebastian, trying to kill him.

Second Aspect: Trine

KEY WORDS:

Active, Idealistic

Teréza had her hands around Sebastian's neck. The bread and the oil spilled all over my father, who'd leaped up to avoid the candle, which now rolled across the table, dripping wax everywhere.

An inhuman snarl escaped my lips. Lilith coursed through my veins like liquid fire. In a flash, I found myself on top of the table, ready to grab Teréza with all of Lilith's might and toss my rival across the room.

Then I caught my mother's eye. My mother stared at me in horror, like the killer zombie ex-girlfriend was somehow all *my* fault.

Not so long ago, no force on earth could stop Lilith once she'd awoken. Now the ice in my mother's eyes cooled Lilith's reaction. I felt Lilith's strength deep inside my bones and muscles, but the full force of her fearsomeness retracted at my response to my mother's well-honed glare. The Queen of Hell had been stopped cold by "the look."

Just then Sebastian gave a push that sent Teréza crashing into the waitress bringing our food. The two of them toppled into the neighboring table. Plates broke with a crash. Hot food slopped everywhere. People shouted. My dad cursed. The glow of camera phones shone all over the restaurant.

Great. Now this little family disaster would be all over YouTube by morning.

Sebastian stood up. He rubbed his neck with a dark look in his eyes. He talked, and it took me a second to realize that he wasn't speaking English.

Teréza held her hands up in supplication. Sebastian snapped out another command.

Her dead, glassy eyes slid to me. She whispered something in that foreign language, and I felt a chill settle on my shoulders. Lilith flared defensively, ready to strike if Teréza made another move to attack.

Instead, she went toward the door, scuttling like a crab in a jerky, too-fast motion. It was unnatural and creepy. My folks and I watched her go with our mouths agape.

My stomach twisted. Even though Teréza had gone, I felt light-headed and a bit nauseous. It might have been the sensation of the adrenaline flushing out of my system or the smell of all the spilled food on my empty stomach, but I couldn't shake a sickening sensation that something was wrong.

Lilith noticed it too. She hung at the surface of my consciousness like a watchdog ready to strike. I had to take several breaths to convince Lilith to go back into what passed for hiding these days.

Then, Sebastian shrugged, as though he witnessed this sort of thing all the time.

No one in the room moved. We were all stunned silent.

"We should go," he said. His words broke the spell.

"Uh, yeah," I said, suddenly hyperaware that I was standing on top of the table. I slunk quickly back into my seat.

My mother cleared her throat as I was sliding out of the booth. The sound stopped me cold. "I think you have some apologizing to do first," she said, her eyes flicking in the direction of the waitress and the patrons who were untangling themselves.

But Sebastian was already graciously helping the waitress to her feet and making offers to pay for damages. Trying not to glance at my mother for approval, I told anyone who would listen that I was very, very, *very* sorry for everything. Several times.

My father watched the whole thing with his hands on his hips and a shake of his head. I felt completely chagrined.

My dad took out his billfold and started rummaging through the bills. "We should pay for dinner," he grumbled, with a glance at where the waitress and I were mopping up bits of ravioli and linguine.

"No, let me," Sebastian insisted, making a move for his own wallet.

My dad tossed three twenties on the table defiantly. Dad

pinned him with a look that dared Sebastian to insult his manhood by not allowing him to pay his own damn way. I prayed to the Goddess that Sebastian would let it go.

Sebastian's lips thinned, but he must have sensed this was not a good time to argue over the bill. "That's very generous of you," he said through clenched teeth.

Satisfied, my father pulled himself upright, took my mother's hand, and marched out with as much dignity as he could muster, covered in olive oil and candle wax.

I sat back on my heels in a pool of cream sauce. Though the smell made my stomach growl, all I really wanted to do was throw up. Sebastian offered me a hand up. I let him lift me to my feet and propel me toward the door, where he casually left two hundred-dollar bills with the maître d'.

"Men." I sighed.

Outside, a blast of freezing air made my nostrils stick together. The restaurant had a small, sheltered courtyard out front. Thick ice clung along the twisted, dry husks of Virginia creeper that lined the walls looking like lace on brick. Tough, blackened stalks of purple coneflower seed heads poked up through the blanket of snow.

"What the hell was that?" my dad asked, his voice tight, controlled.

"I believe that was my dead ex-girlfriend trying to kill me," Sebastian said drily.

"Oh," Dad said, as if that explained everything to his satisfaction. Shoving his hands into the pockets of his parka, he added, "Well, heck. I'm starving."

We moved carefully along the shoveled path, cautious of slick cobblestones.

"Dad's right," I said. "We still need dinner." I slipped my hand into the crook of Sebastian's arm. "Any ideas?" I asked him.

He gave me a small smile, but his mouth was set in a grim line. I could tell he was still thinking about Teréza. His eyes roamed the corners of the courtyard as if expecting her to leap out again.

"Let's go home," he said, meaning his farm. "It's warded. Safe."

Except Mátyás was there.

Mátyás was Sebastian's 150-year-old magically perpetually teenage son. I hadn't gotten around to mentioning him to my folks either. "Sure," I said with a shrug, "Why not?"

I mean, really, could this get any worse?

Thankfully, we decided to take separate cars, with my folks following behind Sebastian's new-to-him 1968, two-door Javelin in their rusty truck.

Sebastian kept an eye on them in the rearview mirror, but he drove at regular speeds and made no other special effort to make sure they were behind us. I thought for sure we'd lose them, but he pointed out that the cherry red paint job he'd had custom done was easy to spot.

After a few moments of silence, I finally asked. "Isn't Teréza supposed to be, you know, dead?"

Sebastian chewed on his lower lip. "I thought so."

"Mátyás had the pope exorcize her," I remembered. Mátyás

and I had become tentative friends when Sebastian had gone missing a few months ago. "He told me it worked."

Sebastian snorted. "An exorcism? That's just great." His hands were white-knuckled on the steering wheel.

"You seem really upset," I said waiting for him to say more. "What's wrong?"

"An exorcism is something you do to the devil, a demon, to an evil spirit," he said. "Not magic."

For the second time in so many hours, I felt like a world-class idiot. I should have guessed what made Sebastian so particularly upset. Any time a Wiccan came out to a non-magical person, the first thing they usually had to do was explain that witchcraft had absolutely nothing to do with Satan or evil or any of the various and sundry things that went bump in the night. Of course it would bother Sebastian that an exorcism seemed to have had positive results. He'd always told me that he felt horrified that his magically enhanced and alchemically transformed blood hadn't been sufficient to turn Teréza. But if his special brand of vampirism was actually linked to Satan? Well, for Sebastian, I imagine that would feel like a nightmare come true.

"This means they were right about me, Garnet."

"No, it doesn't," I replied. Sebastian had grown up in some remote part of the proto–Austro-Hungarian Empire at a very superstitious time. He had been born on Christmas, which was considered supremely bad luck, because it meant your parents were fornicating on the same night the Holy Mother was getting the Big News from the archangel Gabriel or something crazy like that. Why this was considered bad any time after A.D. zero, I never really understood. But what I did know was that it mattered to Sebastian. It haunted him, actually, because people had lost no opportunity to remind him his whole life that he was dirty, evil, corrupt . . . and cursed. In fact, he'd studied all the "dark arts," partly because it was what people expected of him.

When he didn't say anything, I asked, "You know that, right?"

He made a noncommittal grunt.

I reached out a hand and squeezed his knee. The sun had set, even though it was only just a little past seven. The dashboard lights illuminated his angry, twisted scowl.

"God didn't curse you because your birthday was Christmas, Sebastian. If everyone who was born on Christmas was turned into a vampire, my vet would be one."

"Maybe she will be when she's dead," Sebastian said grumpily, though he wasn't being serious.

"You told me yourself you only started studying alchemy because people expected you to. Their prophecy was self-fulfilling. Not the other way around. Anyway, I thought we got over this last winter."

"You mean when we were attacked by the frost demon on my birthday?"

"Um, well, yeah."

"Because *that* didn't seem cursed," he said with a sarcastic little eye roll.

Okay, maybe that was a bad example. It would be just our luck to be jumped on by something supernatural after I'd cajoled and begged Sebastian into going out on his birthday.

15

I tried to shrug it off. "Well, it all worked out in the end, didn't it?"

"Garnet, that's like saying you're lucky to have survived a car accident. True luck is not getting into one in the first place."

"Excuse me, Mr. Half-Empty."

It was hard to believe we weren't already married, the way we bickered. Sebastian must have had the same thought, because he smiled fondly at me. "I suppose the parents weren't terribly impressed with Teréza, eh?"

I shook my head. What a disaster. "I can't wait until they meet Mátyás."

"That boy really needs to get his own apartment," Sebastian muttered as we turned onto the highway. I craned my neck to see if my folks made the turn. They did.

I nodded. Having Mátyás live with us was completely cramping our style, especially given that the guest bedroom was haunted, so he slept in the middle of the living room on the couch. Sebastian had offered several times to buy him a place in town, but Mátyás refused any charity.

It wasn't that Mátyás wasn't willing to work. The problem was that his résumé hadn't been updated since the turn of the century. I'd been working on my friend Izzy, who managed the coffee shop next to my bookstore, to take him on as a barista, but so far she'd chosen to date him instead. Talk about awkward: your best friend dating your fiancé's son. Double-dating was out of the question, believe me.

"You don't think Mátyás had anything to do with all this, do you?" I asked. I mean, Mátyás had never made any secret of the fact that he preferred his mother to me.

Sebastian shrugged. "The boy loves his mother."

And mostly hated me—although that wasn't an entirely fair assessment. Lately Mátyás and I had a kind of détente that involved only the occasional volley of insults over breakfast. I'd actually kind of grown fond of it all. After he'd helped me exhume Sebastian some months ago, I'd given up imagining Mátyás was actively trying to get me killed. But then again, he had stood by while Vatican agents put an arrow through my leg, and, well, memories like that were hard to shake. My calf twinged at the thought. I rubbed at it absently. That night had revealed something else though, I remembered. "Yeah," I said. "But he loves you too."

I heard Sebastian's soft sigh in the darkness.

Without a doubt I was marrying into a complicated family. We rode in silence for a little while.

"What was it that you said to Teréza, anyway?" I asked, remembering the creepy-crawly feeling that came over me when she cursed us. Lilith perked up as though interested in the answer as well. "What language was that?"

"Romany," he said.

"You speak Gypsy?"

"Gypsy isn't really the polite term these days," Sebastian reminded me, which was funny if only because normally I was the one who had to admonish him for his use of outdated, politically incorrect terms. "But yeah, I speak it. Teréza and I were together a long time. Her father was quite adamant that I learn when he discovered she was pregnant with my child."

I waited for him to say more. Despite being a thousand years old, Sebastian hardly ever talked about the past. I always figured that he coped with the cumulative effects of all the mistakes made and loves lost by living in the present as much as possible.

I laid my hand on my tummy. Underneath my fingers, I felt the electric hum of Lilith. She no longer slept inside me the way she once did. Since bonding with her in order to defeat a thieving Trickster God, Lilith's entire being whispered across my skin in a much more present way. I was no longer entirely human, myself. I'd become a demigoddess. In fact, I might live a thousand years now too.

What would it be like to live on while friends died around me? Shaking my head, I dismissed the tumult of fears that threatened to overwhelm my thoughts. I'd only barely begun to cope with the fact that my magical abilities had quadrupled since the bonding . . . and the fact that my temper was a lot shorter. No need to start freaking out about the future when I had enough problems right now.

At least my new perspective on my own life gave me a lot of sympathy for Sebastian's situation. Teréza hadn't been around long, but she was someone with whom he had capital *H*, History. As much as I'd like him to be able to shrug off his relationship with her as so yesterday, I knew that was unrealistic. I gave his thigh another sympathetic squeeze.

"At the restaurant," I asked. "How did you get Teréza to leave? Where do you think she went?"

"It was a spell. It was supposed to send her back to her grave."

"You can do that?"

"She has my blood. She's a part of me."

I hadn't really thought about that. I knew the history, of course, but I hadn't thought about the consequences of the fact that Sebastian's magic-laced blood was the only thing keeping Teréza from the grave. "So, you have blood power over her?"

Parrish, my ex, who was the only traditional vampire I had any significant contact with, used to talk about his maker in hushed tones. She had a kind of power over him that was akin to glamour, the vampire's ability to charm the pants off anyone, only ten times more powerful.

Sebastian lifted his shoulder in a shrug. "I honestly don't know, but I suspected that any spells I cast would have a strong effect on her magical blood since I am, in essence, her Sire. Anyway, it seems to have worked."

I nodded. That made sense. "Okay, so she's headed back to her grave—but which one?"

Sebastian lifted his shoulder lightly, like he didn't care, but I could see his lips press into a thin, tense line.

My understanding was that Teréza had been interred a number of times. Before the pope's exorcism apparently woke her, Sebastian believed Teréza "rested" better underground. Mátyás, meanwhile, felt that putting her in the ground was akin to burying someone alive. So, the times Sebastian had possession of Teréza's body, he'd arrange a grave. When Mátyás discovered where she was planted, he'd play grave-robber and "liberate" her corpse.

It was particularly morbid, especially since I'd gotten the sense that Mátyás tended to go all Norman Bates about his mother. Sebastian had alluded to the fact that Mátyás would keep Teréza in a nice room and talk to her as though she wasn't dead, merely sleeping.

Mostly, I tried to ignore this particularly creepy aspect of

Sebastian and Mátyás's relationship. Now she was up and in my face.

We pulled into the driveway in front of Sebastian's small farm. The tires crunched on the gravel and ice. Despite the fact that I'd been living here since my apartment was attacked by a tree, I still thought of it as Sebastian's place. I might have been born on a farm, but I had the soul of a city girl, and all the quiet of rural living was alien to my sensibilities.

However, my cat Barney loved it. Sebastian had a tendency to think of cats as farmhands. Thus, despite my constant reminders that Barney was to continue the life of a pampered indoor feline, she'd been put to work in the barn catching mice. Sebastian constantly nudged her out the door; I always let her back in. She'd gotten over her initial dislike of Sebastian and was now sleeping on his chest most nights. To me, she gave her mutilated rodent "presents."

I tried not to be jealous.

Sebastian cut the engine. "We need to tell Benjamin that we're having guests."

Right, another complication: Sebastian's house had come with an overprotective ghost. I suppose technically Benjamin was a poltergeist, since he was more than capable of flickering lights and tossing things around when he got cranky. Which was often.

"You tell him," I said. "Benjamin likes you better."

Sebastian nodded, but what I'd said wasn't entirely the truth. Despite the fact that we're pretty certain Benjamin axe-murdered his wife in what is now the guest bedroom, Benjamin had started sleeping next to me from time to time. Sometimes at night I felt his arms around me or saw the depression of his body on the edge of the bed. I figured Benjamin's new interest in me had something to do with the time we met in the spirit realm, but I found him especially scary up close. I hadn't told Sebastian about Benjamin's sudden familiarity, because I didn't want to worry him. Anyway, I was sure it could all be cleared up with a little chat on the astral plane, though I hadn't quite figured out how to tell a serial-killing ghost I wanted to "just be friends."

Between Barney, Benjamin, Sebastian, and me, the bed was starting to get a little crowded.

The headlights of my parents' car flashed as they rounded the corner. Sebastian headed inside to convince Benjamin to be on his best behavior, and I stepped out of the car into the cold to greet my folks. A hostile ghost and a half-vampire son waited for them inside. I sighed. And they thought they'd had a lot to deal with at the restaurant.

"Hey," I said, as my dad came up beside me. The wind rustled through the white pine windbreak and brought with it the scent of woodsmoke. I could almost see my father's shoulders relax.

"You've been living here?"

He sounded surprised, as well he should. I fled farm life the first moment I could. Even before that, every chance I got, I snuck away to Hinckley or any town with a population over forty. "Yeah," I said, smiling.

Unlike most Minnesotan farms, Sebastian's property encompassed several hills. The stubby remains of the corn that poked up through the snow cover followed the curving contours of the land.

"Oh, it's lovely," my mother said, joining us. She tucked

her hand into my father's parka pocket to hold his. My smile broadened. They were always an affectionate couple. "How much land do you have?"

"Not much," I said. A yard light glowed brightly on the country graveyard just over the side fence. "Sebastian owns the outbuildings and a couple square acres. The rest belongs to a commercial operation."

My dad gave a nod of understanding. It was how a lot of farms ran these days. Of course, their chicken ranch stretched acres and employed workers. But, in the grand scheme of modern farming, they were considered quite small.

"So, is that where he buries his victims?" Dad asked, jerking his thumb in the direction of the headstones.

Mom gave Dad a jab in the parka-covered ribs. "Honey!"

"Well, she says he's a vampire, doesn't she?"

Did they think I was making it up, even after they met the zombie, half-dead girlfriend?

Then I remembered how difficult it was for the uninitiated to accept the magical world. They'd probably found some rationalization for Teréza's odd appearance and behavior. She was drunk. Homeless. Insane. Anything other than a living corpse hell-bent on choking Sebastian to death.

Since it seemed we couldn't get along for more than ten minutes at a time regardless of how hard I worked, and they thought I was making all this stuff up anyway, I decided to go for honesty. "Sebastian doesn't have to kill to get enough blood to survive."

"That's a relief," my mother said, her lips a thin line. "The fiancé isn't a murderer, at least."

My father harrumphed, unimpressed.

An eddy of snow drifted in a lazy circle across the driveway. The snow had turned dusty in the cold, and the wind eroded miniature canyons in the mountains of ice on either side of the drive. "I know this is a lot to take in. How about we talk about everything inside? Sebastian has a fireplace," I added hopefully.

"I'd rather work it out here. Privately," Dad said. "I don't want to embarrass the young man, who otherwise seems nice enough, I guess."

Wow. From my taciturn father, "nice enough, I guess" was tantamount to approval. Did he actually like Sebastian, despite everything?

"Why must everything be such drama with you?" Dad continued. "We don't hear from you for years, and suddenly it's 'I'm marrying a vampire'?"

Oh, okay. Sebastian might be "nice enough," but I was still the weirdo who pretended magic was real. The biggest hurdle, of course, was the fact that my parents had never had contact with real magic.

There is a kind of veil of denial most people never pass through, which is how most vampires and other denizens of the night manage to say hidden in plain sight. Until my parents experienced the touch of real magic firsthand, all my talk of Vatican witch hunters, etc., would seem like the ramblings of a madwoman.

Of course, the moment they walked through Sebastian's warded doors and had any kind of significant contact with Benjamin, they'd be able to see what some part of them always knew existed. Probably their interaction with Teréza was already unraveling their worldview, which might explain why my father sounded so hostile.

Cold nipped at the tip of my nose, while a blush warmed the rest of my face. "Sebastian didn't want me to tell you, either," I admitted. "Maybe we could pretend I never said anything?"

I was still holding out hope for the do-over button, I guess. Instead, my dad shook his head in a way that made it obvious he wasn't done chastising me, but he was willing to wait for a different moment to discuss things. "Let's go inside."

Indoors, oak logs crackled and popped in the fireplace. Sebastian had tidied up. He must have used his preternatural speed to pull out our Yule log and some evergreen boughs, which he positioned artfully in the center of the Mission-style coffee table. Candles were lit around the room, and a few of the floor lamps had been switched to low, so pools of warm light added to the room's general coziness.

I pulled off my boots and set them on the thick rug underneath the coat-tree. I shook the snow off my shoulders and hung up my jacket. Beside me I heard my mother murmur appreciatively, "Look at all the books." She sighed. My mother was a serious bibliophile.

And, to be fair, Sebastian had a truly impressive library. I tried to see it as my parents did. Glass-fronted bookcases lined one entire wall of the living room, and still others were tucked in nearly every available space. Books were piled on the floor, in particular next to the leather wing chair he favored close to the fire. After removing her coat and boots, my mother moved into the room in order to greedily run her fingers over the titles.

"Is this German?" she asked.

"That one is Old German. The majority of the titles on that shelf are probably Germanic in one form or another." Sebastian came in from the kitchen at that moment, a silver tray in his hands bearing what looked like tiny tea sandwiches.

He offered the tray to Mom. She took one a little hesitantly.

"I feel it's a gentleman's duty to always have the makings for proper tea about the house. That's cucumber and cream cheese." Sebastian pointed, Vanna White–style, to the rest of the spread. "These are egg salad with dill. There's some hummus and, for the meat eaters, some liver pâté. I hope they'll tide you over until I can make something more substantial."

After my mom made yummy noises, my dad took an experimental bite of the pâté. He nodded and scooped up three more.

Sebastian set the tray down in the middle of the table. Barney came out from under the couch to sniff at the edges of the plate. "You'd better eat up all the liver, Dad," I said. "You've got competition."

Dad chuckled a little as he settled down into the big couch. He affectionately scratched Barney's ear. I could hear her purr from where I stood by the door. Could it be? Had we turned the evening around finally?

Sebastian flashed me a you-can-relax-now smile, and headed

back into the kitchen to whip up some culinary delight. Sebastian was a fantastic cook. I had no doubt he'd conjure up something tasty out of the leftovers in the fridge. His skill in the kitchen was one of the many, many things I loved about him.

Mom noticed my adoring gaze. "A man who can cook," she said almost kindly, "that's nice."

I nodded and settled next to my dad on the couch. Barney fluffed her substantial girth around my father's stocking feet and lay down on his toes. In a moment, her eyes closed in satisfaction; her claws kneaded the Persian rug. My dad had a strange kind of natural animal attraction. Even our chickens liked him, and he stole their eggs on a regular basis.

I leaned back into the plush suede and let the warmth of the room soothe my nerves. My mother continued to peruse the books, and my father munched sandwiches by the handful. Barney began to snore.

Our familial bliss was interrupted by the clomp, clomp of engineer boots on the staircase. Mátyás descended wearing tailored black pants and a matching Armani T-shirt. His hair was a stylized mess, which just added the final touch to his general Eurotrash fashion statement.

My mother looked up and took him in from head to toe. Her expression became instantly disapproving. My father sat up like a predator threatened by the approach of another male into his territory. Barney hissed.

Mátyás glanced over the rim of his tinted glasses and sneered. "Ah, this must be the Lacey family. Somehow I expected you all to be naked, given that was how I first met you, Garnet."

Nice.

My parents looked at me for an explanation.

Disheartened, I waved a hand in the direction of the smug figure poised on the staircase. "Mom, Dad," I said, "This is Mátyás Von Traum, Sebastian's son."

"Son? Sebastian has a teenage son?" My mother asked, her tone full of outrage.

"Naked?" My dad sputtered. All the color had drained from his face, and he had a sort of stricken look, as though it just occurred to him that anyone might ever see his only daughter without clothes on. "Naked?"

"Oh, yes," Mátyás purred. "And I'm no teenager. Certainly, older than Garnet here. Oh, and talk about awkward," Mátyás said, continuing his way down the stairs.

"How much older?" my mother asked quietly yet firmly, as though she didn't really want to know the answer but she had to ask.

"Naked," my dad repeated. This time it was a bit louder and less of a question.

"What difference does it make how much older he is?" I asked no one in particular. My father turned to watch Mátyás shrug into his leather trench coat. My mother clutched the book she'd been looking at to her breast with white knuckles. Barney jumped up on to the arm of the couch and dug her claws into the upholstery angrily. I continued, "I mean, so what if Mátyás is older than me?"

"Significantly older," Mátyás answered. "Much like dear Papa."

"What are you implying?" My mother said, and then turning to me, she repeated, "What is he saying? How old is

Sebastian? He doesn't look that much older than you, but his son says he's your age at least. Is Sebastian *our* age? Exactly how old is he?" By the time she reached the end of her tirade, my mother's voice was nearly a screech.

"Naked." My dad's eyes were narrow slits now. He was really steamed.

Just before heading out the door, Mátyás caught my eye and flashed me a "gotcha" smile. I returned an "I'll get you later" stare.

"Garnet, your mother asked you a question," my father said, still standing. Barney had fled back under the couch. Her tail stuck out. I wished I could join her. "And explain this whole naked thing."

"Uh," I started, but then quickly lost direction. I mean, my dad wasn't going to like the image of Mátyás walking in on me after I'd had sex with Sebastian for the first time.

Then again, it wasn't like I needed explain my sex life to my parents. I was a grown woman, over thirty, for Goddess' sake. My sex life was my own business, wasn't it? Gah, I hated how I always felt like a kid when my parents were in the room.

"Well?" Mom prompted. "How old is Sebastian?"

A thousand years old—yeah, you could say Sebastian's my older man. Ha. Ha. Sure, I could lie, but these were my folks. If anyone was going to see through me, it was them. I was considering muttering something noncommittal like, "There's a definite age difference," when Sebastian came back in the room with an easy, relaxed smile that indicated he had no idea he was wandering into the lions' den.

Sebastian misinterpreted the sudden attention. "I just put dinner in the oven. I hope you like veggie soufflé."

"He doesn't look old enough to have a twenty-year-old son," my mother told my father as if Sebastian wasn't standing right next to her. "Maybe he's had work done. You know, like plastic surgery. I understand that's very popular."

"Maybe he was a young father," my dad offered. "How old does a guy have to be, anyway?"

"Well," my mother scrutinized Sebastian like she was judging a chicken at the state fair, "he'd have to be at least sixteen, I would think. I suppose he could be thirty-six. Does he look thirty-six to you?"

Sebastian looked to me for an answer as to why he was being talked around. I mouthed, Mátyás. Sebastian's expression instantly darkened.

My father shrugged. "He looks seventeen to me. His kid looks older than he does."

It was starting to be true. Sebastian never aged; Mátyás did—only very, very slowly.

"Would you like me to be thirty-six?" Sebastian asked in a silky smooth voice. I smelled cinnamon and baking bread, and I knew Sebastian was using glamour on my parents. Even with Lilith bonded to me, I felt a keen desire to believe anything he said right now. My mother's tight face relaxed into a soft smile. My dad sat down. Barney sneezed wetly under the couch. "Then I am thirty-six."

"Did you say dinner would be ready soon?" my dad asked, as though he'd forgotten the entire encounter with Mátyás.

Sebastian nodded. "About fifteen minutes."

I wasn't sure how I felt about Sebastian using his magic to delude my folks, especially since I'd been working so hard to try to tell them the truth. Still, I had to admit it was disaster averted for now. I only hoped they didn't remember this moment when their nonmagical worldview came crashing around their ears. "I'll help you set the table," I said.

"I already . . ." Sebastian started until he saw my I-want-to-talk-privately eyebrow arch. "Sounds great."

"Talk among yourselves," I jokingly said to my folks, who still looked a little dazed. My mother groggily went back to looking over the book she had in her hands. My dad reached for another sandwich. Barney pulled her tail in under the couch and sniffled.

"We could have told them the truth," I said, munching on a carrot stick from a tray of appetizers Sebastian had arranged on the table. I leaned against the counter and tried to stay out of his way as he cooked and fussed.

Sebastian's farmhouse didn't have a formal dining room. We usually ate at the kitchen table, on which Sebastian always had a variety of tinctures, essential oils, and the like, brewing, steeping, or infusing. He'd cleared all that away and put on a red and white checked tablecloth. Simple white china plates had been set at each place. He'd broken out the good silver and linen napkins. It looked elegant but not overdone. My folks should like that.

The soufflé smelled great. I could detect the scent of onion, garlic, and something green like asparagus. My stomach growled in anticipation.

"I think we've got enough to worry about, don't you?" Sebastian said, as he straightened out his pile of recipes on top of the refrigerator. "What possessed you to tell them about me, anyway? I thought we'd agreed not to bring that up."

We hadn't actually agreed to anything, but I didn't feel like arguing the point. Clearly, telling them *had* been a mistake. "Mátyás started the age thing, and anyway, do you plan to use your glamour to have them forget Teréza too?"

I knew he couldn't actually do that. Glamour only worked in small doses, and he couldn't retroactively make someone forget something with which they had actual physical contact. I only made the snide comment because I was cranky about how the whole evening had turned out, and I was getting tired of talking around all the important stuff in my life. I kind of wanted my parents to get in the know sooner rather than later.

"Teréza's out there," Sebastian said.

"Yeah, I know, we have to deal with her."

"No," Sebastian said. "I mean, out there. In the yard."

I felt the hairs on the back of my neck rise at the thought. I pulled aside the curtain on the window over the sink. "What, you mean like right now?"

Sebastian nodded. "We need to get your folks back to their hotel soon. I have to deal with her."

There was a "once and for all" that hung, unspoken in the air. Sebastian's jaw twitched as if in grim determination.

"What are you planning to do?" I asked, glancing back at him. "I thought she was supposed to be headed to her grave."

"Apparently not. She showed up ten minutes ago." His eyes didn't quite meet mine as he fussed around the kitchen.

I doubted Sebastian actually "forgot" digging a grave for his ex. Clearly, he was embarrassed that she'd been next door while we were dating.

The window rattled in the wind. A carrot piece lodged itself in my throat. Still holding the curtain in my fingers, I leaned over the sink to look in the direction of the little cemetery in the adjacent lot. In among the tilted, crumbling, snow-covered headstones, I saw her. She stood just beyond a waist-high monolith, staring hungrily at the farmhouse. The yard light made her skin pale and hooded her eyes. With her ragged coat and straggly hair, she looked like a specter.

"Shit," I said.

"Yeah, that pretty much sums things up," Sebastian agreed.

"She can't get past the wards, can she?" I asked, quickly closing the curtain.

Sebastian's answer didn't hearten me. "Maybe. But I sent Benjamin out to guard the property as added protection."

My brain stalled on the first part: " 'Maybe'? What do you mean 'maybe'?"

"It's my blood magic that set the wards; the same that keeps her alive." Sebastian flicked on the oven light to check on the soufflé. Satisfied, he turned back to me. "I don't really know how it all works, but since I can pass through the wards, I suppose it's possible she could too."

"We re-warded the place when I moved in," I reminded him. "Lilith's magic is here too."

Sebastian nodded, pulling aside the curtain over the back door's window to peek out at her. "I think that's why she looks so pissed off. She probably doesn't like the scent of another witch in my house."

Step back. Had I known Teréza was a witch? That creepy feeling crawled across my stomach again. I felt dizzy and had to grab onto the counter for support. "Uh, 'another'? How powerful a witch was, er, *is* Teréza?"

Just then the door from the living room swung open, and my dad leaned in. "Everything okay in here? You guys aren't fighting or anything, are you? Hmmm, smells delicious."

As it happened, the oven timer chose that moment to go off, so we ushered my folks in. Even though the glamour should have worn off, my mother seemed to have completely fallen under Sebastian's spell and made very appreciative noises about the table setting and the coziness of the kitchen in general. My father complimented the chef after nearly every bite. Barney muscled the kitchen door open and then brazenly licked soufflé batter from the bowl in the sink.

Throughout the meal, I kept my eye on the back door. I half expected Teréza to come stumbling through any minute and destroy the evening again. The December wind, or maybe it was Benjamin, groaned around the gables.

Sebastian was much better at acting relaxed. He smiled and joked easily with my parents. Meanwhile, I couldn't shake the image of Teréza rocking back and forth mournfully among the headstones. How were we going to get my parents past her without incident? Would she attack them? What did she want anyway? Teréza seemed quite determined to kill Sebastian at the restaurant. Was she just a mindless corpse bent on destroying her creator? It might be unkind of me, but I certainly hoped so for Sebastian's sake.

I watched him smile while my mother recounted a story she'd heard on NPR about the history of soufflés or some such related topic. I wasn't really listening. I was thinking back to the dark pain in Sebastian's expression when he suggested he had to finish things with Teréza. No matter what she was after, dealing with Teréza wasn't going to be easy on Sebastian. All the times he had possession of her completely lifeless body he'd never been able to send her to the final death, even when he thought it might be preferable to her twilight state between living and dead.

If there was even the tiniest spark of humanity left in Teréza, I knew Sebastian would be honor-bound to rescue it. The image of Teréza standing forlornly among the headstones flashed through my mind, and my heart sank.

Our wedding was supposed to be in two weeks.

"Have you picked out your dress?" my mother asked. Apparently while my mind wandered, the conversation had also turned to our upcoming nuptials.

"Uh, yeah, of course," I said.

My mother raised her eyebrows. "I see," she said icily.

That'll teach me not to pay attention. My mind started racing: Was I supposed to have shopped for it with her? Did she have an heirloom dress in the attic? Had she hoped to sew it for me? Oh God, this was worse than the idea of Teréza bursting through the door with a foaming mouth and a butcher knife. I didn't know what to say. Should I offer to throw mine out? Start over? "Uh," I started. "Er."

Unknowingly, my dad came to my rescue. "Are you getting married in a church? What religion are you, anyway?" he asked Sebastian.

"Catholic," Sebastian said.

"Really?" My dad was astonished. I'm sure he was expecting Sebastian to also be Wiccan or maybe something even more oddball. Although my dad was enough of an antiestablishment sort to be a little skeptical of organized religions, I think he might have preferred me to find a nice secular humanist or atheist to settle down with. "Like, Roman Catholic?"

"Well . . ." Now it was Sebastian's turn to be in the corner. When Sebastian was born there really was only one version of Catholicism, but shortly after his "death," the church split, and Eastern Orthodoxy and its various regional expressions was born. Politics and religion shifted over time, but Sebastian always stayed true to what he'd been raised, even though there was no church that existed today that held his precise beliefs. "Not exactly."

Because everything was going badly tonight, my dad misinterpreted. "Are you with one of those ultraconservative groups?"

Why did he go there? "Do you think he'd be marrying me if he was?"

"Will you be wearing white?" My mother interjected, clearly still obsessed with the dress.

"No, Mom," I said. Was this the issue with the dress? Did she have dreams of me in white? "Uh, that's not really fashionable anymore."

My mother gasped. "Please tell me you're not wearing black."

"Cream," I insisted. Then I wondered, was I supposed to still be a virgin? Was that the deal?

My mom and I never really had the birds-and-bees conversation. When I got close to puberty, I found a book on my bed stand with all sorts of clinical terms for various body parts. Luckily, thanks to my mother's book obsession, I also had access to *Our Bodies, Our Selves*, which had much cooler pictures and a lot more modern language, if you considered anything written in the seventies "modern"—although it was definitely "mod."

So maybe she thought I should wear white? "Uh . . ." I started, but didn't really know where I was going.

Barney barfed up the soufflé batter on my dad's shoes. I'd never been more grateful for my cat's sensitive stomach.

After cleaning up the mess, Sebastian and I managed to steer the conversation back to safer and more mundane topics. The smell of cinnamon and baking bread almost made me cough.

At last the meal was over. My dad pushed back his plate and folded his hands over his stomach. He looked full, satisfied, and ready to settle in for a long after-dinner nap. My mom too seemed sated. At some point during the meal, she'd kicked her shoes off. Her stocking feet stretched out under the table. Barney twined around my legs, hopeful for another handout or two.

The window rattled. I jumped, my eyes seeking out Sebastian nervously.

"Sounds like a storm is coming in," Sebastian said. "You should probably head back to your hotel before it gets bad."

There was enough residue glamour in the air that my mother quickly got the hint. "I'm sorry we can't stay," my mother said. "But I think that storm *is* really picking up."

My dad, who must have been slightly more impervious to Sebastian's magic, sighed. "What about dessert?"

"It's been a long night. We should let these kids get some rest," my mother said. She winked at me. "We can order something from room service."

"Seriously?" my dad said. My mother ordering room service was a rare extravagance. "Well," my dad said, making a show of looking at his pocket watch. "If that's the time, you're probably right. Let's get on the road."

We herded them into the living room to gather coats and boots and such. Sebastian whispered in my ear that he was going to send Benjamin along to guard them until they were safely off the property. So he made an excuse to duck back into the kitchen for a few moments.

"He's all right after all, isn't he?" Mom said, wrapping her pumps in a used plastic bag that she'd had in her coat pocket. She stepped into her tall, faux-fur lined boots.

"I'm rather fond of him," I agreed.

My mother smiled. "You know, honey, you're going to need a lot of help with the wedding planning and organizing. Maybe your father and I should stay in town."

"But that's two weeks!" I protested. Besides, the idea of my mother's help made my blood run cold. I looked to my dad for assistance. He was busy lacing up his boots.

"I think it's a good idea," my mother said, "don't you, Glen?"

My dad looked up. "Yeah, you bet."

"Good, then it's settled." My mother looked genuinely cheerful, the happiest she had all night. I tried to smile back.

When Sebastian returned to the room, the proper good-byes began again in earnest. He caught my eye and nodded, letting me know my folks would be protected by our house ghost.

Being Minnesotan, however, my parents had to repeat the good-bye ritual several more times before they actually made it out the door. Mom had to first make a few more complimentary comments about Sebastian's library. Dad had to discuss the advantages of using firewood for heat. I made sure my folks could make their way back to the city and their hotel. Sebastian drew them a map on a sticky note.

All the while, I bit my lip and tried not to shoo them out. Twenty minutes later the door finally closed behind them.

I looked to Sebastian. "Now what?"

He was already putting on his coat. "Now I go out there and face her."

"You think she's still there?" I asked. I peered out into the lightly falling snow, ostensibly to wave a last good-bye to my folks, but their car was already around the bend and on the county highway. I glanced in the direction of the graveyard. At first, I thought Teréza had gone, but then I saw her sitting in the snow with her back resting against a crumbling marble marker. She looked like a child, huddled there. If you didn't know what to look for, you wouldn't know she was there. At least I wouldn't have to try to explain *that* to my folks. "What are you going to do?"

Sebastian had told me time and time again that even though there were moments when it would be easier to "let Teréza go" and destroy her body, he hadn't been able to do it.

He'd loved her once, and she was the mother of his only son. More than that, he felt so much guilt about her current condition. He wanted to make things right. His voice was almost a whisper. "I don't know."

"I'm coming with you," I said, taking his hand.

Outside, the wind had picked up. Snow creaked under our feet as we made our way across the lawn to the cemetery. The moment the door of the house opened, Teréza stood up expectantly. I held tightly to Sebastian's hand, but his eyes focused on the ragged, swaying form that hovered among the gravestones.

Something icy touched the back of my neck. The wind whispered in my ear, "I'm here." Sensing a presence beside me, I turned. Even though I saw nothing but an added set of footprints in the snow, I knew Benjamin had joined us. Although I made a mental note to have that relationship chat with him sooner rather than later, I was glad to know we had supernatural backup.

We were getting closer to Teréza. Dark circles ringed her manically glittering eyes. The icy wind reddened her cheeks and pulled the skin of her face into a taut, gaunt smile. Brittle-looking clumps of jet black hair swirled around her face.

Her eyes darted back and forth between Sebastian and me as we approached. Sebastian's face was grim, and she seemed frightened by it. My heart pounded in my throat. She raised a skeletal, clawlike hand to ward us off.

My stomach got all queasy again.

Lilith perked up, as if she sensed trouble. I could feel her fire just under the surface, ready.

Then my cell phone rang. The ring tone was Ricky Martin's "Livin' La Vida Loca."

Everyone, even Teréza with her bugged-out eyes, stared at my coat pocket. The phone continued to ring. I reached for it automatically.

"What?" Sebastian asked. "You're going to answer it? Now?"

Thing was, I'd set all the wedding related calls to that song. I'd been having such a hell of a time connecting with the band to discuss play lists and such, I didn't want to miss it.

Teréza moaned.

I glanced at the screen. It *was* the band. "I've got to take this," I told Sebastian. "It's about the wedding."

"You're fucking kidding me," he said, throwing his hands up in the air.

"Sorry." I mouthed. I turned away slightly and connected. "Hello?"

There was good news/bad news, the band's manager explained. The good news was that the band got a record contract. The bad news was that the stress was breaking them up. The good news was they had a replacement lined up for me. The bad news was it was a polka band.

"How is that good news exactly?" I shouted. My guest list was under the age of sixty, mostly, and I'd desperately wanted a band that could play our song. I doubted Rob Zombie's "Dragula," sounded the same on an accordion.

"Hang up," Sebastian demanded. "Hang up the damn phone."

Sebastian was right. I couldn't cope with this right now, not standing ankle deep in snow in a graveyard. "I'll have to call you back," I told the manager. I hung up.

"Sometimes I rue the day I gave you that blasted contraption," Sebastian said.

"I had to answer it. I'd been trying all week to get ahold of those people, and now they've canceled." Turning around, I noticed Teréza was gone. "Wait, where'd she go?" I asked Sebastian, as I slipped the cell back into my pocket.

Sebastian, who had been watching me with his mouth agape, turned to where Teréza had been standing. "Oh, great," he said. "I can't believe you answered the phone. Now she got away!"

"And we have an oompah band!"

He opened his mouth and then closed it a few times. Finally, he said, "What, like, polka music?"

I nodded.

"Well, this is a disaster," Sebastian muttered, though I didn't think he meant the band. Leaning his butt against one of the marble monuments, he crossed his arms and glanced over the cornfield, no doubt using his preternatural senses to check for signs of Teréza's escape.

I hugged myself as well. I was upset about Teréza, of course, but my mind kept returning to the music situation. The wedding was only two weeks away, and I'd already started having nightmares about it. My hands started shaking. For once in my life, I'd had every detail all planned out. In advance. Now everything was falling apart.

"I just don't see her," he said.

All I saw was dark and more dark and the impressive array of the Milky Way above, but I knew Sebastian could see miles in this light.

"That's strange," I agreed. "She moved all creepy crawly at the restaurant. You wouldn't think she could go far like that."

I closed my eyes for a second and reopened them in second sight. Before I bonded with Lilith, using my magical senses always took a few moments of prep and visualization. Now it came, quite literally, in the blink of an eye.

I could see more too. For instance, though it was black on black, I noticed instantly the huge bend Teréza's leaving had folded into the fiber of time and space. "She disappeared," I said.

"I know," Sebastian muttered. "It's weird."

"No, I mean she vanished. Teleported. Poofed!"

"Oh," Sebastian said in a tone that was both intrigued and spooked.

Teleportation was a major skill for anyone corporeal; I have never heard of anyone who could do it. I glanced at Benjamin, who I could see clearly with my magical eye. I was about to ask him what he saw in the astral plane, but I thought better of it. He stood in front of a tilted headstone that simply said, Wife. He looked alternately saddened and angry. Every time his expression turned angry, his face became that of a monster: hollowed cheeks, empty eye sockets, and twisted, furious lips.

I had a feeling the house was going to get a good tossing around tonight.

I took a deep breath, reminding myself to deal with one thing at a time. "Just how powerful is Teréza, Sebastian?"

He shrugged his shoulder and glanced off to the side. Through my magical vision, Sebastian always seemed paler, hungrier—more dead, actually. The black hole where his aura should be stood out starkly with its absence. "Stronger than me," he said.

"Seriously? Is that possible? You're a vampire!"

"There are things stronger than vampires. Remember the Trickster God?" How could I forget him? Micah had been the one that triggered my bonding with Lilith—plus he was a total hottie. "Anyway," Sebastian continued, "Teréza's people have been practicing magic for a long time."

Gypsy magic: If there really was a famtrad—a family tradition of hereditary magic—Romany blood would be one. I blinked myself back to normal vision. Lilith rippled across my skin, itching for a fight. The band might have canceled, but if we didn't track down Teréza soon, we could have a scene like this at the church. I could live with a polka band. My friends would think it was retro and hip. But the teleporting zombie ex was another problem, one I did not want popping in on my wedding day.

"We have to find Teréza, Sebastian. Now. But she could be anywhere," I said, considering out loud. "I say let's go to the source."

Sebastian perked up. "You mean blood magic?"

"No," I said. "Mátyás."

Third Aspect: Square

KEY WORDS:

Combative, Individualistic

We found Mátyás at Holy Grounds. Besides hanging out with Izzy, Mátyás and William had taken to playing games like speed chess and Go at the coffee shop. Their obsession with those sorts of tactical/intellectual pastimes had gotten so intense that I'd begun to suspect William's latest new religion was strategy. My theory was bolstered by the fact that just the other day I'd caught William poring over Sun Tzu's *The Art of War* during his lunch hour.

The coffee shop was nearly empty. After the briskness of the evening air, the peppermint-mocha warmth felt a bit stifling. The heat steamed the ice particles in my hair.

Snowflakes had been stenciled on the window in that ubiquitous powdery spray paint. The rest of the place had been

decorated with everything from Santa-cap-wearing Buddhas
to Chanukah menorahs. The only thing traditionally Christ-
massy was the electric faux fireplace set up in the back by the
couches and the constant Christmas music that streamed over
the speakers.

Izzy looked up from behind the bar when the door swung
open. Izzy always reminded me of that famous bust of Nefer-
titi, especially now that her dreads had grown to reach her
shoulder, and she often held her hair away from her face with
a scarf. Her skin was the warm color of the mochas she
served, and her features had a regal cut I deeply envied. She'd
been experimenting with fashion too. Tonight, Izzy went for
that whole naughty British schoolgirl look and wore a man's
button-down shirt, a necktie, and a knee-length pleated wool
skirt.

Seeing us, she smiled. I waved back, but I couldn't quite
bring myself to smile in return. I was on the warpath. My
wedding was potentially at stake, and someone was going to
pay.

Mátyás and William perched on opposite chairs hunched
over a game of Risk. William's hair was short-cropped and
frosted blond. I wasn't quite sure what kind of image he was
going for, but with the little round glasses perched on the
end of his nose, he looked a bit like a sexed-up Radar O'Reilly
from *M*A*S*H* or James Spader in the movie *Stargate*.

Izzy came out from behind the bar to join Sebastian and
me as we approached them. "What's going on?" she asked.

Mátyás glanced up. From what I could tell, he'd taken
most of Europe and Asia and was clearly advancing on the

South Pacific. William's extracurricular reading didn't seem to be helping him.

I opened my mouth, but Sebastian beat me to it. "Where is she?" he demanded.

"Who?" You'd think Mátyás would know better than to try the innocent act on his father.

Sebastian ground his teeth together angrily, and I wasn't sure he was going to say anything constructive, so I said, "Your mother." Then, just to be crystal clear, I added, "Teréza."

Mátyás quickly looked over his shoulder as if worried she might be hovering there. Then he glanced from Izzy to me, avoiding looking at Sebastian. "Uh . . . I don't really know. I sort of lost track of her."

"Lost track?" Sebastian sputtered.

"You have a mother living around here?" Izzy asked with a tone that implied she felt she should have heard about this before now, and Mátyás was down a couple of relationship points. I smiled.

"Living? I thought your mother was dead," William said, his attention still divided between the conversation and the game. He had the kind of vaguely guilty look of someone who really wanted to take advantage of Mátyás's distraction and change the board.

Meanwhile, Adam Sandler serenaded us with "The Chanukah Song."

"Either way," I said. "Teréza certainly found us."

Mátyás's face tightened for a moment, but then he smiled up at us. "Seriously? She was up and walking? That's fantastic. Did she *say* anything?"

She had cursed Sebastian and me. Was this some kind of breakthrough Mátyás was hoping for? Actually, she had said, "I curse you." She could have talking to both of us . . . or to *me*.

"That's not the point, Mátyás," Sebastian said. "Your mother tried to kill me."

Mátyás sat up, clearly excited by the news. He wasn't winning any points with his father, however, whose face grew darker.

"I can't believe it," Mátyás said happily. "You're suggesting she was strong enough to try to hurt you?"

"You sound a little creepy when you say things like that, honey," Izzy said drily, like she'd talked to him about this sort of thing before.

"I still don't get how she could do any of it dead," William said, his eyes still on the board.

My phone rang. "Livin' La Vida Loca" again. "Oh, what now?" I was tempted to let it go, but I knew it had to be a wedding thing. What could be going wrong now? I took a few steps away from everyone, even though I could hear Sebastian telling Mátyás to cut the crap and start telling us what was going on with Teréza.

It was the dress shop. They were calling to confirm that my bridesmaids' dresses were salmon-pink taffeta. "No!" I shouted. "Silk. Ice blue."

I looked at Izzy. She was meant to be my maid of honor, and I'd picked a color that not only went with the season but that would also complement her skin tone. "The color is really important," I explained, not to mention the fact that the style I'd chosen was a simple sheath that could be reused as a cocktail dress. The ones the shop described had a giant butt-bow.

I moaned. They could replace them, but it would take time. "How long?"

A couple of weeks, they thought. Maybe. "Maybe?" I repeated, horrified. "My wedding is in two weeks *exactly*."

They'd do their best. My hand was shaking when I slipped my phone back into my coat pocket. Lilith surged through my veins, a hot pulse at my throat.

"All right, I've had it," I snapped. Before I knew quite what I was doing, I'd swept Mátyás out of his chair. Balling his shirt in my fists, I shoved him hard against the bookcase. "What's going on? Am I cursed or something? Did your freaky stalker mother hex me?"

I moved so fast that the chair hit the floor two seconds after I heard the air leave Mátyás's lungs.

Did I mention Lilith's hair trigger?

It was all I could do to keep Lilith from battering Mátyás's head against the shelves. Over the roar of emotion, Sebastian's voice shouted for me to stand down. Izzy was yelling something too, but it was William's calm, soothing tones that reached me: ". . . you are wise, oh Goddess. Mátyás is truly an idiot, but I humbly beg you to spare his worthless life."

I took in a breath. I felt Lilith's anger recede as William continued to purr platitudes into my ear. Mátyás's eyes bugged out a little less as my grip on his throat loosened.

The funny part in all this was that Mátyás outweighed me by at least fifty pounds. He was also nearly six feet tall. When I realized I was standing on tiptoe to hold him up, I uncurled my fingers and lowered myself back down. A blush slid across my cheeks.

William, who had been creeping closer and closer to me, rushed in to support Mátyás when I released him. Mátyás clutched at his throat and concentrated on breathing. Sebastian's face was impassive, but I could tell he was watching Mátyás and me with concern. Izzy had stopped yelling, but as she slipped past me to comfort Mátyás, she was still muttering about anger-management courses and unmedicated craziness.

A random female customer hooted out a "You go, girl." But when I turned around to see who said it, everyone suddenly found newspapers and lattes endlessly fascinating.

With an apologetic shrug, I smiled weakly. This sort of thing had been happening a lot more than I liked since Lilith and I bonded.

At first, I'd imagined the change in my relationship with Lilith as entirely positive. I mean, I found I could tap into Lilith's magic instantly. My spells kicked ass now. Plus her physical strength was available upon request, which came in very handy that time the delivery guy dumped all the stock for my store at the wrong loading dock. I'd found too that I was much less afraid of really losing control. Used to be, if I accidentally triggered Lilith's wrath, I could wake up to find myself with bodies to bury, literally. Now I was conscious during the outbursts, and she was easier to rein in . . . at least so far.

But the outbursts, while no longer the nuclear option, were a whole hell of a lot more frequent. It was crazy-making, Izzy was right. It unnerved me how unpredictable I was becoming. Mátyás had gotten hurt. Only thanks to sheer will-power was he not more damaged.

"I'm sorry," I said.

Mátyás looked up at my words. Wounded pride burned in his eyes.

"It's okay," William said. "We all know how Lilith is, right, guys?"

Izzy didn't look so sure. Mátyás's jaw twitched. Sebastian, however, came to stand beside me. "Of course we do," he said. He took me under his arm and swept me over to the plastic water cooler that hung over the edge of the bar. The dispenser made a loud *glug-glug* as he pressed down on the spigot. I gratefully accepted the cool glass he handed me. "I'm sorry. I can't control it." I looked over my shoulder to where Izzy was fussing over Mátyás. Noticing my inquiring glance, Mátyás glared at me. "He hates me."

Sebastian stroked my hair. "He always has, my darling. Anyway, Mátyás is just pissed right now because he had his ass handed to him by a five-foot-tall, perky Goth."

I laughed a little at that image, but my smile quickly faded. "I didn't mean to hurt him."

"Everyone knows that," Sebastian said kindly. "Even Mátyás."

"He's going to have bruises."

"Not for very long. He's a dhampyr; he heals fast."

I nodded, but I didn't feel comforted.

We'd perched on the tall stools near the bar. I could hear the others starting to talk, though I couldn't make out any individual words over "Santa, Baby," which played on the speakers.

"What happened to the dresses?" Sebastian asked.

"The order is completely screwed up. They got pink taffeta."

Sebastian made a face to show his opinion of that. I couldn't have agreed more. We laughed, even though my stomach lurched at the thought of the disaster my wedding was turning into.

The door opened to a couple of UW students with books under their arms. As they picked seats and shrugged out of their parkas, Izzy came back around the counter to take their orders.

"Mátyás is prickly," Sebastian said, watching as Izzy made small talk about finals and cold weather with the students. "But you'll make things up with Izzy."

"I hope so," I said, but just then Izzy saw me out of the corner of her eye and gave me a soft "we're okay" smile.

"See," Sebastian said. Letting his hands slide from my hair to my shoulders, he gave me a soft massage. It felt really great, and I could feel Lilith relaxing as well.

William came up beside us and plunked himself down on one of the stools. "Hey," he said to me. "Thanks for ruining my game. I was totally getting the smack-down."

"Yeah, I saw that," I said with a smile.

Sebastian craned his neck around. "Where's Mátyás? Isn't he going to join us?"

"He's sulking," William supplied. "Sore loser, as always."

"He never did tell us where his mother is," Sebastian said grumpily.

"That's because I don't know," Mátyás said, coming to sit

beside me on the other side of the water cooler. "And I don't sulk."

"You totally sulk, man," William said with a teasing snort from where he sat on the other side of Sebastian.

"I find it difficult to believe you don't know where your mother is," Sebastian said, giving Mátyás a glare. "It's not like you." To not hover over her like a mother hen, he clearly implied. I had to agree. Mátyás did have that whole attachment issue with Teréza.

"I don't have her tagged with a GPS collar for chrissakes," Mátyás said.

I cringed and seriously considered ducking. Sebastian had a very old-fashioned sense when it came to swearing. He wasn't a prude. Not in the least. He said *shit* and *fuck* and some of the even nastier words from time to time as the situation demanded, but he didn't really approve of taking the Lord's name in vain. This was never a problem between us, because, well, I wasn't Christian. Not only did he respect that it didn't have the same impact coming from a nonbeliever, but I purposefully avoided mentioning a certain son of a carpenter when I was mad. If I was going to take a lord's name in vain, it'd be my own.

But Mátyás was Catholic like his father.

Sebastian's teeth were clenched, and I could see the tips of fangs. That boy knew all the buttons to push with his father.

I decided to intercede. "I think you at least owe us some kind of explanation. I mean, the last time any of us knew about it, Teréza was still out . . . well, out cold, as it were."

"Dead," William offered.

"Trapped," Mátyás clarified.

"Whatever," I said. "The point is, she wasn't up and walking around."

"She got better," Mátyás said.

William laughed. We all looked at him blankly. "That's the line from Monty Python—the 'Bring Out Your Dead' skit? Or was it the witch one? Anyway, you remember. . . . Uh." He looked sheepish when we all continued to stare at him. "Sorry, dudes, it's just kind of surreal all this casual talk of animated corpses and whatnot."

I turned back to Mátyás, who was getting a glass of water for himself.

Izzy had finished with the customers and came over to where we were all seated at the far end of the bar. "Who's got a casual corpse?" she asked, setting down two cups of black coffee—one for Mátyás, the other for Sebastian. "Yours are coming," she told William and me. We both preferred, as Izzy mockingly called them, "froufrou" lattes.

"Mátyás was going to explain to us how his mother recovered from being dead," Sebastian said, handing over a twenty to cover all our drinks. "Weren't you, son?"

Oooh, "son." Sebastian only ever used that particular designation when he was pissed off.

David Bowie and Bing Crosby softly sang "Little Drummer Boy" as we waited to see what Mátyás would say.

"You're not going to be happy," Mátyás said.

I glanced over at Sebastian, flashing him the try-to-be-supportive eyebrow. "He knows about the exorcism," I told Mátyás.

"And you're right, I'm not happy about it," Sebastian said, taking a sip from the cup.

"It worked," Mátyás said.

"How does an exorcism work on a dead lady?" William wondered. Izzy set frothy drinks in front of William and me. I got a honey latte and William a soy mocha with sprinkles.

"Apparently, the pope drove my evil out of her," Sebastian said. "Do you know how irritated that makes me? The sitting pope! I totally supported the wrong faction if his magic is stronger than mine."

I exchanged a do-you-know-what-he's-talking-about glance with William, but he shrugged. Mátyás and Izzy looked just as lost.

"There was the whole Avignon schism?" He started, then shrugged. "Never mind."

I slurped the foam from the top of the coffee. It had just a hint of sweetness. "But you told me about the exorcism months ago," I said to Mátyás. "She waited until now—right before my wedding—to show up and start laying claim to Sebastian?"

"I might have actually mentioned the wedding," Mátyás mumbled into his cup.

Sebastian roared, "You what?!"

"She'd been so listless before. I needed to put some fire in her belly," Mátyás said defensively. Despite his bold tone, he sat up straighter and eyed the door, as though making sure he had a clear escape route in case Sebastian pounced.

Sebastian, meanwhile, clenched his hands around his coffee cup so hard I was afraid it might break. "So you mentioned our wedding. I knew you were against it, but I never thought you'd use your mother this way. Hasn't she suffered enough?"

Mátyás stiffened. "What would you know about her suffering? You've been trying to deny her existence for the past hundred fifty years."

"That's unfair," I said.

"The hell it is," Mátyás snarled. "He shoved her underground time and time again." Turning his anger back at Sebastian, he said, "You've been buried alive. Tell me it was 'peaceful.'"

Sebastian always claimed that Teréza rested better underground. I'd always been a bit dubious, myself. But Sebastian was a lot closer to dead than I was. What did I know about it?

"When was Sebastian buried?" William whispered to Izzy. She raised her eyebrow as if to say it was news to her as well. I made a mental note to fill them in on the whole thing later.

"That's not the same," Sebastian said after a grim, considering silence. "The last time I was buried, it was against my will. I was transfixed by a wooden stake."

"I remember," Mátyás said in a tone that dripped with and-you-should-be-more-grateful-I-dug-you-out-and-offered-my-blood.

Speaking of which . . . "Is Teréza a vampire now?" I asked. Because how much would it suck to have a vampire, zombie, and Gypsy witch all rolled into one after us?

Mátyás's jaw twitched. He didn't meet my gaze.

"Oh great Goddess, she is, isn't she?"

If I weren't already sitting down, my knees would have

buckled. As it was, it made my stomach tingle to think about all that magical power at the disposal of someone who was so clearly unhinged.

"So, wait," William said. "What did the pope cure, if she's still a vampire?"

Good question. "Consumption?" I wondered. "What was she dying of?"

"The pope can cure sickness?" Izzy seemed impressed but a little skeptical. "I thought the Evangelicals did that."

"So the vampirism wasn't the sin," I said to Sebastian, although it was clear by his faint smile that he'd already come to the same conclusion.

"She's not exactly healed," Mátyás muttered.

Well, there was that.

We all sipped our coffee. The lights above the bar blinked in tune to George Michael's "Last Christmas."

Sebastian frowned intently. Every once in a while, he'd glance at Mátyás. I was just about to ask what was eating at him, when Sebastian reached over and pulled up Mátyás's sleeve to the hollow of his elbow like he was looking for needle tracks. I wasn't sure what Sebastian was expecting until he said, "Are you feeding her? Where are you keeping her?"

Mátyás pulled his arm away. There were no bite marks; his arm was clean, but there were other places he could be feeding her from. "I don't need to answer your questions," he said.

But in a way he already had. Mátyás was too responsible to let his mother wander the streets trying to hunt up blood. The way she looked, it would be hard for her to use guile to lure victims in the usual way. It seemed most likely that he was feeding her, so there had to be a ghoul and a house somewhere.

Sebastian immediately headed for the door.

"You'll never find her," Mátyás said, standing up.

Sebastian didn't even turn around to respond. The bells over the door jingled as he headed out into the night.

"Where's he going?" William nudged me.

"To tap the ghoul community to try to find who's feeding Teréza," I said. I'd stood up too with the intention of following Sebastian, but he was already down the street. I could hurry to catch up to him, but it seemed clear that he wanted to deal with this on his own. Besides, I had a sort of "don't ask, don't tell" policy with Sebastian and his ghouls, so it was probably best that I let him deal with this on his own. He didn't need my complicating jealousy to slow down his search.

On the stereo, a country singer wailed out "Beep, beep, bye, bye, Santa's got a semi."

"I don't understand why you're keeping Teréza a secret," Izzy said from behind the counter. I turned to hear Mátyás's response.

"You saw how he reacted. He was happier when she was dead and buried," Mátyás said, eyeing me.

I didn't want to argue with him, and anyway, I wasn't sure I could make a good case in Sebastian's defense. We rarely talked about Teréza, but when we did, Sebastian often cut the conversation short. He didn't know what to do with Teréza, and yet he felt responsible for her. I rubbed my eyebrow, overwhelmed by the whole thing.

"Uh, hey, you look tired. And your ride just left," William said, putting his hand on my shoulder. "So I'll bet you need a lift home now, eh, Garnet?"

We left Izzy and Mátyás to their own conversation.

William and I were cruising down the highway, half-way back to the farm, when he casually dropped a gigantic bomb in my lap. "Hey, I saw Parrish the other day."

Parrish, my vampire ex-boyfriend—the one who sacrificed himself to save me a trip to federal prison and about whom my feelings were complicated at best—back in town? "What? Where?"

William rubbed his nose thoughtfully, and then returned his hands to the ten-and-two position on the wheel. "Club 5."

"Isn't that a gay bar? What were you doing there?"

"Dancing," William said without guilt.

I smiled devilishly. "Alone?"

"No. I went with Jorge."

Ah, the cute ambulance driver he'd met when I'd had a little run-in with a possessed wind chime. "Was it a date?"

William shrugged. "I had a great time dancing."

Another thing William was clearly undecided about. "Cool. But are you sure it was Parrish?"

"Oh, yeah," William said. "He came up and said hello. It was weird because I think Jorge thought he was *my* ex and got all jealous, which just made everything kind of weird. Anyway, didn't you invite him? He said he was in town for a wedding. I assumed he meant yours."

Had I invited Parrish? Thing is, I might have.

I'd been stuffing our wedding invitation envelopes a few weeks back and feeling kind of sad about how few people would be officially sitting on the bride's side of the aisle. Oh sure, I had the new coven Sebastian and I had started. But my old friends—the ones who knew me before the Vatican witch hunters killed my previous coven—thought I was dead. In order to stay hidden from the hunters and the FBI, I'd had to keep them in the dark about my new life. But the threat was over. I'd used magic to fool the Vatican into believing I was no longer a problem, and the FBI had closed its case.

So in a fit of spontaneous nostalgia, I sent out a call on the astral plane. I wove a spell that asked my old friends to dream of me and to receive the message that I was getting married. I even "sent" specifics and a way for them to get ahold of me to RSVP.

I knew it worked, because my oldest friend from high school called the next day. She'd Googled my folks and pried out my information from them. She wasn't even Wiccan! We caught up, and she agreed to be a bridesmaid. Others called throughout the whole week. I felt really good about it, but I'd kind of forgotten about Parrish. Of course, of all the people I'd ever known, Parrish would listen to a dream. Hell, a dream like that might have woken him, literally, from his grave.

This was just bloody lovely. Now not only did I have Sebastian's ex to deal with, but I also had my own.

"Did he say where he was staying?" I asked.

"So, you didn't invite him?" William ascertained. "I kind of wondered."

"No," I said. "I think I did. Magically—in a dream."

"Oh yeah, I think I had that dream," William said with a nod and a bit of surprise.

"You did? Cool." I said. It hadn't occurred to me that everyone would get it, even my local friends. "But I should make sure he's not planning on making a scene at the wedding."

"He won't be able to come, will he? I mean, he's a nightwalker." Unlike Sebastian, Parrish was restricted to nighttime hours.

"Our wedding is on Solstice. The sun is setting at four twenty-six." I happened to know the exact time, because we'd considered having a later wedding so that some of our nocturnally oriented friends could attend. But in the end we went with a more traditional afternoon wedding. We were getting married in a church. "He could easily crash the reception."

"What are you worried about? I thought you and Parrish were over."

Except he'd given me his wedding ring.

William pulled the car into Sebastian's drive. I scanned the graveyard, looking for signs of Teréza. William let the engine run, and I steeled myself to head out into the cold. Despite the fact that I knew that I was looking at a spell, Sebastian's house still appeared abandoned. The porch seemed slumped by age. The bulb that threw glittering light on the snow looked bare and harsh.

It hadn't fooled Teréza, though. I sighed.

"You guys should buy a new house," William said. "No offense."

I laughed. "It's just the wards that make it look that way," I said. "It's actually really well kept up. You know that."

William gave me the sure-if-you-say-so nod.

After fluffing my scarf closer around my neck, I thanked William for the ride, and really, for interceding between Mátyás and me.

Before I shut the door, William leaned across the seat to ask, "What do you think Sebastian is going to do when he finds Teréza? Do you think he'll really kill her?"

"I really don't know," I said. "I hope not. He loved her once, and I think he still does. But I'll tell you, having seen the state she's in, it might be a mercy."

"Oh." William's expression paled a little, but he nodded. "Take care," he said. "Keep warm."

I waved to his retreating taillights.

The moon shone overhead, and I could see the bright pin-point of light that was Mars nearby. The sky was clear and dark. The Milky Way twinkled in a broad, hazy swath overhead. Lilith expanded the stillness in me until I could feel myself becoming one with the universe . . . and, of course, that's when I felt an icy hand grip my shoulder.

Fourth Aspect: Opposition

KEY WORDS:

Overstimulation, Dissonance

Clenching my hand into a fist, I swung around full force. Lilith added her strength to my momentum, and we sucker punched Parrish right in the gut. By the time I recognized him, it was too late to pull back. Parrish landed hard on his ass in the driveway, fifteen feet away.

I stared in shock of recognition, while Parrish flailed around on the ground, his boots unable to gain purchase on the slick surface. Finally, I thought to walk over and offer him a hand. "Parrish? Are you all right?"

Recovering his dignity, he quickly got to his feet. Despite the minus-degree windchill, Parrish's only nod to the weather was a leather biker jacket. He didn't even bother to zip it. Underneath was a thin cotton T-shirt and faded blue jeans. If it wasn't for the ice that frosted the edges of his shoulder-length auburn hair, you'd have thought he was out for a summer buzz around the lake on his motorcycle.

"Your skills as a pugilist have improved since we last met," he noted, rubbing the spot on his abdomen where I'd bashed him.

"Lilith," I said, flexing my hands inside my wool mittens. I expected to feel the beginnings of bruises on my knuckles, but there was nothing beyond a pleasant warm buzz just under my skin. "Were your ears burning?" I asked him. "William and I were just talking about you. And, oh, are you stalking me or something? What are you doing here at this time of night?"

He laughed. "At least some things haven't changed. You're still as effervescent as ever, I see."

"And you're still evasive as ever," I said, though I smiled.

"Are you going to invite me in?" Parrish asked theatrically, indicating Sebastian's house.

"Absolutely not," I said. "Besides, it's still Sebastian's. He'd have to do the honors. And, anyway, Benjamin the attack ghost would probably kill you on principle."

"Then I'd best make this quick." He took my mittened hand in his and cleared his throat. "You're making a mistake. No one will ever love you as I do."

I smiled. "I know," I said quite sincerely. "You'd sacrifice your life for me."

"Time and time again," he said with a nod.

"I love you," I admitted, "but we'd never make it together— not long-term. The things I love about you are also the things that'd break us up in the end." I'd had a long time to think about all this while Parrish was gone. Parrish was the kind of man that instantly turned me on: a bad boy. He was strong, impulsive, and more than a little bit crazy. "And even if you could somehow change to suit me, well, then you'd lose the essential you-ness I adore. We'd never work."

Parrish leaned down and kissed me. His lips were as cold as ice. "I had to try," he said. "One last time."

My body heated to his touch, but my toes slowly went numb in the cold. Even so, I held Parrish's hand and looked deeply into his storm gray eyes. "If you want the ring back, I'll understand."

"No," he said. "I want you to keep it. Besides, there's no one else for me."

Aw. A tear welled in my eye, and I was completely ready to risk Sebastian's wrath and try inviting Parrish in, when I heard the moaning.

Teréza stood about fifty feet away, swaying in the ankle-deep snow piled near the edge of the road. "Oh, God," I murmured.

"What in heaven's name is that?" Parrish asked. His head moved in sympathy to her rocking, and I was starting to get seasick watching the both of them.

"A vampire zombie. A vambie? A zompire? Anyway, it's Teréza, Sebastian's . . . well, Mátyás's mom."

"Who's Mátyás?"

"Sebastian's son."

"Ah, I see." After a moment's consideration, Parrish added, "The man you prefer comes with a surprising number of extraneous family members."

Parrish had a point, and I was definitely starting to see the downside of that.

Teréza lurched forward.

Like a gentleman, Parrish put his body between Teréza and me. She hissed at him, like something out of a B movie.

Parrish frowned down at her, his arms crossed in front of his chest. "She seems rather harmless," he noted, as she continued to make booga-booga noises at him.

I cowered helplessly behind his back. I peeped around his torso, and Teréza lunged at me. Her fingernails raked my cheeks.

Parrish used that super-ninja speed of his to grab her wrist in his hand. She squeaked. He held her firmly, casually. "Your vambie is unimpressive," he said.

Teréza made a few swipes at me, but Parrish deftly kept her from reaching me.

"Don't underestimate her," I said. "She's a witch."

As if in response to my words, Parrish let go of her like his hand was on fire. Actually, it was. Bright whitish yellow flames leaped from his fingers and palm. He stared at it, horrified. I could smell burning flesh.

Teréza made a grab for me, but I ducked. Grabbing a handful of snow in my mitten, I quickly pressed it into Parrish's hand.

Teréza snarled, as she came around again for another attack. I watched her warily as I continued to dump snow on Parrish's still-burning hand. Our eyes met. I thought Teréza was going to make another jump at me, but she held her fingernails up to her lips and licked them, as though licking my blood from her fingers. Then she blew me a kiss.

Lilith sparkled under my skin and began to rise in defense—to what, I wasn't sure. I felt myself begin to surrender to Lilith's control. But just before I lost consciousness, Teréza winked. A moment later, she disappeared.

I almost got magical whiplash from the speed at which Lilith retreated back into me. I turned my attention back to Parrish. The skin on his hand had puckered and swelled. My astute medical opinion was, "That looks bad."

"Hurts like a sonuvabitch, too," Parrish said with a weak smile. I could tell it really did pain him.

Hospital was out of the question. The guy was a two-hundred-year-old vampire. They wouldn't know what to do with his physiology. "Will it get better? I mean, like, soon?"

He shook his head. "Takes time."

"Should we wrap it or something?"

"That would be helpful," he agreed.

So I needed to get him into the farmhouse. Problem was, Benjamin the killer ghost would fricassee another vampire in Sebastian's house.

"Hang on," I said. I ran up the drive to the door. I put my hand on the ward and opened the door with my key. Stepping over the threshold, I felt the heat of the interior on my cheeks. "Benjamin?" I called softly. "I need to let another vampire in for a moment. He's a friend, he . . ."

The lights flickered.

"It'll only be for a second."

A lamp tipped over and smashed onto the floor.

"Okay, I'll just get what I need." I ran upstairs to the bathroom. In the cabinet, I found some gauze and medical tape. I grabbed them, even as I felt a cold breath at my neck. "He was burned," I told Benjamin. "By Teréza."

The atmosphere changed instantly. The cold at my neck

disappeared and was replaced by a pleasant warmth. I got the sense Parrish would be welcome. Apparently Benjamin disliked Teréza more than the idea of another vampire.

"Should I go get him? Bring him in?"

Nothing broke or flickered. That seemed like a good sign. I grabbed the stuff and bounded down the stairs.

"I think you can come in," I told Parrish.

Parrish appeared at the door using that freaky undead speed again. "Shouldn't you be more formal?"

"Like you really need that," I muttered. I knew he didn't. Previously, he had a tendency to break into my apartment on a regular basis. "Please come in, Daniel Parrish," I said. "But only tonight."

He snorted, "A caveat, I see."

"Like any of it matters," I said with a roll of my eyes. "You don't really need an invite. Do you?"

Parrish gave me an I'll-never-tell-you smile. Cradling his hand, he stepped in the door. He looked around the room slowly, no doubt taking in the multitude of books and expensive furniture. "Well," he sniffed, plopping himself down on the suede sofa. "Isn't this cozy?"

Yeah, he was jealous. He might have the accent, but Parrish was never aristocracy. In life, he had been a carriage robber, a highwayman. I could almost see the dollar signs in his eyes as his gaze calculated the value of each object in the room. The books must have baffled him. I'm not sure Parrish had ever learned to read beyond a sixth grade level, if that.

Barney, who had always been fond of Parrish, came out from wherever she'd been hiding and plopped herself down in his lap. He reached down with his uninjured hand to pet her. She purred loudly.

Benjamin rustled the curtains. He might have decided to let Parrish stay, but apparently he wanted me to know that if Barney liked Parrish, he most certainly did not. I shook my head at the absurdity of the ghost's rivalry with my cat. "Let me see your hand," I said to Parrish.

Parrish offered me his hand. The skin of his fingers and palms had puffed up and seemed weepy and wet. His hand was an angry red mess. "I'm afraid to touch it," I said.

The door opened. Cold air rushed in, and I looked up to see Sebastian frowning at the tableau of me kneeling before Parrish. I stood up quickly, despite how guilty it made me look. Before Sebastian could even open his mouth, I said, "I can explain."

Sebastian's eyes strayed to the shards of broken vase on the rug, and his frown deepened. His jaw flexed, but he turned to hang up his coat. "Okay," he said.

"Teréza was here," I said. Touching my cheek where Teréza's fingernails had scratched, I continued quickly. "She attacked me and burned Parrish with her magic."

"It's true," Parrish said, standing up. "I'd come to congratulate you both on your upcoming nuptials."

"I'll bet you had," Sebastian's voice was tight with anger.

Parrish ignored his tone. Though he closed it, Sebastian stood at the door with snow melting on his boots. I hadn't moved either. I held the gauze and tape outstretched in my hands as if to say, "Here's proof my intentions were innocent." Parrish was the only one of us who managed to look the least bit comfortable. Though he cradled his injured hand close to his chest, the other stroked Barney. She stood on the arm of the couch and bumped her cheek against his knuckles, undaunted after having been dumped off his lap when he'd stood up suddenly.

"The zompire is quite the creation," Parrish said. "Yours, I take it?"

"The what?" Sebastian said, looking to me for explanation.

I was about to answer, when Parrish said, "Zompire. Or do you prefer vambie?" A bit of an evil smile quirked at the edge of Parrish's lips as he spoke. "I take it you had some trouble turning that one?"

"It's no joking matter," Sebastian snapped.

"No, I imagine not," Parrish said. "An undead wife makes marriage a bit complicated, doesn't it?"

"That's none of your business," Sebastian said, taking a step forward. "And we were never married."

"Ah, so the child is a bastard," Parrish said casually, as though he were remarking on the color of the curtains.

Sebastian momentarily started, as though slapped, but then quickly regained his composure enough to offer a wry smile that implied he might be inclined to agree, but he wasn't willing to give Parrish the point. "Keep my family out of this," he said. "You're uninvited, nightwalker. I suggest you leave."

I cleared my throat. "Uh, actually, technically I invited him in." Sebastian's face tightened as though he'd suddenly contracted a headache. I moved to quickly take Sebastian's hand. "Look, honey, Parrish just needs to bandage his hand. Then he's leaving."

Parrish flashed me a hurt expression as if I'd all but chucked him out into the snow on the spot. I gave him the what-did-you-want-me-to-say? eyebrow quirk in return.

Sebastian glanced at Parrish's wound. "It looks bad. I served as a medic in World War Two," he said, taking the bandages and tape from me. "I'll dress it for you."

Parrish offered his hand, though there was a trace of sarcasm in his tone as he said, "You're a true gentleman, sir."

Sebastian snorted but gently inspected the burn. Slowly, carefully, he wrapped it in a clean bandage. "You're a fool to come here," he said, as he taped off a very neat turn of gauze. "You have no claim to Garnet."

"Yet your heart is divided," he said quietly as he admired Sebastian's ministrations.

"No, it's not," Sebastian said, looking directly at me.

The intensity of Sebastian's look made my heart flutter. Despite myself, I doubted him a little. I knew Sebastian loved me, but Teréza was more than just some past fling. She was his son's mother.

Parrish's nod was curt. "I see. Well, I look forward to the ceremony. I wish you both well." He tipped an imaginary hat and made his way to the door. With his hand on the knob, he paused. Over his shoulder, Parrish said, "A medic in the Second World War? Hitler was an Austrian, too, wasn't he?"

Sebastian stiffened, and his eyes narrowed. "I believe you were leaving."

Parrish nodded knowingly. "Well, then, good night to you both."

* * *

Sebastian was agitated the rest of the night. Over a midnight snack of peppermint ice cream with hot fudge, I told him all the gory details of my encounter with Teréza. He nodded absently as he cleared the dishes. In bed, after we'd changed and done all our settling in rituals, he finally said, "I want you to know I was never a Nazi."

"I never thought you were, Sebastian," I said quite honestly. In fact, I tended to forget that Sebastian had actually lived through things I'd only skimmed over in my high school history textbook.

"I fought in Africa with Rommel."

I blinked at him.

"The Desert Fox," he tried.

It still wasn't ringing any bells. I stretched my knowledge of the events of World War Two, until I had a vague inkling. "That would make you on the wrong side, wouldn't it? I thought you just said . . ."

"Things are more obvious in hindsight," he said, perching on the edge of the bed. He wore blue and green flannel pajama bottoms. I could see the scar from the sword that pierced his heart. "If I had known . . ." He shook his head. "I thought . . . the economy, you see. National pride . . . I never saw. . . . No. No. There are no excuses."

I stood there with my mouth agape; I couldn't quite believe what I was hearing.

"Do you want me to sleep on the couch?"

"No," I said reflexively. "I will." I grabbed a pillow.

As I passed him on my way out, without looking up, he said, "What have you done about Guantánamo or Abu Ghraib, eh? What horrors have you allowed?"

"That's different," I said.

"Is it? Only time will tell."

I hated to admit he had a point. "I'm still sleeping on the couch."

"And I'll be here in the morning."

Turns out, Sebastian didn't have to wait until morning for me to forgive him. The couch has never been terribly comfortable, and the temperature dropped in the middle of night, making the skimpy blanket I'd dragged out of the hall closet completely useless. Plus I could feel Benjamin watching me. I woke up at one point when he was stroking my hair. I'd been dreaming about some strange combination of the Inquisition and the Nazis. When I startled awake at Benjamin's touch, I realized this whole issue was so terribly complicated even my subconscious couldn't untangle it. I believed Sebastian when he said he wasn't involved in Nazi politics, but it was hard to jibe the idea of him fighting for Hitler with the man I knew.

I rubbed my face. I wasn't going to resolve my feelings about it tonight. I might as well sleep in the comfortable bed.

The stairs creaked as I climbed them, and the blanket I'd wrapped around my shoulders trailed behind me like the train of a wedding dress. Benjamin followed behind, making the floorboards pop a second time in echo. Pale squares of moonlight checkered the hall.

On the bed in our room, Sebastian's body stretched under the covers at an awkward angle. He lay completely still. He looked dead. Other vampires slept in coffins or underground, but Sebastian lay exactly as he'd fallen in battle, his head twisted to the side and his hands cradling the spot where he'd been run through by the enemy's sword. It was as though he died again every night.

Barney had curled up in the crook of one of his arms. Her chin rested on his elbow.

When I started sleeping over, I wondered if I'd ever get used to seeing him that way. I crawled in my side and spooned up against his partially arched back as I always did. When he was like this, his body was heavy and stiff, but I'd found I could move him a little with some determination. So I shifted him onto his side and held on tight. It seemed to me that, even though he slept at night like I did, this was the time when Sebastian was at his most vulnerable. I tried to shield as much of his body with my own as I could. After tucking the extra blanket around us without disturbing the cat, I fell asleep.

Sometime after two A.M. **I heard Mátyás come in.** I used to be a sound sleeper, but ever since Benjamin started paying extra attention to me at night, I found even the slightest thing woke me. I slid out of bed and padded down the stairs with the blanket around my shoulders.

He was getting bedding from the linen closet when I came up to him. He jumped when I cleared my throat.

"Jesus, Garnet, I thought you were Benjamin!"

I put my hands on my hips. "Your mother set Parrish's hand on fire. She scratched me. This is getting ridiculous. Call her off." I almost added: "Oh, and did you know your dad fought for Hilter?" But then I thought better of it. I needed to keep focused on Teréza.

I needn't have worried. He completely ignored me anyway. He tucked a pillow under his arm. "Hey," he said, pointing. "You've got my favorite blanket. Give that back."

"What are you hoping to gain by siccing her on us?" I asked, even as I handed over the blanket.

Mátyás absently folded the blanket over his arm and then set it on the couch. He moved over to the fireplace and began setting up the makings of a fire.

Exasperated, I followed behind. I watched as he crumpled up some newspaper to tuck under a pile of sticks. "You can't seriously hope that Sebastian will abandon me in favor of your mother. We're getting married in two weeks. The invitations have been sent. The food is ordered."

Placing a heavy, seasoned log on top of the paper and kindling, he struck a match from the box Sebastian kept on the mantel. The paper caught immediately. The sticks crackled. Mátyás crouched in front of the fire, watching it burn. "She needs him more than you do," he said.

I frowned at his back. "What do you think Sebastian can do for her? Isn't it his fault she's the way she is?"

Using the blackened steel poker from the stand, Mátyás jabbed at the log. Sparks flew. "She needs a Sire," he said. "She needs guidance. She needs someone to teach her how to be what she's become."

Despite myself, I understood. From what Sebastian and Parrish have told me, I knew becoming a vampire wasn't an easy transition. There was that whole life-after-life thing, and I couldn't even begin to imagine how to deal with procuring victims, not to mention the fact that Teréza had the handicap of major culture shock having been functionally dead for a hundred-plus years. I nodded. "Yeah, I'm sure she does need help to adjust," I said. "He should be there for her."

Mátyás turned to look at me.

"What?" I asked, seeing his shocked expression. "Is it such a surprise I'm sympathetic?"

He laughed. "Actually, it is."

"Well, get over it," I said. "I don't have a problem with Sebastian wanting or even *needing* to help Teréza learn how to function as a vampire. What I have a problem with is her trying to kill him. And me. And setting Parrish's hand on fire. Are you sure she's—well, up for all this? I mean, she was dead a long time. That might have affected her emotional state a little bit, don't you think?"

Mátyás dropped his smile. "She's fine. She's just having a little trouble adjusting."

Hello, denial. "Oh," I said, because as someone well-practiced with denial, I knew that there wasn't much else I could really say. "Okay."

"She'll be fine," he insisted as he put the grate in front of the now-roaring fire. "If Papa would just spend some time with her, everything would be all right."

Sure it would, I thought, after Teréza kills us all. But I didn't say that. Instead, I put a hand on Mátyás's shoulder. He stiffened under my touch, but I gave him a quick squeeze before dropping my hand. "Everything is mostly taken care of for the wedding," I said. "I don't see why Sebastian couldn't spend some time with Teréza. You know, see if there's anything he can do. I'll talk to him about it in the morning."

It actually sounded like a good idea. I mean, who's to say it wouldn't help her? Unlike Parrish, Sebastian seemed to be able to hold his own against her. He had the advantage of blood magic or whatever his hold was over her. Plus, as long as nothing else with the wedding fell apart, it wasn't like there was that much to do at this point. I'd been feeling as though Teréza cursed me, but maybe I was being silly and superstitious about that. And even so, I could always do a spell of protection to ward off any negative energy she might be sending. Heck, that was probably a good idea anyway.

Mátyás looked at me as though he wasn't quite sure he believed this sudden burst of generosity, so I added, "Seriously, Mátyás. I'll talk to him."

"Okay," he said, as he stood up. "I guess that's a start."

"Where is Teréza now?"

He shook his head and gave a rueful laugh. "I told you before: I don't know where she goes."

"Don't you have a safe house for her or anything?"

"Yes, there's a place she's supposed to go, but my mother has been somewhat"—he searched for the right word for a moment, before deciding on—"unpredictable, lately."

Unpredictable? Try crazy. But I just nodded. "Will she freeze? Outside, I mean? Is her physiology like Sebastian's? She's going to be okay out on her own, right?"

"Are you honestly worried about her?"

I shrugged. I couldn't exactly tell Mátyás that I was probably more concerned that Parrish would run into Teréza again and get completely torched, so I said, "Sebastian cares for her," I said. "He loved . . . loves her. You and I both know that."

Mátyás squinted at me. "You're so understanding."

"Weird, isn't it?" I laughed. Then I sighed. "Seriously, it's not like I don't realize Sebastian and Teréza have history," I said. "There's not much I can do about that, is there?"

"No," he agreed, turning away to fluff up his pillow. I wasn't sure, but I thought he sounded a bit hostile again. With a sniff, he added, "The role of supportive wife suits you."

He didn't mean it as a compliment, I could tell. I had no idea what I'd said to piss him off. "Yeah," I said, "fuck you too," with as much sarcasm as I could, and stomped back upstairs to bed.

When I got back upstairs, Sebastian was awake. He sat propped up against the headboard. His long hair spilled loosely around his face. "Mátyás is back?"

I nodded. "And in fine form. He seems to think the only thing wrong with Teréza is that she's in desperate need of vampire education from you."

He raked his fingers through his hair, "That would be great if I could find her. She seems much more interested in you."

I sat at the foot of bed. A thin layer of ice crusted the inside edges of the windows. Frost laced the rest of the glass. "Yeah." I nodded, frowning. "Although she clearly wants to hurt you too."

"True enough." He smiled grimly.

"I think I want to ask the coven to help do a protection spell," I said.

"What, like for a bachelorette party?"

I laughed. "That's a good idea, actually—a spell and a party. Works for me."

Somehow I felt like all the tension I'd been carrying around with me since dinner with my folks melted away with our laughter. My shoulders relaxed. "Hell of a day, huh?" I asked.

"Come here," he said patting the spot in front of him. I scootched forward. He made the "turn around" motion with his finger. I obeyed.

Sebastian began to massage my neck. His touch was firm and confident. I could feel the stress melting under his fingertips. I made appreciative grunts and ahhhs.

"You should take your shirt off," he said. "Then I could do your whole back."

Like I could resist that offer? "Let me get the oil from the bathroom," I said.

I quickly dashed to the cabinet and pulled out some massage oil I'd bought at Soap Opera, my favorite bath and body shop on State Street. They let you design your own scents, and I'd had them concoct the perfect mixture for me that reminded me of Sebastian. It had a bit of cinnamon and musk. I grabbed the bottle and hurried back to the bedroom.

I tossed the bottle to Sebastian. He caught it deftly. I stripped off my shirt. Normally, I would tease Sebastian a little with the sight of my naked body, but this was Wisconsin in the winter. I plopped myself facedown on the bed and pulled the comforter around my sides. Sebastian laughed at my lack of ceremony and straddled my butt.

I felt myself getting aroused simply from the pressure of his body pressing against my backside. I heard him uncork the bottle of oil and shivered in anticipation. After rubbing the oil between his hands to warm it, his palms glided across my naked back. I sighed deeply. Encouraged, he began rubbing my shoulder blades in slow, steady circles. I groaned as I heard my muscles pop beneath his ministrations. The smell of the scented oil relaxed me even deeper. A warm tingle spread along my body to settle deep between my thighs.

"Have I told you how much I love you?" I murmured into the pillow.

"It's funny how you always say that when I'm giving you a massage," he teased, leaning down to playfully kiss my ear. His breath tickled, and my eyelids quivered in response.

I heard him chuckle low, predator-like.

"What's funny is how your massages always lead to sex," I reminded him.

"Yeah," he said, running his fingers up my rib cage in a way that made me shudder uncontrollably. "Funny thing."

He kissed the spot between my shoulder blades. Sitting up once again, his hands continued to smooth and work my body. I could feel him getting aroused as well, which only made me want him more.

I swiveled my hips, and he lifted himself so I could turn to face him. Pouring another drop of oil into his hands, he cupped my breasts.

Arching my back, I allowed him full access. His palms were slick with oil and slid easily across my breasts to my nipples. Sebastian leaned down and kissed my lips. His mouth covered mine, firm and hungry. My tongue darted into his mouth.

Sebastian was a good kisser. I liked the way he never hurried through a kiss. He lingered over every contour of my mouth and tongue. Somehow he made every kiss feel like a first.

As Sebastian gently squeezed my breasts, I suddenly wanted much more than kissing. My nipples hardened, sending a spike of pleasure all the way to my core. I felt myself growing moist.

I ran my palms over the flat planes of his chest. I loved the feel of his taut stomach. He didn't have the six-pack abs of someone who lifted weights to intentionally sculpt his body, but he was hard from a life lived on the sword's edge. It was damn sexy.

And suddenly kind of awkward, because it reminded me how long Sebastian had been alive.

That made me think of Teréza.

Had he smiled possessively like that when they'd had sex? Had she wriggled out of her sweatpants like I was doing? Of course they didn't have sweatpants back then, but I wondered if his fingers had stroked her inner thigh the same . . . Oh!

I let out a moan. The sheets twisted in my fingers. Sebastian kissed my breasts, licking at the oil. I forgot about everything except his tongue and hands.

Frantically, I grasped for the drawstrings of his pajama bottoms. He was ready, and so was I. He glided into me easily. Even after all the times we've found ourselves in this position, I reveled in how perfectly we fit together. I wrapped my arms around his shoulders and pulled him closer, deeper. We moved together, faster and faster, until we came together in a rush. Sweaty and satisfied, I kissed Sebastian on the mouth. "I can't wait to be married to you."

He smiled, and I noticed his fangs.

"Oh," I said. "We forgot to . . ."

"It's okay," he said.

I touched his cheek, and he leaned into my hand. "No," I said. "I want to."

Leaning back on the bed, I offered my throat. The sweat on my body began to dry, and the room felt chilly. I shivered from cold and anticipation.

Sebastian laughed low. "You're cold," he said, pulling the comforter up over me. "And, uh, if I bit your neck, I'd probably kill you."

I blushed all the way to my ears. It's not that I was paying that much attention when Sebastian bit me during sex; my mind was usually on other things. "I knew that," I said, with a little shrug.

He smiled and ran a finger along my shoulder. Leaning in, he nipped my exposed flesh. Then, moving downward an inch, he took another light bite. Despite everything we'd just finished, I felt my body responding instantly. "I thought I'd just go on a little exploratory mission," he said.

"Uh, um, yeah," I said as encouragingly as I could. "Nice. Yes."

Sebastian slowly pulled the comforter down, as he moved on to my stomach. I twitched and moaned with every nibble. It didn't take long before I started begging Sebastian to bite and bite hard.

When he finally sank his teeth into a tender spot on my inner thigh, I came again.

* * *

I woke up to the sound of the phone ringing. My hand groped the bedside tabletop, trying to find the receiver. I mumbled a "Hello," while squinting at the numbers on the alarm clock. I was disappointed to discover it wasn't nearly as early as it felt. Someone was talking, so I had to say, "What?"

It was the bakery. Their cake maker quit. No one else at the store had training. They were very sorry. I could try the other place across town.

"But," I said, "you're the only place in town that does organic, vegan, locally produced . . ." Words failed me. I couldn't believe this was happening again.

They were sorry; a lot of people were inconvenienced.

I thanked them for letting me know. With trembling fingers, I returned the receiver to its cradle. "Well, that sucks," I said to Sebastian's sleeping form. "Now we have no cake to go with the polka band and the pink taffeta."

He murmured in his sleep. I gave him a kiss on the head, but it didn't rouse him. I considered poking him until he got up, but he looked so peaceful lying there, and besides, I had other things to do, not the least of which was go to work. Getting up made the springs creak, and Sebastian grunted an "I love you."

"I love you too," I whispered. Grabbing some clothes, I headed off to the bathroom to dress and get ready.

In the kitchen, Mátyás nursed a cup of coffee and stared, bleary-eyed, at the *New York Times'* front page. He hadn't shaved, and his hair hung over his eyes. The way he continued to focus on the paper, I thought for a second something spectacular must have happened overnight. But a peep over his shoulder on the way to the coffeemaker revealed nothing more than the typical unrest in the Middle East.

"You look rougher than usual," I said, reaching for my favorite mug. It was hand thrown and had a nearly rude depiction of a peach on it. That's not what I liked about it, though. I appreciated its size. The cup was fat and deep. I could put almost two regular cups inside. "Didn't sleep well?"

"You two could learn to be quieter."

I blushed but tried to hide it behind my cup. I leaned against the counter near the sink. Once I thought I could look him steadily in the eye, I said, "You could move out."

He snorted. I waited for some kind of retort, but instead he flipped to the next page.

Barney twined her girth around my leg. A plaintive meow reminded me that she had not yet been served her breakfast. I shook some kibbles into her bowl and refreshed her water. As I was setting the bowl down, I saw it. On the Welcome Kitty mat lay the dead and decapitated form of a brown mouse. "Oh gross," I moaned in disgust.

Barney chirped and purred happily as she munched her food.

"Kind of late in the season for that," Mátyás said, as I wrapped the carcass in huge wad of paper towels. I didn't reply. I was too busy cursing my cat under my breath and stomping into the pair of boots I left by the back door. I had to take the mouse corpse out to the bins in the back. I didn't want it stinking up the kitchen garbage.

I didn't bother with a coat. The shock of the cold nipped

my nose. Where water had splashed my hair while I washed my face, ice crystals began to form. The sky had turned a dusty gray, anticipating the sunrise. The bare trees were stark silhouettes. Everything was shrouded in a predawn hush.

I hurried down the icy steps and across the yard to the barn. The big plastic bins were lined up against the far wall. My hands were freezing as I tossed the paper coffin into the first one. As I slipped and slid back toward the warmth of the house, movement caught my eye. A crack between the barn doors revealed the passing of a shadow. There was something—or someone—in the barn. Despite the acreage, Sebastian didn't keep any animals. The barn was mostly filled with his classic cars and the rusty farm implements left behind by previous tenants.

I didn't know why it never occurred to me before. The barn made a perfect hiding place for someone impervious to the weather but who needed protection from the sun. I paused with that thought. Was Teréza more of a vampire now that she was awake? Could this be why Mátyás was nervous about the idea of Sebastian finding his mother? Was she right under our noses this whole time?

Was Mátyás keeping his mother in the barn?

I thought I'd better take a closer look in the barn just to be certain, but then I saw the parted curtain in the kitchen. Mátyás was watching me. I waved, and the lace fell quickly back into place. He knew I knew.

The aluminum door handle was frigid on my exposed skin, and the sudden warmth from the kitchen brought tears to my eyes. Mátyás stood by the stove with his arms crossed defensively in front of his chest. His set expression told me he was ready for my arguments.

Just then Sebastian came strolling into the kitchen with a cheery, "Morning all."

He crossed right between us, making a beeline for the coffee. Mátyás and I stayed locked in a stare.

After filling his cup, Sebastian turned to regard both of us. He gave me a quick smile and offered me my cup, which I'd left on the counter. The porcelain seared my skin. "Business as usual, I see," he said drily. "Although it seems early in the game to be at stony silence. Don't we usually save that for Saturday afternoons?"

I felt like I should say something about Teréza. As I opened my mouth, Mátyás's eyes betrayed a tiny hint of fear. I frowned. Didn't he just tell me last night he wanted Sebastian to talk to her? What was with the look? Was he still afraid Sebastian would actually kill Teréza?

"Seriously, the fight can't be that bad. I only took a fifteen-minute shower."

I shrugged. "Can you give me a ride?"

Mátyás looked away, still clearly nervous. He opened the cupboard and rummaged through the cereal boxes.

Sebastian frowned at him and then at me. "Yeah, okay."

Sebastian started up the car. We sat for a moment as our breaths fogged up the inside. "All right, what's going on?" he asked, as he took the scraper out from under his seat.

After taking the other one from the glove box, I met him outside. He started removing the frost from his side of the windshield. I worked on mine. "I'm pretty sure Teréza is living in the barn," I said in a hushed voice with a glance over my shoulder.

I expected swearing, maybe some banging of fists on the hood of the car, or some other eruption of emotion. Instead, Sebastian just nodded. He continued sliding the scraper over the glass. Peels of frost curled up under the plastic blade. "Yeah, makes sense. I should have thought of that."

"Are you okay with that? I mean what do you plan to do about it?"

"I'm not sure." He chewed his lip. We'd worked our way around the car to the rear window. Sebastian's side was meticulously clean; mine had uneven stripes on the window.

Once the windows were clear, we got back in the car. The interior had warmed some. I shook off the cold with an exaggerated shiver and rubbed my gloved hands together, trying to warm up my fingertips, which had gotten chilled. The sunlight glared brilliantly, glinting off fields of ice.

"She tried to kill us both," Sebastian said. "Do you really think talking will help?"

"Don't you have to try? She's his mom." I buckled myself in as he pulled the car out of the driveway.

He nodded. He sounded a little defeated as he said, "I know."

Exhaust-blackened crust covered the snow piles on either side of the highway. A murder of crows burst into noisy flight as we passed a raccoon carcass on the side of the road.

"I think you should wait," I said. "Let me gather the coven first. We'll do our spell of protection and make sure to include you."

"Maybe you could ask the Goddess for some guidance," he said. I thought he sounded tired.

"You could try praying."

"I don't believe in the Goddess," he said.

"I wasn't suggesting that," I said.

He glanced at me briefly. "I haven't prayed to . . . not since the excommunication."

"I've been thinking. If the exorcism drove out Teréza's illness—not her vampirism—well, what if . . . What if you could be a Catholic again?"

He shook his head. "I still am Catholic. I'm just excommunicated."

"You *know* what I mean."

Sebastian's jaw twitched. He reached for the sunglasses he always kept in the cup holder, and his lips were tight. I'd been with Sebastian long enough to know what that meant: time to change the subject.

I shielded my eyes as we turned eastward, directly into the sun. I felt like I must look like Nosferatu in that old, black-and-white movie. How ironic then that I sat next to a real vampire who looked relatively comfortable in the harsh light.

"You know what's weird?" I said, grateful that we'd gotten into the city, and the buildings and tall trees now occasionally blocked out the glare. "It seemed to me that Teréza was slinking off to hide this morning. Given that she's your progeny, shouldn't she be able to daywalk?"

Sebastian's frown deepened. "What are you suggesting?"

"Well, you always told me that the change didn't work, and Mátyás is pretty desperate to have his mom back. Vampires have that mutant healing factor. Maybe he thought if someone else turned her, you know, more-or-less 'all the way,' she'd get better, you know, faster."

"So you think the pope healed her illness, but some other vampire got her up and walking, as it were?" His knuckles flexed on the steering wheel.

"It makes sense, doesn't it?"

Sebastian's jaw clenched. Clearly, he didn't like the idea. "I suppose it does."

"I'm just saying it's not unlike Mátyás to hedge his bets."

"She responded to my spell well enough," Sebastian muttered under his breath.

"What do you mean?" I asked. "What difference does that make?"

"I was just thinking that if Teréza has another Blood Sire, then my power over her would be diluted. That would explain why she could try to kill me at all, I suppose."

"I don't know anything about this whole Blood Sire thing. Parrish would hardly talk about his."

"Well, I don't have one," Sebastian reminded me. "I'm just making guesses."

"But you knew a spell over her would work. How did you know?"

Sebastian gave me a sidelong glance through his sunglasses. "I've been around for a thousand years. You think I never met another vampire in all that time?"

"So you do know something," I said. A stand of oak trees that had firmly held on to bronzed leaves blocked the sunlight momentarily.

"Not really. The vampire I met was very . . . cagey about

her traditions. Plus it turns out vampires are very territorial. She saw me as a threat."

"She?" I asked. I knew Parrish's Sire was actually a lady, but I had no idea Sebastian had ever met one. I was feeling a little jealous.

Sebastian nodded; not picking up on the subtext, he stared at the road. "I learned, though, that one thing Hollywood got right was that a vampire increases in power the more progeny they have. It's because they have power over the other person—the power of life and death."

"So, what are you saying? A Blood Sire can kill their progeny, what, with a stern glance?"

Sebastian laughed. "No, by breaking the bond with a spell."

"Can you break with Teréza?"

"Didn't you hear what I said?" he asked sharply. "If I did that, it'd kill her."

"Oh." And that would be bad because? "But there's another vampire's mark on her," I pointed out.

Sebastian glared at me. "It's too risky."

I nodded. I was right about Sebastian. He still cared enough about her not to want to hurt her. Perhaps I should try Mátyás's tack. "Well, maybe if we can find this other Sire, we can enlist their help. Mátyás seems to think all she needs is some direction."

"If that's even the case." Sebastian reminded me, as he adjusted his sunglasses. "No, Teréza's problem is that she's been buried too long."

"Still, maybe this other Sire could, you know, take her under his wing."

"His?" Sebastian asked. "You have a reason to think it's a man?"

Unfortunately, I could think of one likely suspect right away, one that was known to trade his bites for hard, cold cash.

It didn't take long for Sebastian to come to the same conclusion. "If it's that Daniel Parrish, he's going to wish he'd stayed dead."

Fifth Aspect: Semiquintile

KEY WORDS:

Difficult, Blocked

At the curb, I gave my dark and brooding vampire a quick kiss good-bye. He hardly noticed me for the bloody murder in his eyes. I suspected he was going to spend the morning hunting down people who might know where Parrish slept during the day.

My only comfort was that I knew the type that Parrish attracted as ghouls; they tended toward fierce loyalty. Not only that, but I was sure any sort of bullying of another vamp's ghouls would get Sebastian in trouble with whatever weird, shadowy organization controlled the Suppliers' Guild. He wasn't going to get very far, but he'd be able to let off some steam on a wild-goose chase. As I watched Sebastian drive away without even a wave, I thought he might need it.

* * *

I strolled the half a block up to my store. State Street is a pedestrian mall, so Sebastian had let me off at the nearest cross street. The sky was a brilliant blue. I could see the white marble dome of the Capitol building a few blocks farther up. My breath crystallized into white puffs in the air. The tip of my nose was red by the time I saw my reflection in the door of my store.

Flipping on the lights, I went through the routines of getting the store ready for opening. I had the till counted and in place by the time William came in with two large cups of coffee from Holy Grounds.

"Froufrou drink?" he offered.

"Thanks," I said, and we clinked the tops of our plastic lids in a faux toast to our girly lattes.

"Izzy's in a bad mood," William said, sipping his drink. "I think she and Matt had a fight."

"Matt?"

"So much easier to say than Mátyás. Anyway, I heard her call him that once as a pet name."

Somehow I couldn't quite imagine Mátyás as a Matt. That sounded like someone who was the captain of the football team in high school, not some Eurotrash son of a vampire. "Did he like it?"

"He did when she said it. I haven't quite had the nerve to try it to his face for myself."

"Wise move," I said. William followed me as I went to unlock the front door and flip on the neon Open sign in the window. "What do you think their fight was about?"

"You're kidding, right? What do *you* think?"

"His mom."

William nodded. We walked back to the register and the little circular alcove that surrounded it. "Plus, I don't think Izzy likes being on the business end of you and Sebastian."

"Did she say that?" I was shocked. I never thought of myself as having a "business end," though Sebastian could be scary when he was intent on something. Still, if she spent any time at all with Mátyás she must be aware that what he and his father shared didn't exactly qualify as a functional relationship.

"She didn't say anything. She was really grouchy."

That wasn't much like Izzy. I resolved to go talk to her during my break to see what was going on. Maybe she knew something about the possibility of Parrish's involvement in the whole Teréza thing . . . or maybe I could convince her to help me try to find out.

A customer came in looking for a good book on magical journaling, and soon I was knee-deep in the usual Saturday business.

In no time, it was noon, and I'd missed my break.

I thought I might have lunch over at Holy Grounds and see about chatting with Izzy now. But when I went into the back office to file a few of the bills that had come in with the post, I saw the note I'd left myself on the calendar. Today was the day I was supposed to go down to the courthouse to pick up the application for our marriage license. I was also supposed to check in with the Unitarian minister who would be officiating our ceremony to arrange getting the programs printed up.

Izzy would have to wait.

Changing out of the Converses I kept in my bottom desk drawer, I stomped into my heavy winter boots. I wrapped a fluffy pink and metallic yarn scarf around my neck and shrugged into my down-filled ski jacket. A matching pink hat snuggled in tight over my ears. Pulling my bright orange Tigger gloves on, I was set.

I let William know that I might be a little long at lunch and then braved the outside. The temperature had warmed up to a comfortable thirty degrees, but the sky had gone gray and overcast. I could smell the promise of snow in the air, and the breeze that touched my face was heavy with moisture. Nervous flocks of house sparrows pecked at the sand and salt pebbles along the edges of the sidewalks.

The bus to the courthouse was overheated with stale, claustrophobic air, but the ride was mercifully short. I phoned Sebastian from the front steps and reminded him to meet me at the church. Getting the application involved navigating a maze of government offices and prying information out of overworked and underpaid bureaucrats. Even though the whole affair took less than a half hour, it seemed to last forever. I felt drained by the time I found myself waiting for the bus to take me to the church.

I checked my watch. Either the bus was late, or I'd just missed it. I phoned Sebastian and told him just to get started with the minister and that I'd be there as soon as I could. He offered to pick me up, but I was sure the bus was coming any minute.

He snorted. "I sure hope someone buys you a car as a wedding present. If you're not careful, it's going to be me."

"How'd it go?" I asked him. "Did you find out whether Parrish turned Teréza or not?" I stepped out into the street to see if I could see the bus.

I heard Sebastian sigh. "No one is talking, but the less people say, the more suspicious I am."

"Could you do me a favor?"

"Of course," he said. "Anything."

"Would you call the coven about tonight? Maybe pick up some munchies and beer so we can have a bit of a party?" After all the hassle at the courthouse, I really wanted to have some fun.

"Leave it to me, darling."

"Thanks," I said.

He must have heard the tension leave my body slightly, because he added, "Look, why don't you go back to the store. I can handle this program thing on my own. I know how it's all supposed to go. We've talked about all the readings and hymns a million times. Besides, if I'm unsure of anything, I can always give you a ring."

I chewed on my lip. I wasn't sure whether it would make me more or less stressed *not* to be there. Sebastian was right, though. We'd gone over the events of the day a thousand times. "Yeah, okay," I said. "I haven't had lunch yet."

I left the bus stop and considered the options for places that might have decent vegetarian fare. As I settled into a window booth at a Chipotle, I watched the bus roll by. Ah, well. Munching on a burrito full of beans and rice and all the works, I pulled a pen from my jacket. On a napkin, I started trying to salvage my upcoming wedding plans. I reconstructed my timeline of all the people I needed to check in with—catering staff, bartenders, ushers, church musicians, outfitters—and a baker for that damn cake!—anyone I could think of, and I started a list of ways to fix what had already gone wrong.

When I left the restaurant, I was feeling pretty confident that I had things in hand. I was going to get through this. That, of course, is when my mother called. She was in tears.

"It has to be your grandmother's dress," she sobbed. "It just wouldn't be right if you didn't have your grandmother's dress. I've always dreamed of seeing my baby in the dress I wore. My little baby girl," she sniffed.

Oh great Goddess. I'd had no idea. Never in my life had she ever told me about this dress. I'd seen her wedding photos, of course, but she'd never made a big deal of it then. "Mom? Where are you? Do you want to talk about it?"

"I want you to wear the dress." She was hysterical. It sounded like she'd been holding on to this emotion for the past few days, and it was all finally bursting out. "Say you'll wear the dress!"

"I'm on my way over to your hotel, okay?" My folks were staying at the Concourse, which was just off State Street, only a few blocks from my work. I said good-bye, told her I loved her, and hung up. I started booking for the bus. Just what I didn't need: a Mom meltdown!

The black-and-white photo was grainy, and it was dif-ficult to really see the details, especially since it had been folded several times to fit in her wallet. In the picture my mother looked happy in a very, very old-fashioned dress—

Victorian, even. It was high-necked, long-sleeved, beaded, with a veil and everything. I sat on the edge of the hotel bed. My mom leaned against me, arm around my shoulder. My dad sat at the desk, his stocking feet propped up on a footstool. He gave me a little I-don't-get-this-girl-stuff shrug when I gave him an appealing glance.

"It's beautiful," I said, though it was totally not my style.

My mom rubbed my shoulders. "Oh, honey. You'd look so lovely." She stopped and stared at my head. I had sticky, sweaty, hat head. My mother tsked her tongue and touched the frayed tips of my hair. "If we did something with your hair, of course."

I was about to tell her that I had all that arranged. My guy, Paul, had blocked the whole morning for me and my bridesmaids.

"I called around. Your aunt Edith knows someone here in town who can get your hair back to its natural color. Then maybe we could add some curls—a nice, light perm. What do you think, dear?" She asked my dad.

"Hmm," he said noncommittally. He'd picked up a copy of the tourist magazine and was leafing through it. "Sounds nice."

I'd look like a Goth Shirley Temple. "I already have all that taken care of, Mom."

She nodded suspiciously. "You are planning on going back to blonde, though, right? It's just that it suits your coloring so much better."

"If I tried to bleach the dye that's already in my hair, Goddess only knows what color I'd end up . . . if all my hair didn't fall out first."

My mother looked stricken.

I thought she might start to cry again, so I blurted out, "Do you think the dress can be shipped and altered in time?"

She brightened. "You'll wear it?"

"If it means that much to you," I said, "of course, I will."

William was shoveling the sidewalk as I came down the block. He had on the classic shapeless parka most Midwesterners sported half the year, but he accented it with one of those extra-long tipped elf hats that hung almost to the back of his knees. It was bright yellow with black stripes and a big pompom at the end.

"Who's minding the store?" I asked.

"I called in Slow Bob. I was starting to get worried about you."

"I'm sorry. I should have called. Family crisis." I thrust the picture at him. "My mother wants me to wear this."

He leaned up against the shovel and adjusted his glasses. "It's . . . uh, it's very nice?" He looked at me, and I shook my head.

"It's beautiful—gorgeous, even, but it's not what I wanted. I'll look ridiculous in that. I spent hundreds of dollars on a trim silver evening dress. It's modern and stylish, and it took me three months to find it."

"Oh. So, uh, can you say no or something?" He handed the picture back and tucked the shovel into the crook of his arm. Together we headed for the door.

"I don't know. My only hope is that it's so old it can't really be fitted to me." I sighed. "My mother was hysterical, though. I've never seen her like that. She's usually such a stoic Norwegian, you know?"

William nodded, but I knew he had no idea. He'd told me his family was Irish and typically loud and boisterous.

Slow Bob looked visibly relieved when we walked in. Bob was an excellent employee. Punctual, polite, and often available for short-notice shifts, he was a master alphabetizer, and I swore he read every single title we purchased. Slow Bob's biggest drawback was that he would not be hurried, regardless of how many people might be waiting. I suspected that he became so slow on the register because he really hated that particular aspect of the job, and he seized up with intense shyness whenever he was forced to deal with a customer.

William stepped into the back room to put the shovel away. Slow Bob gave me a little happy wave and retreated to the shelves. I took the spot he vacated behind the counter.

I looked at the photograph again. It wasn't so bad. At least it wasn't pink taffeta, like poor Izzy was going to be wearing if I didn't fix things.

I spent the rest of the day at work dividing my time between my duties to the store and trying to solve various personal crises. The wedding, however, remained a Gordian knot. I couldn't untangle the damage. I must have called every band and music agency listed in the phone book. Nearly everyone was either already booked or unavailable so close to the Christmas holiday. There was one called White Wedding, a Billy Idol tribute band, but I couldn't decide if that was better or worse than polka. The vision of my dad and me sharing "Rebel Yell," just didn't quite work for me. For now, we were stuck with "Roll Out the Barrel."

I got my mom on finding a cake. I thought that giving her a job might help distract her and soothe her ruffled feathers. She seemed eager, and even though I told her I'd like to try to find local and organic bakers, I also gave up any reasonable hope she could find what I wanted on such short notice. I told her I'd be happy with anything she could find, and I meant it.

As for the bridesmaid's dresses, I had a thought. After William and I fended off a brief rush of customers buying Solstice cards and Goddess-themed ornaments, I turned to him. "Say, do you still have a lot of friends in the Society for Creative Anachronism?"

He looked a little embarrassed. "Why?"

"I remember that girl you dated. She was an amazing seamstress, and she made that one awesome dress with all the beadwork in, like, two weeks."

"Lady Candice, yeah," he said with a fond smile.

"Are you on speaking terms?"

"Again with the 'why'?" he asked.

"The dresses for the bridesmaids," I said. "The order is all screwed up, remember? I've got the right dresses on back order, but, well, the way things are going, I'd like to have a backup plan."

"I think she's expensive when she does work for non-SCA people, but I'll give you her number."

"That's great, William. Thanks," I said, and then I set out on the Internet to find a possible pattern for the lady to use.

I hummed while I surfed. I felt, briefly, like things might be back on track again.

It was dark by the time we closed up the shop. Since William was coming to the bridal shower/coven meeting, he offered me a ride home.

I was turning the key in the shop's lock when a figure stepped out of the shadows. I almost did my ninja-Lilith thing again before I recognized Parrish. I showed him my keys in my fist, "You're going to have to stop doing that. I'm going to end up killing you."

He smiled devilishly. "Sorry, it's in my nature, dear Garnet. Hello, William," he said in a rather predatory tone.

William scratched his neck nervously, and said, "Uh, hi," huskily.

I stared at the two of them. It was clear there was history between them I didn't know. William watched the neon marquee light flicker on the snowdrifts without meeting Parrish's eyes; all the while Parrish stared hungrily at him.

"Uh, anyway, I'm glad you're skulking about," I said to Parrish. "I wanted to have a word with you."

"Oh?" Parrish glanced away from William long enough to give me a raised eyebrow. "What about?"

"Teréza. You did a great act the other night, pretending you didn't know her or what she was. I think you turned her."

"Why would I do that? She belongs to Sebastian, doesn't she?"

"Yeah, exactly." That was precisely the sort of thing that would motivate Parrish beyond hard, cold cash: getting one up on Sebastian.

"Uh, we're going to be late," William said quietly.

"Did Mátyás pay you to vamp her?"

Parrish tried to look offended. "You think I'd sell the Dark Gift?"

"Yes," I said with a smile. "You'd sell your own grandmother if the price was right."

Parrish laughed. "You know me well, indeed."

William tugged my sleeve. I nodded that I knew we needed to be going, but I just wanted a few more seconds with Parrish. "Did you? Did you turn Teréza?"

Parrish shook his head. "You'll have to look for another scapegoat. If I had, do you think I would have let the vambie do this?" He held up his injured hand. It looked better, though still a bit puffy. He'd removed the bandage, and the swelling was down. I thought the color looked better, but it was hard to really tell much in the harsh electric light.

"Vambie?" William asked.

"Vampire zombie," Parrish supplied. "I rather like the term. Likewise, zompire."

"I don't know," said William. "Vambie sounds like something starring Jane Fonda, you know?"

"Like *Barbarella*?" Parrish laughed. For a second, the boys seemed to bond, but then William got all scared-like and stepped back.

"We're late," he reminded me.

"We'll talk later," I said to Parrish, and I let William drag me off to his parked car.

William's car didn't start right away. The below-zero temperature made the battery sluggish. It took three tries, but the engine finally caught.

"So . . . ?" I asked after William stopped complaining about Wisconsin winters.

"So what?"

"What's with the tension between you and Parrish?"

"Nothing," he said too quickly.

This was the moment where I had to decide if I really wanted to know the details or if finding out would push this conversation into that gray area of "too much information."

I was pretty sure I understood what transpired, anyway. After discovering that vampires were real, William had gone through a Goth phase of his own, complete with lots of black clothes and eyeliner and fingernail polish. At that time Parrish had been hanging around the university crowd, doing a little blood fetish work for hire. It wasn't impossible to imagine the two of them hooking up.

Uh, except for the actual imagining part . . . William and Parrish naked together? My brain hurt.

"Did Sebastian tell you what the coven is planning on doing tonight when he called you?" I asked, allowing the subject to change.

"Not really. It was a short conversation. He said something about a hex-breaking spell, though. Is that against Teréza? Are you still convinced she's cursed you?"

I shrugged. "There are just too many things going wrong. I mean, I know every wedding has its disasters, but these just don't seem to stop." I ticked off the list on my fingers. "The dresses, the band, the cake, my mother . . . okay, that last one was probably inevitable, but—oh! Where's the application?"

I dug around frantically in the pockets of my coat.

105

William, who almost pathologically never took his eyes from the road, glanced nervously at me. "What did you lose?"

"The application for our marriage license, and I spent all afternoon going to get it too," I said, and despite myself, my voice caught a little. "Maybe I left it at work or at my parents' hotel room."

"Should I turn around?"

"No," I said, although part of me wanted him to. "It'll be okay."

I just had to keep convincing myself of that. Besides, the sooner we got to the coven meeting, the sooner I could put an end to this damn curse. Or whatever it was.

There was a line of cars in the driveway when we pulled up. I saw Griffin's beat-up station wagon with guitar cases piled in the back and Xylia's stylish yellow VW bug covered in leftist political bumper stickers. I recognized some of the others as well.

When we stepped in, I smelled chili and cornbread. My mouth watered. People sat on the couches. Xylia came over from where she'd been perched by the staircase and gave me a hug. "Congratulations."

"Really?" I was kind of surprised to hear her say that. She was totally the type to call traditional weddings "giving in to the patriarchy." Xylia had a flattop and, despite the chill, she wore a muscle shirt that showed off fairly sculpted arms and a tattoo of a gecko.

"Yeah," she said with a smile. "I'm looking forward to the wedding. I love weddings."

"You do?"

"She'll probably cry," Griffin said, throwing an arm around Xylia's narrow shoulders. Griffin had classic metalhead, Norse God looks. Long, slightly straggly blond hair framed a stubble-studded square jaw. He pretended to dab his eyes. "I'll probably cry too."

"You guys," I said with a shake of my head.

They laughed. "I do like weddings, though," Xylia said with a little shy smile that made her nose stud glitter. "There's a little traditional in me, I guess."

I nodded. I could understand. All the things I wanted when I was a dreamy tween became so important when I started planning the wedding.

"Not me," Griffin said, letting his arm drop from Xylia. "It's going to be a simple handfast in the woods for me."

"If anyone will have you," Xylia said with a poke.

"Ha. Hey, William," Griffin said. "What about you? What's your dream wedding?"

"I don't know. Don't I have to keep a girlfriend longer than six months first?"

Sebastian came out with a stack of bowls. He leaned in and said, "It's a must."

"Oh! Does that mean chili is ready?" Xylia asked, reaching for a bowl.

We all descended on the kitchen. Sebastian had whipped up both vegetarian and meat versions of his fantastic chili. There was also homemade cornbread. He'd set out all sorts of munchies as well: carrot slices, broccoli florets, sliced radishes. There were potato chips, popcorn, and pretzels in bowls all around the house. Enough food to feed an army, which was good, since I doubted there would be a crumb left after everyone was satisfied.

"So what's the plan of action?" Blythe asked after we'd licked the last of the chili from our lips. Blythe was a leggy, model-gorgeous comparative religions major at UW. She was a British national, and Sebastian found her cosmopolitan and charming. I spent a lot of time and energy trying not to hate her. After months of working with her in the coven, however, I had to grudgingly admit she made a good addition to the crew.

"I think I might have gotten cursed by Mátyás's mother," I said.

"She was dead, but she got better," William muttered next to me. Our elbows touched, and I gave him a little hey-now-none-of-that nudge in the ribs.

"So you want to turn the hex?" Blythe asked.

I nodded. "Mostly, I just want to deflect the energy."

"I don't know," William said. "I've been doing my reading, you know, and this seems like bad juju to me." William was voluntarily studying Wicca for a year and a day. He said he didn't quite feel qualified to be in the coven and proclaimed himself a novice. "Every time you cast a spell against someone, you bind your energy to them."

"But the woman has to protect herself," Griffin said.

"Damn straight," agreed Xylia.

"I'm not sure it's precisely the same when used in defense," Blythe said. "I mean, after all, the person who cursed Garnet already bound them together. Garnet is trying to break that bond and free herself."

As if I really could. I looked over at Sebastian, who was

silent through this entire discussion. He seemed lost in his own thoughts, studying the pattern of the Persian rug.

"What do you think, Sebastian?" I asked.

Barney wandered into the room. She made a beeline for the empty chili bowls on the table. Putting her front paws on the edge of the table, she put her nose into one of them. Sebastian edged her away with a gentle nudge from his toe.

"If Teréza hasn't cursed you, then all this energy we're raising tonight most certainly *will* bind you to her," Sebastian said. I opened my mouth to protest, when he continued, "But it seems obvious she has. I'm not sure how much more can go wrong with our wedding plans."

I made a mental note to tell Sebastian about my mother's meltdown and the missing application later.

"You've convinced me. Let's do this," William said.

It was nearly midnight once we had everything planned and ready. We'd brainstormed and consulted several of the spell books that Sebastian and I had in our library. Plus William used his BlackBerry to Google hex-breaking. Nearly every source we found agreed that curse-breaking spells needed to be performed at a crossroads. We all piled into Robert's van in search of a suitable site.

Sebastian called shotgun, since he had a road atlas and a pen flashlight. William, Xylia, Blythe, and I piled into the next row. The others filled in behind us. Robert's van rumbled to a start, and we all bounced down the county roads. In my bag I had four oversized black votive candles, a compass, several boxes of matches, a charcoal brick, a strip of paper, and a pen. I also had a plastic bag full of homemade incense that the coven had whipped up in the kitchen. It consisted of frankincense, myrrh, pine needles, and dragon's blood.

Sebastian and Robert argued good-naturedly about the directions in the front. Meanwhile, William tried to convince Griffin that "real men" used a mortar and pestle to grind their herbs, not a Cuisinart. Someone in the backseat hummed "O Tannenbaum."

With everyone in full arctic gear, we were packed in tightly. My hips tended toward ample anyway, but add in a layer of cotton long underwear and a fluffy parka, and I felt like a stuffed hippo. It didn't help that Blythe sat next to me in her fashionable knee-high boots and slim tweed jacket. Her mittens, scarf, and hat all matched.

The windows fogged up from the heat of all the bodies wedged together in the van, but through the haze I could see the twinkle of stars in an inky black sky. Snow-covered hills rolled past the window. The dark shapes of bare, twisted oak branches and bramble patches slashed the crystalline land-scape. Highway lights lengthened shadows cast by fence posts and wire.

Lilith stirred in my belly. I felt her tingle along my nerves.

"Deer!" someone in the back shouted, and Robert hit the brakes just in time. A buck sprang onto the road. The deer stopped in front of the van for a second and stared at us with big, glossy black eyes. His ears flicked, and he turned his head, as if sensing something in the wind. With a single bound he cleared the road and darted up over the hill. We all watched breathlessly as his retreating white tail reflected the light of the headlights.

No one said anything for a long moment.

"Wow," William breathed.

"Better than wow," Sebastian said. "We're at a crossroads."

We tumbled out of the van, our boots crunching the snow. The air was cold and crisp and clear. The hairs in my nose stuck together with my first breath. A crescent moon shone faintly over a line of pine trees on the eastbound side of the road. On the opposite side, I could see cattails dusted with snow bent low in a brown pool of frozen marsh water. A short distance up the road, a small, log cabin–style mom-and-pop bait shop was illuminated by a yard light. The plastic letters on the portable marquee spelled out, "Closed for the Season. See U in April."

Given Lilith's sudden presence earlier, I wasn't at all surprised when the compass revealed that not only had we arrived at a crossroads but that it was perfectly aligned to the cardinal directions. Green street signs informed us that we were at the junction of County Highway L and road number 107.

Robert pulled the van into the parking lot of the bait shop next to a semi trailer that clearly hadn't moved in decades. We huddled around each other in a tight circle, working out the last bit of logistics. "We're going to need a sentry," I said, looking at everyone in turn. "Someone willing to skip out of the spell in order to alert us if someone's coming."

"I'll do it," Sebastian said.

I frowned. As a vampire made from magic, Sebastian was the second most powerful witch in the coven. I only trumped him because I harbored a Goddess.

Sebastian could sense my hesitation, so he added, "I'm the only one who can handle Teréza if she shows."

I was going to say something about how far she'd have to travel on foot to catch up with us, when I remembered she could pop up wherever she wanted to. "Oh, all right," I said. "It makes sense."

I set everyone else on task. We placed our candles in the center of each arm of the crossroads. A member of the coven stood by each with a box of matches. The rest of us took handfuls of snow from the ditch to make a little mound of snow in the middle of the intersection. I made a little depression in the snow with my fist and then dumped in half of the bag of herbs. Then I lit a corner of the charcoal brick and set it on top of the heap. In a moment, scented smoke began to rise. The herbs burned dully, casting an eerie, shadowy light in the almost completely darkened intersection.

Griffin, who stood in the north arm, bent down and lit his candle. It took a couple of tries before the wick caught, but soon it was flickering in the slight breeze. In the east, Xylia lit her candle, followed by William in the south and Blythe in the west.

Once the candles were going, we began to hum. We'd been working together as a group for several months now, and we'd discovered that we all centered quickly when we sang or hummed the "Circle Song." It had a very simple tune and a repetitive chorus of "We are a circle, within a circle, with no beginning and never ending." As we sang, I took pinches of herbs and tossed them onto the charcoal. Their impact made a dramatic puff of aromatic smoke.

I let Lilith rise slowly. The tangy scent of frankincense mingled with the sharper odor of pine sap, putting me in mind of all the times I'd practiced magic and smelled such smells. Above, the blackness of the sky seemed immense and as endless as the circle in our song. The cold air kissed my exposed cheeks, focusing me on this moment.

When I felt that Lilith and I were together, I took the sheet of paper and black felt marker out of my bag. On one side I wrote, "Return to Sender," on the other, "Break this curse." I held it up for the coven to see and for them to add their energy to. Once they had, I tossed it onto the smoldering pile of herbs. The paper caught quickly and soon burned to ashes. I visualized the smoke taking the hex back to the one who originally cast it.

The last step in our spell was to raise the energy of protection and then, finally, those of us in the center would stomp on the remains of the incense pyre and thus fully break up the curse.

Someone started singing the words to the circle song again to begin our traditional way of raising energy. One by one, each person joined in. Xylia's bright soprano, William's baritone, Griffin's gruff base, Blythe's warble, and finally . . .

A car horn let out a wailing honk. Headlights blinded me as a vehicle came barreling around the curve. Xylia dove for cover.

I raised my hand. My only thought was, Stop the car! Lilith's energy shot out of me like a hammer. I heard the engine stall. The truck plowed over a candle, and the brakes hissed. Lilith continued to push against the oncoming force. The vehicle skidded on the ice but stopped less than a foot from my outstretched palm.

Lilith retreated. My hand trembled, and I dropped it to my side, feeling spent. All the energy we'd raised had dissipated into stopping the truck. Suddenly I felt a bit like that deer, staring into the battered grill of a Chevy pickup truck. I could see the startled expression of a man in a cap through the windshield. He slammed his fists on the steering wheel and said something I couldn't hear. When the door opened, he was still cursing. He stumbled awkwardly out of the vehicle. His words were slurred. "What the hell you kids doing out here in the middle of the road?" His eyes narrowed in on the plastic bag in my hand. "Is this some sort of drug party? Are you people crazy or something?"

The guy had the uniform of a Midwestern farmer down pat: work boots, faded jeans, and a plaid shirt with a parka vest over it. Sandy brown hair stubbled his head and merged with a slightly grayer five o'clock shadow. I totally expected him to have a gun rack in the cab of his truck, but instead I thought I saw a Feingold for President button on the collar of his vest.

I continued to stare at the interloper with my caught-in-the-headlights look. Where the hell was Sebastian? He was supposed to be our lookout! Had he gotten into some trouble?

"Hey," the farmer guy said, his eyes darting from the candles to the smoldering herbs. He swayed unsteadily on his feet and gripped the handle of his truck door to steady himself. "What's going on? What are you doing in the middle of the road?"

Griffin swaggered over, his shoulders squared. "Practicing magic. What are you doing? It's the middle of the night. This is the middle of nowhere."

Farmer-guy was taken aback. He blinked rapidly. I thought

he might have a heart attack. Instead he stammered, "I was going home. It's bar close. Did you say magic? Are you a cult or something?"

Griffin shook his head, his long hair bright in the head-lights. "Wiccans."

William came up beside me. In a loud whisper, he asked, "What's Griffin doing? Do we have one of those mind-wiping pens the men-in-black guys have?"

I snorted a laugh. I kind of wished we did. "We should get out of the road so you can get on your way, eh?"

The farmer glanced at me as if he just realized I was there. He looked at Griffin, who nodded like he thought that might be a good idea. Finally, the farmer tipped his hat. "Yeah, that'd be good."

I motioned for everyone to move off to the side. He started up the engine, looking at me through the windshield with a baffled expression. He kept shaking his head, as if trying to banish us all like a bad dream.

The truck rolled gingerly past us, scattering the ashes in the snow mound under a tire. I rubbed my nose, which was starting to feel the effects of the cold. "Well, that spell was officially screwed."

"Fucked up, more like," said Griffin, coming over to where William and I stood watching the taillights retreat in the darkness. The others gathered around. "Should we do it again?" someone asked.

Xylia checked her watch. "It's well past midnight now. Does the spell have to happen at midnight?"

"Maybe it was still good," said Blythe. "We were almost done."

"Almost isn't all the way," Griffin said.

"I'm hungry," someone said. "Can we skip to the cakes and ale part?"

"Where's Sebastian?" I asked out loud. "He was supposed to make sure that no one interrupted us. Do you think Teréza followed us?"

My question was answered by a bloodcurdling scream. My heart jumped in my throat. I couldn't tell where the noise had come from. The whole woods seemed silent now. Ice glinted dully on the straw in the marsh.

"What the hell was that?" Xylia asked.

"Trouble, I'd wager," Blythe said.

"Let's hope Sebastian can take care of whatever it is," William murmured.

I closed my eyes momentarily and called up the second sight, my magical senses. When I opened my eyes, the crossroads glowed with the energy the coven had raised. A purplish glow made a giant X marking the spot of the ritual. The flickering flames of the remaining candles were white-hot dots. Each coven member's aura glowed around them like a soft blanket, blending with the purplish power that surrounded all of us. I scanned the forest. Sebastian had no aura, because he was dead, so I wasn't expecting to see any sign of him.

However, Sebastian and I were connected by a silver thread, thanks to a blood-bonding spell we did long ago. Searching for it revealed a thin line heading in the direction of the woods, but it seemed to be obscured by a more powerful magic.

Teréza.

If Teréza was out there, I figured she'd light up like a Roman candle. She was dead—or used to be, and she had so much magic coursing through her, sustaining her. Plus, I knew she left a signature. I'd seen it before, when she disappeared at Sebastian's farm.

There was nothing. "Sebastian!" I called out. "Where are you?" Nothing. Then, I thought to try: "Teréza?"

A flash! A golden stab of magical light flared through the trunks of the pine trees. "There," I pointed, though I knew I was the only one who could see it. "He's over there."

Without question, the coven followed me as I ran toward where I last saw the glint of magic. The snow crunched underfoot as several sets of boots slid down the ditch and took us into the trees. Tall grass dragged at my legs, and I sank into snow up to my knees.

I pushed myself onward as fast as I could. The soft, slippery stalks stymied my progress. I strained to hear any noise of struggle, any sign that Sebastian was alive—okay, upright—and fighting.

If she was hurting him . . . My teeth set. I'd kill her. With a mighty burst of strength aided by desperation and Lilith, I cleared the tall, tangled weeds. Under the shelter of the tall pine trees, the ground was hard-packed. In places, dirt was even exposed. Passing a ragged, hand-printed Trespassers Will Be Shot sign, I ran into the stand of trees.

In a clearing, I saw them. They were pressed close together. The smell of pine was sharp in my nose. Sebastian's back was up against the trunk of a pine. Teréza's hands touched

Sebastian's throat and, for a second, I thought she was trying to choke him again. Then I watched as her hand trailed slowly down his shoulders to his waist.

They weren't locked in mortal combat. They were kissing. I was going to *kill* him.

Sixth Aspect: Inconjunct

KEY WORDS:

Poor Judgment, Insecurity

My eyes widened, and my breath came in short, angry huffs as Sebastian and Teréza continued to kiss while the entire coven looked on.

Lilith grew hot under my skin. I could feel her proverbial claws descending. I tried to counter her presence with some deep breathing, but I kept snarling. That wasn't helping.

"Dude," someone said reproachfully.

Sebastian broke away. "Oh," he said, his eyes scanning the bevy of disapproving looks. "Uh, I can explain."

My snarl sounded a bit like a tiger's. I had a bad feeling that my eyes glowed like lava.

William, ever sensitive, started to hum the "Circle Song." I could hear others picking it up slowly. They were trying to ground me—to help me keep Lilith from emerging and slaughtering Sebastian and Teréza where they stood.

Despite the fact that I wasn't entirely sure I didn't want to see some blood, I could feel myself calming to the sound of the familiar tune.

I raised my hand to let everyone know I felt in control and to stifle further disparaging commentary from the peanut gallery. I was curious, after all. How did Sebastian think he could explain away this hello-we're-supposed-to-be-married-in-a-week-and-a-half transgression?

Sebastian wriggled desperately in Teréza's clutches, likely trying to get some respectable distance between them. He looked really nervous. He knew exactly the disaster the coven's humming had averted. Teréza, meanwhile, held on tightly.

"It was the only way I could get her to calm down," Sebastian said.

"Huh." I grunted, my eyes watching the way his arm continued to cup her waist distractedly.

Lilith lifted my lips in a sneer. I could feel her pulling away from my control. She wanted to throttle him. And Teréza. And everyone here.

Hmmm, it was the last part that reminded me why I couldn't let her all the way out. She never cared who she killed, just as long as someone died . . . hard and often.

The humming intensified.

Sebastian's eyes darted around the coven. He knew he was in trouble.

"She . . . Teréza was going to kill me," he said. Noticing my glance, he shifted so that both his hands were at his side. Teréza, with her arms still around his waist tightly, laid her head against his chest. She didn't seem all that threatening anymore.

Despite myself, I couldn't help but notice how similar they were.

"I had to defend myself," Sebastian said.

I wasn't listening. All I saw was the way they were together. Similarly pale, unearthly skin glowed faintly in the moonlight. Teréza's long, curling hair had an inky blackness that seemed to blend into the night, like Sebastian's. Maybe it was way they carried themselves, but something about them both seemed to be out of this time, from another era, though they were dressed in regular clothes, even if Teréza's skirt was ragged and Sebastian was underdressed for the weather as usual. For that matter, neither Sebastian nor Teréza shivered, like I did, in the cold.

Teréza's eyes watched me with rare clarity. I saw in her stare the hunger—that strange craving that always came between Sebastian and me. I might understand Sebastian's thirst for blood in theory, but in practice I had to admit it repulsed me. He was a vampire.

So was she.

And they had a kid together.

How was I ever going to compete with that?

"I had to think of something to distract her," Sebastian continued weakly.

Someone jumped in with: "So you kissed her? Dude."

Funny though it was, that was the wrong thing to say. Lilith reared up. I felt fire, like lightning, scorch through my veins. My conscious thought began breaking down into a repetitive phrase: Kill them, kill them all.

But a circle tightened around me like a noose. Raging against the constricting bond, I felt I could break it. Yes, it would be easy. Then they would all die.

Until *his* voice joined in that infernal song of theirs, the one holding me back. His magic wasn't like the others. It was like the cold fire of a diamond facet, and it should be mine. Not hers. I rallied against the circle, but with his added magic, there was no hope of breaking it.

I smiled wickedly. I'd kill her later.

Suddenly, I snapped back fully into myself. The woods echoed with voices. I felt Lilith's evil grin fall. Her heat abandoned me. I stood in a puddle of melted ice on the muddy ground. Around me, the entire coven had formed a physical circle, holding hands. Sebastian stood separated from the others. I could see him over Griffin's shoulder, standing under the pine. Teréza still clung to him, but I could hear his voice clearly above them all.

"I'm cool," I said, but my voice was too hoarse to be heard over the singing. I cleared my throat and tried again. "I'm back."

Slowly, as if not quite trusting my assessment, the song died down.

Out of the corner of my eye, I could see Sebastian step forward, his mouth open, ready to spout some lame excuse when I turned on my heel and started walking back to the van. As I passed William, I asked, "Can I stay at yours tonight?"

"Of course," he said quietly.

I sensed the rest of the coven following behind me in a solemn procession. We left Sebastian and Teréza standing alone in the woods. No one spoke a word; we just filed into the van.

Sebastian came running after us, dragging a reluctant Teréza along. "Garnet! Wait!"

Xylia slammed the sliding door on the sound of his pleas. Robert started the engine.

But I forgot. There was no running away from a vampire.

In a flash, Sebastian stood in front of the van, his hands on the hood. Robert gunned the engine threateningly.

"Run him over," I said. When everyone looked at me in horror, I added, "He's a vampire. It won't kill him."

The engine revved again. "I can't do it," Robert admitted. "My foot won't come off the brake."

"Anyway, he's got the strength of ten men or something," someone muttered from the backseat. "He could probably hold the van back."

"I think your physics is off," William corrected. "Besides there's ice, with the mass of the van . . . I think if we had more momentum or something, we could totally slide him under us."

I got out of my seat, while they continued discussing whether or not Sebastian had the strength or leverage or whatever was needed to hold back our van. I pulled the door open with a jerk and stuck my head out. "Get out of the way, Sebastian," I said.

"We need to talk," he said.

"Go to hell," I yelled.

Teréza hissed at me from the ditch.

"And why don't you take your wife with you."

"She's not my wife," he said.

"Didn't look like that in the woods," I retorted. "Now, get out of my way, or this time I'll let Lilith come out to kick your sorry ass."

The entire van echoed with a chorus of "Boo-yah" and "You go, girl!"

Wisely, Sebastian stepped to the side. He started to say something—no doubt one last appeal to my better judgment. I pulled the door handle. Not being used to these kinds of sliding doors, it bounced a bit against the latch, but I managed to get it shut with a modicum of the drama I'd intended.

The van lurched into motion. The sudden start pushed me back into my seat. Once we rounded the corner, everyone started talking at once. Over my head I heard, "Kicked him to the curb" and "What was he thinking kissing that woman" and "She sure told him."

Without a word, William put his arm around my shoulder.

I started to cry.

Well, I thought, at least now I didn't have to worry about what to tell my mother about the heirloom wedding dress.

I thought I might make it to William's place without anyone in the coven really noticing how upset I was. After the first few tears, I knuckled the rest away and held on tightly to my smile. The initial exuberance had died down. By the time we were pulling onto William's street, everyone was quieter, chatting about their lives and mundane things.

No one mentioned Lilith.

The absence of commentary hung in the air. Every once in a while someone would start to say something about Lilith and stop short. We all pretended not to notice—even me.

Lilith scared me too. If the rest of the coven hadn't been there, Lilith would have killed Sebastian and Teréza. Part of me might have talked about wanting to see him dead, but not like that, not really. I knew what it felt like to wake up with my hands around a dead man's throat. It wasn't something I wanted to repeat ever again.

Lilith hummed under my skin, almost as though she were laughing at me. I got the distinct sense she didn't believe me.

I shoved that thought away quickly. Luckily, we'd arrived. After I unbuckled, there was a lot of jostling, hugging, and saying good-bye. Everyone promised to be there if I needed them. I nodded. I knew they would be . . . hell, they already had been.

I waved good-bye and scurried up the rickety stairs at the back of the house to William's apartment. William's building was a block off Fraternity Row. His house was shabby but well-maintained. The neighborhood, however, left something to be desired. The sidewalk was shoveled, but bits of newspaper and other garbage stuck out from the piles.

Once William let me in, I threw myself on his couch without even taking off my boots or parka. When I heard the door latch, I screamed and hit the pillows with my fists.

"What was he thinking?"

My cell phone rang.

"I imagine he'd like to tell you what happened," William said drily, as he took off his boots and hung up his coat.

"Well, I'm not going to talk to him," I said. The phone rang until it rolled into voice mail. "I'm not ready yet. I need to process this whole thing."

William nodded like he understood. He slid across the floor in stocking feet. "I'll make some hot chocolate."

William had redecorated since my last visit. He still had a lot of India-influenced throw pillows and wall hangings. Bright colors and mirrors and geometric shapes dotted the room. But now, William had added more chrome and sharp edges. It felt a little like a marriage between Ikea and Global Village, but it worked.

It still surprised me how comfortable William had made this shabby space. Where walls were water damaged and cracked, William put up an embroidered quilt that looked Mexican in origin. Accent lamps made warm, comfortable pools of light around the room. Playful pictures of faeries and dragons dotted the walls.

When I glanced at the caller ID on my cell phone, I wasn't surprised at all that it had, in fact, been Sebastian earlier.

Now I just had to decide what to do about him. I rubbed the space between my eyes, trying to banish the image of Sebastian's lips on Teréza's from my mind. Unfortunately, every time I closed my eyes, all I could see was Teréza's arms entwined around his body, which pressed hungrily against hers.

And, worse, how natural they looked together . . .

William put a hot mug into my hands. "You should take your coat off, stay a while."

I'd totally forgotten I was still bundled up. Setting the cup down on a chrome and glass coffee table, I pulled off my coat and stepped out of my boots. William took everything over to the closet by the door and stowed it away. I tucked my feet under my butt and took a sip of the cocoa.

"I wonder how long they were in love," I said to myself. "Did he stay to see Mátyás born?"

William sat down on the couch next to me. He had a cup printed with the Bill of Rights that was slowly disappearing with the heat of his drink. "Izzy says that Mátyás was born after Teréza died."

I crinkled my nose at the thought. "What? How is that possible?"

"Well, I guess it happens sometimes when people are in a coma. And, well, to hear him tell it, she wasn't all the way dead."

"That explains a lot about Mátyás," I said, remembering that he had some magical powers himself, specifically the ability to walk into other people's dreams. "So Sebastian must have been there. To take care of him and stuff, right?"

William shook his head. "Mátyás was taken in by his mother's people."

This conversation wasn't helping. I'd wanted a sense that Sebastian had fallen into Teréza's arms because of some long, romantic history. The more I heard about it from William, the more like a one-night stand Teréza sounded. "That can't be right," I said. "I mean, Sebastian must have courted Teréza for a long time. He said that Teréza's father made him learn to speak their language. He's smart and everything, but that must have taken a while, don't you think? Plus, they were promised to each other—betrothed, engaged, whatever. That doesn't happen overnight, does it?"

"It might when you're pregnant."

"Jeez," I said. "You think Sebastian was that guy? The one who swoops into town and makes a girl pregnant?"

"More like the Gypsy camp."

My mouth hung open for a second. Now I had a line from Cher's "Gypsies, Tramps, and Thieves" in my head about all the men coming 'round and laying their money down. "That sounds really tawdry," I admitted.

William shrugged and took another sip of his cocoa. "Maybe you should ask him about it."

I looked at the drink cooling in my own cup. "I suppose I should."

It seems there were a lot things I didn't know about a man I was about to say "forever" with. In the last couple of days I found out he fought in Africa with Rommel, and, at some point, he hung around Gypsy camps. What else did he have hidden up his sleeve? Did I even know Sebastian at all?

"I guess it's all right to let him stew a bit, though," William said with a little half smile.

I joined him in the grin, and we clinked our cups.

Later, William distracted me with a monster movie. He popped some popcorn, and we drank hard lemonade. When I should have been laughing at the badly dubbed English and the papier-mâché puppet, I found myself staring at the engagement ring on my finger and crying again.

"My wedding's off, isn't it?"

"What?"

"Nothing," I said, pulling my cell out. I swiped away the tears with my fingertips. I'd turned the ringer off when we started the show, and there were several missed calls—all from Sebastian.

William noticed me staring forlornly at my phone. He rubbed his nose. Then he turned off the TV, even though part of Tokyo was still standing. "I'll go take a shower and get ready for bed."

"Okay," I said. "Hey, thanks."

He gave me a tired smile. "You'll do the same for me someday. Now go save your marriage."

My breath hitched. "Do you really think I can?"

"If you really want to, Garnet, you can move mountains."

That was such a William thing to say. My face crinkled into a reluctant smile. "Yeah," I said. "Maybe." But I wasn't sure. I mean, maybe we weren't ready to get married. We hadn't been going out together that long—less than two years—which was what, a flash, in Sebastian's span of a thousand? Even as dead weight, Teréza had been part of Sebastian's life for over a hundred years.

I flipped open the phone. Should I call him? I still couldn't quite shake the image of the kiss. I snapped it shut and stood up. I wandered over to the window. Looking down onto the street, I saw Sebastian standing under a streetlamp. He had his phone in his hand.

I stepped away from the window.

I wasn't sure why I was reluctant to talk to him. Okay, I meant outside of that nagging picture of him lip-locked with his dead-vampire-zombie-Gypsy-queen-ex floating around in my head.

Maybe there was a reasonable explanation, right? I looked out the window again. This time our eyes met. He looked at his phone and then back up to me. I shook my head and pointed to the back of the building where the stairs to

William's door were. My boots were still a little wet and cold, but I put them on anyway. I pulled my coat over my shoulders. Scrunching my hat over my ears, I slipped my gloves over my fingers.

I opened the door to meet Sebastian, but he was already standing at the top of the stairs.

"I'm sorry," he said.

He did look apologetic standing there. His eyes searched mine with a vaguely frantic yet totally sincere look. "Where's Teréza?" I asked.

"Back at the house."

The house? His farm? He took Teréza back to *our* house?

I slammed the door in his face.

Kicking the boots off my feet, I walked back over to the couch and turned the TV on. The DVD began loading. I watched the blue screen without blinking, my coat hunched around my shoulders.

The doorbell rang.

"Okay, I know what you're thinking," his muffled voice said through the door. "But it's not like that. She was already living in the barn. I needed to put her somewhere before coming after you."

The menu came up with loud, jarring music, nearly drowning out the sound of his voice. I pressed pause. Over my shoulder, I yelled, "The coven isn't here, Sebastian. I won't be able to stop Lilith if you tick me off too much. And she really, really, really wants to kill you."

There was silence for a moment as Sebastian considered his options. "I'll call you in the morning."

I nodded. Maybe I'd be ready then. I pointed the remote

with the intention of starting the movie again when I heard his feet shift on the creaky stairs.

"Is William going to be safe?"

My finger hesitated over the buttons. Would he? William had an uncanny ability to calm the beast in me, but what if, blinded by my anger at Sebastian, I lashed out at him? William hadn't even finished his formal witch training. Lilith would squash him like a bug.

Deep in my solar plexus, she buzzed lightly at the idea, like it would be fun.

I put the remote down on the coffee table with a clunk. My hands shook.

"Garnet, did you hear me?" Sebastian asked. "I need to know that William will be safe."

"I can't be here," I said mostly to myself. Lilith was too dangerous tonight. "I can't control her on my own."

"Come home with me," Sebastian pleaded. "I can handle her."

Oh, you only think you can, little man.

"Garnet, please," he said.

"No," I shouted, as I got up to put my boots back on in a hurry. I headed for William's kitchen and the back door. "You're not safe. None of you."

No one ever used William's actual back door. Fire code required a second egress, but it led into someone else's apartment, so most of the time it was locked. The skeleton key hung on the doorknob. It didn't want to turn easily, having been rusted from lack of use.

I could hear Sebastian shouting something, and it sounded like he was coming in to talk to me.

Let him come.

I had to go. Now.

After the briefest knock, I twisted the key hard. The door opened into someone's bedroom. The walls were painted a chalky purple. There were posters of Lynyrd Skynyrd on the wall. CDs and DVD cases lay scattered on the floor and the rumpled futon. A heavy chemistry textbook sat on a cheap plywood desk. A model of the starship *Enterprise* hung on a wire from the acoustic ceiling tile.

Feeling like an interloper, I shut the door behind me quietly, relocking it and taking the key.

The bedroom was the only room on this floor; a short set of stairs led down to the main apartment. I strained to hear the sounds of voices or people moving around, but the only thing I could hear was Sebastian calling for me. I scurried guiltily down the steps and surprised the hell out of a black man in a yellow terrycloth bathrobe.

"Holy shit!"

"Sorry," I said, raising my hands up to show I meant no harm. "I came in through the back door. I'm really sorry, but I had to make an exit," I said, pointing to the ceiling and William's apartment. The warm buzz just under my skin warned me that this guy wasn't safe from Lilith either. "Can I just slip through?"

Above, Sebastian's voice sounded more desperate and angry.

The guy nodded like he understood something. "Got you. Look, just let yourself out that way, okay?"

I smiled my relief and headed in the direction he pointed.

"I hope those boots aren't too wet. The landlord just had

the carpet cleaned," he muttered as I made my way to the door. The scent of industrial soap drifted up with every step, and I knew I was probably tracking around mud from our trip out in the woods.

"Sorry," I said. "Thank you."

"Hmph," he muttered. "I'd better get some good karma for this."

I hoped he would too.

Outside, an eerie, thick fog shrouded the streets. In every direction, the houses disappeared behind a blanket of mist. I started walking. It wouldn't take long for Sebastian and William to figure out I'd slipped out the back way, and I wanted to put some distance between us. Maybe I could walk off my angry mood. Then, if either of them caught up to me, it would be . . . safer.

For several blocks, I just fumed. My eyes on the sidewalk, I muttered to myself about Sebastian. I'd been pretty damn understanding up until tonight. You know, I'd understood that he and Teréza had history. I expected he'd have to work something out with her, but did it have to involve kissing? Two weeks before our wedding?

The wedding! With all the cancellations and mix-ups, it was more like a wedding disaster, anyway. I should have figured it was a sign when I couldn't even get the marriage application without some major snafu. Maybe it was just as well the whole thing was off.

My breath hitched at the thought. Was it really over?

Suddenly, I heard the distinctive call of a cardinal. I searched the bare treetops for bright red plumage. I saw him. A flash of color perched on the tip-top of a bare-limbed cottonwood. As if sensing my eyes upon him, he took to the air and disappeared into the haze.

I stood in the middle of the icy sidewalk and stared at the spot where the mist swallowed the bird. Everything was still in the predawn hour. Even the brightly painted Victorians seemed muted and hushed. The scent of an approaching snowstorm hung in the air.

What would life be like without Sebastian? Like the cardinal in the snow, he was the color in my winter. If I let him vanish from my life, Teréza would win. Her curse wouldn't be broken, it would have broken *me*.

Lilith rattled beneath my skin, but this time it felt more like a rallying cry. I'd be damned if I'd let her take my man.

I hiked to State Street and to Mercury Crossing. Even though the sun rose slowly in the sky, the mist hung on. Where the sidewalks were shoveled, the fog froze, making a thin layer of black ice—nearly invisible and treacherous. I skidded twice, flinging my arms around awkwardly to keep my balance, but my boots had good tread, and I managed to avoid any truly embarrassing falls. I was actually grateful for the spots where lazy landowners hadn't bothered to shovel after the last snowfall. The snow piles, even the packed ones, made for surer footing.

I used my key to let myself into the store. Disarming the alarm, I flicked on a few lights. I took a moment to take in the scent of the place. I loved the smell of books mingled with the sandalwood incense. The whole thing was made sweeter by the fact that several months ago I closed a deal with Eugene, the former owner. Mercury Crossing was mine.

Like nearly all the stores on State Street, it was a narrow, cramped little store. The aisles were barely wide enough to be wheelchair accessible and, consequently, I utilized every space available. Chimes hung from the ceiling, and feathered masks and Goddess art were on the high parts of the walls. Shelves filled the remaining area. There were books, tarot cards, jewelry, ritual knives and cups, greeting cards, prayer mats, Goddess statues, polished rocks, dried herbs in vials and in bulk bins, potted plants, and magical doodads of every conceivable kind. We even had pagan-themed stuffed animals in the kids' section.

After locking the door behind me, I took off my coat and stuffed it into the cubby behind the counter. Pushing up my sleeves, I got to work.

When I was upset, I cleaned and organized. Despite feeling like I needed to fight Teréza's curse, I wasn't resolved about how I felt about Sebastian. Maybe we were rushing things. Since bonding with Lilith, it was possible that I might live an extended lifetime. What was the hurry? Perhaps it would be better to wait until I was sure Sebastian was the one.

It seemed so reasonable, but the thought of all the cancellations made my hands shake as I dusted the counters. My brain started to melt. I took a deep breath. I'd think about that later. I had some bills to take care of in the back room.

Buried in office work, I lost track of the time, and suddenly

William came in the back door. "Hey," he said, tossing my cell phone onto the desk. "You forgot this last night."

"Thanks," I said, distractedly shoving it into the back pocket of my jeans.

William wore a bulky, knit sweater with a cartoon reindeer in the middle of it. On the points of the antlers, someone had sewn little jingle bells that tinkled with his every movement. "Sebastian is probably still out looking for you," he said. "You should give him a call and put that poor boy out of his misery."

"Nah," I said. "Let him stew. Besides, how well does he know me, if he doesn't come looking for me here?"

William snorted. "Good point." He stood leaning against the counter expectantly, watching me. Finally, he asked, "What are you doing?"

"Bills."

"Oh," William said. "I thought you'd be figuring out a way to save your marriage."

I took in a deep breath. "I'm not sure I can."

Turns out Sebastian knew me pretty well, after all. Not only did he walk in the door seconds after we unlocked the front and switched on the Open sign, but he also came bearing gifts: coffee and doughnuts.

He set the box of pastries down on the counter with a slight bow. "A peace offering," he said.

Being impervious to the weather, Sebastian wore only a thin leather coat over a cotton navy sweater. No hat, but gloves covered his hands. He looked like a model in one of those ads where anyone north of the Mason-Dixon Line can tell the "snow" is just soap flakes.

I put my hands on my hips, and my gaze focused on the paper cups in the carrying tray his hands. "I want to see that coffee first," I said.

He handed me the one marked with a *G* in Izzy's handwriting. "Your honeyed latte."

Having gotten no sleep last night, the first hit of caffeine tasted divine.

"I don't think we should get married," I said.

Sebastian's mouth opened. Then it closed. He opened it again. Then he shook his head. "What?"

"This isn't about the kiss," I started. "Well, okay, it is. But it's more than that. The whole thing got me thinking how little I really know about you."

Sebastian's jaw tightened. "If you marry me, we'll have a lifetime to discover each other."

Damn it. When he said ridiculously romantic things like that, it was hard not to fall in love with him all over again. It was annoying. I wanted to be mad.

I frowned at the white plastic top of the latte. Sebastian watched me anxiously.

"Why are you so desperate to marry me anyway?" I asked finally. "You'd think that after all the entanglement of not-dead Teréza, you'd want nothing to do with relationships and commitment and all that."

Sebastian didn't even hesitate. "I'm desperate to marry you because I love you."

I gave him the be-serious-and-less-sappy stare.

William peeked over the top of the *I Ching* section. He gave me a "do you need rescuing?" look. I shook my head. Sebastian noticed our exchange, and William's head disappeared quickly. My hero.

Sebastian ran a finger along the top of his to-go cup. "You want to know why I want to marry you," he said. "I want to marry you because I've never met anyone like you. When I think of something during the day, it's you I want to tell it to. I've never had anyone in my life like that before."

"Never? Not in a thousand years?"

He shook his head. "I've had friends," he said. "Lovers. But, you know, I've never been married before. Not to anyone."

"What?" It seemed incredible that Sebastian could live so long and never get married. "Why not?"

"Because marriage is a sacrament; it's not something to be entered into lightly. I've been a vampire much longer than I was alive, and it would have been a lie to enter into marriage with a mortal knowing that I'd outlive her. I couldn't do it."

"But you asked me before . . ." I spread my hands over my body, where I could feel Lilith's constant presence.

"I know. You're the exception. Besides, you knew what I was almost from the beginning." He shrugged. "Plus you met Mátyás and didn't run screaming."

Well, I wasn't sure if that proved my devotion to Sebastian or my insanity. My cell phone rang. It was "Livin' La Vida Loca." Not what I wanted to deal with now. I let it ring through.

Sebastian's eyebrow twitched. "This is serious. You didn't

take the call. You answered that damn phone when Teréza was standing in the graveyard."

I lifted my shoulder. "It's just another cancellation. Thanks to the fact that you were too busy kissing in the woods to do your job at the ritual last night, the hex-breaking spell was ruined by a guy who tried to run us all over with a truck."

"I'm guessing you're not over that whole kissing thing yet, huh?"

He'd said all the right things, and I did love him. "Nope. Not by a long shot."

"Shit," Sebastian said. His face, which had had a schooled expression of light pleasantness, cracked a little. "I put up with Daniel Parrish showing up at my house—my house, Garnet—and you can't forgive one little kiss?"

"I was bandaging Parrish after he saved me from the crazy zompire you were making out with," I fumed. "Anyway, 'little' kiss? You call that little?"

The top of William's hair was visible over the shelf.

"Yeah, I call that little. Not like the relationship you've had with Parrish for years."

I took in a sharp breath. "I can't believe you're throwing that in my face. I haven't seen Parrish for ages. And since you and I started dating, I've never, ever kissed him." And I said it strongly enough that I almost entirely believed it myself. I hadn't, had I? Anyway, I wasn't going to let doubt ruin a perfectly good argument.

The bells over the door jangled as a grandmotherly woman in a shapeless parka came in. We stared at her. She shook the snow off her shoulders. "It's really coming down, eh?"

I blinked, having completely lost track of my surroundings

during our fight. Huge, storybook flakes fell from the sky. There was probably an inch covering everything already.

I quickly put on my make-nice-for-the-customers smile. Sebastian's eyes flashed angrily, no doubt filled with the retort he had to stifle. "We'll talk about this later," he said in a low voice.

"Oh, we will; don't worry about that," I returned through clenched teeth.

Sebastian turned on his heel and stalked off. The bells chimed as the door closed. Through the window, I watched him stomp over the snow down the street.

Well, that could have gone better. I took a sip of my latte. At least I got some coffee out of the deal.

After directing the customer to the book on witchy needlecraft she was looking for, William sidled up to the register. I was still nursing my latte and frowning at the falling snow. "I thought you guys might actually patch it up there for a while," he said.

"Yeah." I sighed. I shook off my dark mood. I'd been brooding about the fight, and something had been niggling at the back of my mind. I had a half-formed plan, and it included William. "Will you take me dancing tonight?"

William looked over his shoulder, like he thought I must be talking to someone else. "Me?" He pointed to the center of his goofy reindeer sweater. "If your plan is to make Sebastian jealous, well, for one, I don't think it will work, and second, if it did, I'm not sure I want to be around a vampire who's feeling territorial, if you know what I mean."

I laughed. "I want you to take me to that gay bar you and Jorge went to."

"Going gay isn't going to help matters either. You need to work things out with Sebastian."

"I want to find Parrish."

"Oh. Well. That sounds even more insane."

Seventh Aspect: Sextile

KEY WORDS:

Natural Attunement, Openness

Doing anything with Parrish probably *was* a bad idea, but I got it into my head that he was just the man I needed. Mátyás was convinced that Teréza would settle down with a vampire to help her adjust. Well, Sebastian wasn't the only vampire in town.

William and I spent the rest of the time taking care of the usual business. We sold an assortment of tarot, magic books, and incense. I watched for Sebastian throughout the day, but he must have been pretty mad, because he never reappeared.

For my part, I found that when Sebastian wasn't in my line of sight, I was much more ready to forgive him. He had a point, after all. How many times had he walked in and found Parrish and me in an awkward position? I'd always stayed faithful, but I'd certainly been tempted to kiss Parrish from time to time. It wasn't like I couldn't understand the appeal of an ex.

Well, we'd have another chance to talk about it tonight, after I got Parrish in on my plan to take Teréza off Sebastian's hands. "You ready?" I asked William after we'd counted out the till and gotten the deposit ready for the bank.

"Sure," William said. Then he looked down at his sweater, "But I might want to change."

"I think you look super cute," I said.

"Yeah," he agreed a bit dubiously. "I might be impossible to resist."

"The sweater totally screams take-me-home-and-cuddle-me," I said. William blushed beet red, so I added, "I take it you're not quite ready for that?"

"No. I think I should go for something more conservative. So I think I want to stop home. Should we swing by your place too?"

I looked at my own clothes. Winter was tough on my inner fashionista. I'd gone for simple black for the ritual: a turtle-neck sweater and flare-bottom jeans. A heavy silver necklace of skulls and a pair of many-buckled high-heel boots were my only Goth accessories. Still, I thought, even though I hadn't changed in a day, it was an elegant look, which would only be enhanced by my red and black flecked, ankle-length babushka coat. "I think I'm good. Besides, I'm not exactly looking to score," I reminded him.

"Oh, like I am."

* * *

After William showed me the sixth potential outfit, I was beginning to wonder. "Are you sure you're not hoping to pick someone up?" I teased him.

"I just want to look good."

"William, you look good in jeans and a T-shirt."

"Really?"

From the hopeful sound in William's voice, I suddenly realized that I'd stumbled into one of those awkward moments where you want to tell your male friend how hot he is without giving him all the wrong signals. "Really," I admitted. "If I wasn't already engaged, I'd totally date you."

"Don't lie. I'm not your type," he said, finally deciding on a white, button-down shirt.

"Hmm," I muttered, because actually William was totally my type before I met Sebastian. In my younger days, I had an unfortunate tendency to bring home strays that needed a lot of direction and guidance. It was bad match, like the blind leading the blind. Parrish and Sebastian were the exceptions. Apparently, anytime I went for alpha men, I also went for the undead. Explain that one to me, Dr. Freud.

"Well, I think I'm ready," William said.

"Great. Let's go hit the gay bar."

On the drive out to Club 5, I remembered to check my cell phone messages. Turns out, there was a double booking at the reception hall. I'd have to share my wedding reception with a local high school marching band's annual fund-raiser. Nifty.

I guess our hex breaking spell really hadn't worked so well after all.

I closed the cell with a snap. I was a little disappointed that Sebastian hadn't called, so I dialed the number for home. When he answered, I almost hung up, having psyched myself only so far as an answering machine message. "Hey," I said. "I'm sorry." I wasn't entirely over the kiss, but I was getting closer to being ready to hear him out. Besides, I was going to take care of the problem.

"Me too," he said. "Do you want me to come get you? We could have a late dinner. I'll make your favorite: pancakes."

My stomach growled at the offer. "Ooooh, that sounds great, but I was calling to let you know I'm going to be out late. Don't wait up for me."

There was a long pause on the other end. "You're going out? Don't you think we have some things we should talk about?"

I didn't want to start another fight. "We do. But I have a solution to the Teréza problem."

William took his eyes off the road to give me a surprised look.

"You do?" Sebastian didn't sound convinced.

"You gave me the idea, actually. Parrish. I think Parrish should be Teréza's vampire mentor."

There was a pause. Then, "Are you insane?"

"No, listen, it's perfect," I said. "Think about it, Sebastian. I mean, I know they got off on a rocky start, what with the whole burning hand thing, but what if they hit it off? They could be a cute couple."

William almost swerved the car into a ditch.

There were strangled noises coming from the other end of the phone. I could make out the occasional "But . . . I never . . . You. . . ."

"Unless you don't like the idea of Teréza with someone else," I said casually.

The choking sound stopped abruptly. A few seconds of stony silence passed until Sebastian said, "I still think you're insane. I'll leave the light on for you."

His response was cold comfort, but at this point I'd take what I could get. Maybe he'd warm to the idea if it became a reality. "Thanks, honey," I said. "I love you."

"It's never going to work, you know," he said, "But I love you too."

"It's *why* you love me," I reminded him.

"True."

With that we said our good-byes and hung up. William was still sneaking astonished looks at me. "Did I hear you right? Your plan is to play matchmaker with Teréza and Parrish?"

"Well," I said, admitting that it did sound pretty crazy out loud, "if it doesn't work, it's not like we're out anything."

William considered that with a nod. "Yeah, there's no cover. Plus the music is great."

I'd never been to a gay bar. I wasn't sure what I was expecting: maybe strobe lights, mostly naked men in cages gyrating suggestively to a heavy beat, and lots of fashionable people kissing each other on a polished wood floor. The building we pulled up to didn't look particularly impressive.

In fact, it looked a bit like one of those big box stores: flat, windowless, and unremarkable. There was a large parking lot around the whole place, and a few cars were in sight. William pulled in to a spot close to the front door.

The outside didn't look particularly edgy or cool. I had hopes for the inside. After all, Parrish hung out here. Inside, there were polished wood floors, but the people dancing were wearing cowboy hats and two-stepping. Sugarland's "Dear Mom and Dad" twanged through the place. As I shrugged out of my coat, I leaned in to William and said, "It's a country bar?"

"Oh, yeah, on Fridays. Thursday is karaoke."

"And you ran into Parrish here on karaoke night?"

"He's a good singer," William said, finding us a table along the wall.

I folded my coat over the chair. "I need a drink," I said.

I made my way to the bar. A cute, beefy man with dark curly hair and a Celtic knot tattoo on his bicep took my order. I leaned against the bar, took in the very average-looking crowd, and sighed. No hotties in cages. Bummer.

In fact, it kind of made me wonder if we'd see Parrish here at all tonight.

With a wink, the bartender handed me our drinks: a hard lemonade for me and a Coke for William. I smiled back, a bit confused, and asked, "Aren't you barking up the wrong tree?"

"I'm bi." He grinned mischievously.

And somehow he could tell I was straight. I probably had it tattooed in invisible ink on my forehead. I laughed. "Sorry," I said. "I have a fiancé."

The bartender shrugged. "Lucky guy."

When I got back to the table, William was giving me a funny look. "Tony tried it on with you, didn't he?"

"The bartender?"

William nodded, reaching for his Coke. "He's an animal."

I snorted a laugh. I was just about to take a swig from my drink when my cell beeped. It was Sebastian's ring tone, so I picked it up.

"It's your mother," said the voice on the other end. It was a good thing I hadn't taken a drink yet, because I would have spat it out. "I'm at the house, and Sebastian tells me you're out. It's not your bachelorette party yet, is it?"

It took me a minute to regain my breath. "Mom?"

William's eyebrows raised over the can.

"Yes, dear. I came over to talk to you about how things are going with the wedding planning, and Sebastian tells me you've decided to go out."

"Did he tell you why?"

"You had a fight. Don't you think you're being a bit childish? Your wedding is in less than two weeks."

I sputtered. "A fight? Did he tell you I caught him kissing another woman?"

William put down his Coke to stare expectantly. On the dance floor, the two-steppers kicked up their heels to "Suds in the Bucket" by Sara Evans.

For a moment, I thought my mother might have hung up. Then, she said, "Relationships are about compromise. You should be here working things out."

"I'll be home later tonight," I said, and I hung up.

William's hand went to his mouth. "You just hung up on your mom."

I stared at the phone, the audacity of what I'd just done slowly sinking in. "I just hung up on my mom."

"Oh, man," William said with a shake of his head.

I dropped the phone onto the plastic tabletop. "This always happens," I said. "I don't know what it is about my mother, but I always have these great aspirations to, you know, be adult, and I just end up acting like I'm seventeen."

"What did she say?"

I rolled my eyes, though I wasn't sure William could see my expression in the dim light of the bar. "She gave me the whole 'relationships take work' speech."

William gave a little laugh. "Yeah, although with you guys, it's sort of 'relationships take zombies' . . . and voodoo queens, and Vatican assassins, and dead ex-wives, and . . ."

I took a long pull on the bottle in my hand. William had a strange but interesting point. Sebastian and I were always rushing from some supernatural crisis to another. We hardly had time to really have a normal relationship. "It's no surprise I don't know that much about him," I murmured out loud. "When do we have time to really talk?"

"What?" William shouted, as Garth Brooks sang about his "Friends in Low Places." "Did you just say you don't know Sebastian?"

"Parrish said something the other day, and it's kind of been haunting me," I admitted. My finger traced the label on my drink. "I guess Sebastian fought on the wrong side in World War Two."

"He was in Mussolini's army?"

"No, Hitler's." Although, again, William managed to make an unintentional point: there were more than two sides in that war.

William's brow crinkled. "What are you saying exactly? Sebastian was a Nazi?"

"He says he wasn't, and I believe him."

William looked at his Coke like he was beginning to think someone had spiked it. "So, what's the problem, exactly?"

"It made me realize how little I really know about Sebastian. Like, who he is—what's important to him."

"What?" William put his hand to his ear. We weren't sitting terribly far apart, but the music was loud enough that it was difficult to talk. I was beginning to wonder why we were here. I didn't really see country western night as Parrish's scene, anyway.

I stood up. "I should go home."

"You're feeling the mom pressure?"

"Kind of," I said. "Plus I don't think Parrish is going to show."

"Are you kidding?" William asked. "He came in about the time you went for drinks."

"What?!"

William pointed to the dance floor. "He's right there."

I strained to see where William indicated. It took me a while to realize that the guy with the ponytail and black Stetson hat dancing with a tall, mustached guy in a white cowboy hat and vest was, in fact, Daniel Parrish.

Before I even realized it, I was asking to cut in. White Hat looked at me like I had to be kidding. Parrish gave him an apologetic smile and whispered something in White Hat's ear that made him blush and step aside with a go-ahead gesture.

"Do I even want to know what you said to that man?"

"It's not something I'd repeat in front of a lady," he purred.

Weirdly, that turned me on. Even stranger, Parrish looked natural in the cowboy hat. I touched the brim with my finger, "You ever a cowboy?"

He shook his head, "Too much sun for me. But," he said leaning in to my ear, "they taste good. Easy to pick off when they're sleeping around the campfire at night. I miss the days of the open range. It was more like an open buffet."

I punched him in the shoulder.

He twirled me around. I didn't really know how to two-step, so I just shuffled around to the beat as best I could. "What, pray tell, brings you out tonight?"

"I was looking for you," I said.

"And here I thought you were experimenting with alternate lifestyles before settling down."

"So, you said that you didn't turn Teréza—Sebastian's vambie—but, I was wondering, would you be willing to be her Sire, anyway?"

"Are we talking about the crazy lady who burned my hand?"

"Uh," I smiled hopefully, "Yeah. She really needs someone, you know, to teach her how to be a vampire."

Parrish spun me around again. "And I'm performing this as a public service?"

"Because it's the right thing to do?"

Parrish gave me a slight smile that showed the tips of

fangs. "Or because I'm being rewarded handsomely. Surely if she's Von Traum's problem, he'd be willing to finance her recovery."

That's my Daniel Parrish, always looking to make a buck. He put his hand on the small of my back.

"Yes," he said, as though I'd already agreed. "A decent retainer for the duration of my service, say, a hundred dollars a day. Plus combat pay when necessary," he said, lifting up his slightly scorched-looking hand.

I probably should have hesitated. I didn't have that kind of money. But Sebastian did. And I was sure Sebastian would agree that with Teréza occupied, the wedding could get back under way. Besides, maybe Teréza really did only need someone to guide her. Maybe she'd get better under Parrish's tutelage. It was possible, right? "Deal," I said.

Parrish gave me a sideways glance. "Shouldn't you negotiate a little?"

"Probably, but I'm hoping Sebastian will pay."

Parrish laughed. "So am I."

"He owes me," I said, thinking of the kiss in the woods. "I'll make sure he does."

The song was over. Parrish twirled me around one last time and pulled me into a dip. "Do."

Parrish gestured for me to head back to the table. In my brief absence, William had made a friend, it seemed. A young man with spiky, frosted hair had pulled up a chair and was leaning in very closely, like they were discussing something in earnest. I tried to catch William's eye to see if he needed rescuing, but he was too busy laughing.

"Can we join you?" Parrish asked when we were within

earshot. Spiky-hair looked up and checked out Parrish from head to toe. After a glance at William, he stood up, guilty.

"Hey, man," he said, backing away slightly. "No harm no foul."

I've never felt so invisible surrounded by so many men.

William looked baffled. Then it clicked. "Oh, wait, we're not . . ." But spiky hair was already halfway across the bar and never looked back.

Parrish settled in next to William. "Sorry, darling," he purred.

"I liked that guy," William said. "We were talking about *Battlestar Galactica.*"

I picked up my drink. It was warm, but I sipped it anyway.

"Relationships have been based on less," Parrish commented with a glance at me.

"What's that supposed to mean?" I snapped.

Parrish raised an eyebrow. William glanced at me over the rim of his glasses.

"Oh, like that wasn't a dig?" I replied to their accusing stares.

"An innocent remark, I swear," Parrish laid a hand on his chest and inclined his head in a slight bow. It was an odd gesture with the cowboy hat. "But, what's the phrase? If the shoe fits?"

Before I could begin to compose a retort that constituted more than useless sputtering, my phone rang again. I didn't recognize the number, but to avoid Parrish's deliberate stare, I turned my back to him. "Hello?"

It was my high school friend, Jane, the one who'd answered my psychic call to come to my wedding. She wanted to let me know she might not make the rehearsal dinner as planned. Her car had died—something to do with the transmission, or maybe it was an engine gasket, and all the flights were booked due to the holiday season. She'd do her best. She might find a ride with a mutual friend or maybe try the train or Greyhound, but I shouldn't count on her until I saw her.

I told her it was okay, but, by the way she kept apologizing, I could tell she heard through my lie.

"Sounds like you're at a bar or something," she said.

"Yeah," I said, not knowing what to offer in terms of an explanation. I'm here trying to corral my ex-boyfriend into helping me take care of my fiancé's crazy ex–almost wife, didn't sound, well, sane.

"It's a party right up until the end for you, eh?"

More like a nightmare. "Yeah," I murmured. "Good luck. I hope I'll see you soon."

"Oh, I'll get to that wedding come hell or high water, girl. Don't you worry."

I laughed kindly, but I wanted to tell her she was working against a pretty powerful curse. Instead, I said good-bye and wished her luck one more time. Then I hung up.

William, who'd seen this pattern before, instantly asked, "What happened now?" as soon as I tucked the phone away and turned back to the table.

"I'm down one bridesmaid."

"I guess the protection spell didn't work, huh?" William said. "Well, I guess given that it was disrupted by a drunk driver and the whole awkward moment with Sebastian and Teréza kissing in the woods, probably not."

Parrish perked up, like a shark on the scent of blood.

I waved my hands as if trying to turn the direction of the conversation before it could start. "Just don't even ask," I said. "William, I need to go home."

When I stood up, Parrish got to his feet. "I offer my services."

"William can take me," I insisted, even though William still sat looking wistfully at the bar. "Right, William?"

"Huh? Oh, sure," William started to get up.

"No," Parrish said, putting out a hand to indicate William should return to his seat. William obeyed, although he looked a little baffled. "I insist. Besides, I'm on retainer now. We have business to discuss." When I looked at Parrish blankly, he added, "To begin with, you need to tell me where I can find the Lady Von Traum."

"Lady Von Traum? Who's that? Sebastian's mother?" William asked.

"They weren't married," I reminded Parrish.

"Sebastian's parents weren't married?" William asked.

"Certainly I've always thought he was a bastard," Parrish said.

"Parrish!"

"Seriously?" William asked, looking at me.

"No, we were talking about Teréza," I explained. "Parrish, if you want to take me, let's go."

" 'Taking you' has always been my greatest pleasure," Parrish said with a devilish smile.

I rolled my eyes. At this point, being at Sebastian's farm with my mother seemed like the much saner option. Parrish offered me his arm. As we walked out the door of the bar together, I swear I heard the sound of hearts breaking.

Despite the minus degrees and icy roads, I half-expected Parrish to lead me to a motorcycle. Apparently, in the winter, Parrish drove a beat-up Toyota. It was orange red, complemented with brownish rust spots. The rear bumper seemed to be held together with political bumper stickers.

I looked at those, and then at Parrish. "Did you steal this car?"

"Wrong verb tense," he said, wrenching the door open. He sat down in the driver's side and reached across to pop open the lock on the passenger door.

My hand hesitated on the handle. " 'Verb tense'? Do you mean you're *stealing* this car?" My hand flew from the handle like it was hot, which I guess it was—or would be—except not in that sense. I looked over my shoulder nervously. I'm not sure what I expected, maybe a dozen police cars converging on us? The parking lot stayed empty. Snowflakes drifted lazily in the lamplight.

Parrish used a scraper he found on the seat to carve a hole in the frost on the driver's side of the windshield

"Get in," he said. "Unless you can teleport us, we need a car," he reminded me. "Hurry."

At the mention of teleportation, I thought of Teréza, who was probably skulking around the barn while my mother and Sebastian talked in the house. I got in. The interior of the car smelled like clove cigarettes and patchouli. A bunch of empty cans of Monster drinks littered the floorboard. I had to perch my feet on either side of the foot well. Meanwhile, Parrish had pulled the key lock ignition thingy from the steering column. Taking a screwdriver out of an interior pocket, he put it in the ignition and turned it. The car started right up.

I kept turning around in my seat to stare at the bar. I was sure the owners of the car would come out and see us driving away in their ride. Parrish stepped on the gas as we pulled out of the lot, but not nearly fast enough for me.

"Where would I go?" Parrish muttered. He rubbed his chin. I could hear a slight scratch of his hand over stubble. "I'd find a friend. The Lady Von Traum, however, seems more the hiding under the bridge sort."

"She's not his wife," I said suddenly. "And I don't think Sebastian was ever knighted." My back felt itchy pressing into the seat of a car I knew was being stolen. I checked behind us once again. Still no cops on our trail. "How long until they notice their car is missing?"

"Bar closes at two," Parrish said. We turned onto the highway, and he shifted the car smoothly into a higher gear. "I hope to have ditched this by then. Don't worry, it will be miles from your place."

It was probably all my nervous breathing, but the windows were fogging up. Parrish goosed the defroster with a twist of a knob.

"But you're fooling yourself if you don't think Sebastian held a title of some sort," he continued. "Alchemy has never been a pastime of the working class. And nobles, at least the ones I've known, have a particular and well-honed sense of chivalry. A man like Sebastian, think about it. He's not the sort to leave a woman in a delicate condition on her own, without a husband. Is he?"

I had to admit that the thought had crossed my mind—just last night in fact, with the whole Cher thing. "Maybe I don't know Sebastian as well as I thought I did."

"Oh?"

Sure, Parrish sounded innocent enough, but this was a trap. I knew it. If I confessed any weakness here, I was down a road I didn't want to follow. "I caught them kissing in the woods." I sighed. I hated when my mouth didn't obey my brain. "Teréza and Sebastian," I clarified, in case that wasn't patently obvious. Sheesh, why not just tell Parrish I'm not sure about this whole marriage thing?

I stared at the streaks of snow splattering against the window as I waited for whatever I-told-you-so zinger Parrish concocted.

Instead, his hand, cold and heavy, gently tucked a strand of hair behind my ear. He let his fingers stray at the nape of my neck for a moment longer than necessary and then returned his hand to the wheel.

Crap. I would have preferred something sarcastic. Parrish's kindness was threatening to loosen the tears I'd been carefully holding back all day. "It's not like I can't understand it," I said. Then I laughed a little at the irony of explaining this to him, of all people. Parrish was my Teréza. I never seemed to completely get over him, no matter how hard I tried. I knew he wasn't right for me, but we had a history.

"They looked so right together, you know? They're both vampires. And old, like eternally."

"And you're going to grow old and die," Parrish said matter-of-factly. "Sometimes that doesn't matter . . . not if he truly loves you."

The wistfulness in Parrish's tone reminded me that I had a Black Hills gold wedding band of his in my jewelry box at home. He'd married at least once, to a mortal. Though I wanted to hear that story, I felt I needed to explain, "Actually, I'm not sure I *will* grow old and die, not since bonding with Lilith, anyway. That's part of the reason I felt comfortable marrying Sebastian. When we say forever, it's going to be forever."

Parrish gave me an expression I couldn't quite read in the darkness, but I took it to be a combination of surprise and disgust. "Are you insane?"

I felt more than a little insulted. "What do you mean?"

"Forever? Garnet, how many lovers have you had?"

"I'm not telling you that!"

"Even at a generous estimate, probably no more than fifty in your lifetime."

"Fifty! What kind of runaround do you think I—"

He shook his head. "You haven't lived enough to decide on forever."

"You sound like my mother. Well, except she was actually really excited at the prospect," I let that thought drift off and got back to my point. "Look, I know that fifty percent of all marriages end in divorce. But, right now, the idea of spending the rest of my life—however long it ends up being—with Sebastian feels right. I love him. I can't imagine life without him."

Parrish shook his head and frowned at the passing countryside. The windshield wipers slapped out their rhythmical beat, and I realized I meant what I said.

I was still plenty mad about the kiss. And I felt that I still had a lot to learn about who Sebastian is, and was, all those many years of his undead life, but I was anxious to find out . . . with him. I was willing to try to work things out between us, because the idea of life without Sebastian seemed impossible.

The landmarks were beginning to look familiar. We passed the Fieldman farm, though I could hardly see their traditional white farmhouse through the falling snow. That reminded me. "Teréza's been living in the barn, I think."

"He's been keeping his ex-wife on his property?"

"To be fair, I think the barn was Mátyás's idea. And they were never married."

"Keep telling yourself that," Parrish said. "But, wait, this Mátyás, that's Sebastian's son?"

"Yeah," then I laughed, remembering what Parrish had said, "the bastard."

"How is it he's still alive? Did Sebastian turn his whole family? He's sicker than I thought."

Sick? It sounded like maybe Parrish had some issues with being a vampire. "No, Teréza's the only one Sebastian tried to turn. Mátyás is a dhampyr."

"What's that?"

Here was a curious situation: me, explaining to a four-hundred-year-old vampire some esoteric lore. "Uh, from what I understand, Mátyás was conceived the old-fashioned way, only Sebastian was already a vampire."

"That's not possible," Parrish said, driving past Sebastian's farm at fifty-five miles an hour.

"That was the turnoff. We just missed the house," I pointed out.

"Vampires cannot have children the traditional way." Parrish slowed the car down and pulled a U-turn that bumped us a little way onto the shoulder. The undercarriage scraped on the ice-packed snowdrifts on the side of the road.

"Sebastian can, I guess," I said. "It's probably because of how he was made. He can walk in sunlight too."

"You hardly need to remind me of that," Parrish said with a sneer as he drove past Sebastian's farm a second time. "Well, it seems you've inherited a ready-made family. How nice for you."

"Uh, you missed it again. The driveway," I said, watching the adjoining cemetery retreat in the distance.

Parrish hit the brakes. They screeched as we slid a couple of feet before coming to a stop. "Get out," he said curtly.

I started to argue, but I got the sense I'd better open up the door right away, or he was going to toss me out himself. I stepped into the cold, blustery wind. Wet snow stung my cheeks.

"And you can tell Von Traum I'm not cleaning up his messes. Not for all the gold in England."

I clung tightly to the doorframe. "No, wait, Parrish, it's not Sebastian's mess, it's mine. You have to help me. I can't seem to counter her spells, and I need someone to distract her from Sebastian. Please!"

"No," he said simply. He looked straight ahead. His jaw clenched, reflecting the bluish light of the dashboard.

"Parrish, please. I'll double your wages. Triple them."

"No," he said. Revving the engine, he glared at me with a look of pure hurt. "He already has everything I could ever hope for. Why should I make things easier for him? In fact, maybe if I team up with Teréza, I can make sure the wedding never happens."

Even though the passenger side door was still open, Parrish stepped on the gas. The car flew past me, and the door slammed shut.

Taillights disappeared into the night. Snow fell on my head.

By the time I got to the front door, my hair was sop-ping wet. No one greeted me at the door, not even Barney. The living room was dark, but there was laughter coming from the kitchen. I slid out of my boots and hung my sodden coat on a hanger.

My mother's laughter rang through the house again. I don't know why, but the happy sound depressed me. I wanted to crawl into bed and hide my head under a pillow. Maybe when I woke up, I could pretend like nothing had happened.

After all, nothing else I'd tried helped. My wedding plans were in shambles. The protection spell ended in disaster. And now somehow I'd managed to piss off Parrish so much that not only did he no longer want to help, but he'd also decided to join forces with the person determined to destroy my life with Sebastian.

Teréza.

I peered up at the piano window beside the stair. It was too high up on the wall for me to see the barn, but I knew it was out there. And so was she.

I should just go kick her ass.

Eighth Aspect: Sesqui-Square

Before I knew it, I had my coat and boots back on. The snow fell in huge, wet clumps. In the spotlight of the lonely lamppost in the cemetery, flakes rained down in a glittering white sheet. As I slogged my way along the side of the barn, I was grateful I'd taken a moment to find my pink wool hat and fluffy blue scarf.

I tried to be sneaky, but each footfall made a splashing, spattering sound. The air, at least, had warmed slightly, but that also meant that the snowpack was melting into slush.

I was sure Teréza knew I was coming.

The barn was the classic, two-story wood structure. It had even been painted brick red at one point, though not much evidence of that still clung to the aged gray boards. Part of the roof had collapsed and, during the summer, barn swallows made their nests in the rafters.

But now, in the dark of winter, the place looked cold and dark and forbidding. At the door, I could smell the rot of accumulated years. The scent of hay mingled with skunk musk and the iron tang of rusted farm equipment.

Slowly, I creaked the door open wider. If Teréza hadn't heard me sloshing up the hill, the loud groan of hinges gave my presence away. I could care less. I was done playing games. It was time for the direct approach.

"I know you're in here," I said into the cavernous darkness of the barn's interior. "We need to talk. Woman to woman."

Something skittered in the gloom—a soft, scraping sound of tiny claws on flagstone. I stepped farther inside.

I left the door wide-open, since the only light came from the yard light. Dirt-encrusted rakes and hoes hung on pegs along the wall. The rusted curved blade of a two-handed scythe blended into the shadows. Chains hung from the ceiling.

"Hello?" I ventured, a little less certainly. Then, hearing the timid echo of my own voice, I cleared my throat and tried again. "Get out here. I'm done playing games with you."

An amused, condescending chuckle drifted out of the darkness.

What I really wanted to do was crawl under a rock and hide. Instead, I squared my shoulders. She was dangerous, but so was I. Closing my eyes, I formed the image of a circle of protection around me. It surrounded me like a soap bubble, though there were tiny holes at the top and bottom. The bottom hole drew up energy from the earth. The top was there as a release valve, if I needed it. And I had a feeling I would.

"I'm not afraid of you," I said, this time with the knowledge there was an invisible ring of protection around me, sounding like I believed it.

"Who's afraid of the big, bad vampire?" Teréza's voice intoned from beyond my sight.

"Show yourself."

"I'm here. Can't you see me, little mortal?" Slowly, Teréza's features emerged from the dark. Shrouded by long, black hair, her pale face seemed to hover in shadows. The hanging chains swayed as she walked under them, clacking softly.

O-kay, she definitely scored more points in the creepiness department.

Now it was my turn to show off at bit. I took a deep, calming breath. As I breathed in, I visualized Lilith swelling up inside me. Her heat raced along my nerve endings. I began to sweat. My clothes felt heavy and steamy, like I'd spent an hour cross-country skiing. An electric spark skated around the circumference of the protective sphere.

People told me that when I was at this stage, with Lilith barely below the surface, my eyes glowed ruby red. When I spoke, though I couldn't hear it in my own ears, I know my voice took on a strange timbre, like two people speaking at once. "It's time for you to back off, Teréza. Leave my family alone."

Teréza stepped forward, and now I could see the dim outline of her form. She still wore the ragged remains of a black evening gown, but she had added a calf-length, military-style coat. It had some kind of dark fur at the collar, reminding me of a Russian soldier's uniform. "Your family?" She asked, seemingly unimpressed by my display of power. "It's my son and his father in that house."

After everything Parrish had said in the car, I was strangely relieved she didn't say "husband" when referring to Sebastian. "You're dead. You've been dead for over a hundred and fifty years," I said. "They're mine now."

I couldn't believe I'd just claimed Mátyás as family, but it was already out of my mouth. I wasn't going to take it back.

"Dead?" Teréza sounded surprised. "Sleeping. Terrible dreams."

As always when she seemed lost, I felt a deep stab of sympathy for her. It wasn't her fault that Sebastian's attempt to turn her into a vampire had failed. "I'm sorry," I said. "I'm sure no one meant for this to happen to you."

Apparently, apologizing was the wrong thing to say. Teréza's brow furrowed. The moment her lip pulled back into a snarl, I was ready for it.

Or at least I thought I was. I was expecting a physical attack, but instead, Teréza's grimace became a sly smile. She bowed her head slightly and murmured something. I thought I heard "mote" or maybe it was "smote," but the next thing I knew, dust from the floor began to rise.

A wall of dirt and hay bits took form before my startled eyes. For a moment, the particles became a crudely human shape. There was a head and two arms, but it didn't hold together terribly well. Just as it seemed nearly solid, it would melt and need to be re-formed.

I was impressed. She'd called up an earth elemental, mostly. That was serious magic and certainly not something

I could do on the fly. When she was alive, she must have been the kind of witch that struck terror into people's hearts. I could see why Sebastian had been attracted to her.

Teréza's eyebrows drew together in concentration. Whatever was wrong with her mind seemed to be keeping her from holding it together, literally. Every moment I thought for certain the dust golem was ready to attack, it would shatter. Finally, she gave up with a frustrated cry and jumped on me.

I snapped my hand forward with my palm out, like a traffic cop signaling "stop." Instantly, the protective shield became an opaque electric blue.

When Teréza's body hit the bubble's barrier, she flew backwards. Sailing through the air, she crashed against the far wall of the barn. Dislodged farm tools clattered onto her head. The hoe, the scythe, a rake, and two shovels banged onto the stone floor.

While she shook her head, dazed, I prepared my next move. I didn't want her to have time to cast another spell. The elemental demon might not have held together, but something else might.

Stepping forward, I traced the shape of a pentacle in the air. A door appeared. When Teréza pulled herself upright, I grabbed her by the lapels of the coat. My fingers touched the silky material, and my brain registered it as real animal fur. Oh, now I'd take great pleasure in strangling her to death.

Meanwhile, she had taken the scythe in one super strong hand. The next thing I knew, I felt the blade slide across my shoulder, cutting my coat. Surprise focused Lilith like a laser. My hand snapped up and grabbed Teréza's larynx and started crushing.

I smelled human rot. Something slimy and squirmy slithered onto my hand. White, wriggly insects crawled up my wrist. Maggots! I pulled my hand back in disgust. The instant I let go, the bugs disappeared. An illusion? I shook my hand to get rid of the creepy-crawly feeling.

Teréza stumbled out of the circle, grasping at her neck. The scythe fell to the floor with a clatter.

Lilith sneered in anger. Teréza tricked me with her magic. Lilith did not like being fooled. I had to move quickly to regain my advantage.

The barn doors flew open with a crash. "Stop!"

Even though our blood bond had weakened over the years, Sebastian still knew any time I triggered Lilith. My fingers were already knotted in Teréza's hair. My other hand was poised to jam her throat.

"Oh my, Garnet!" a voice shouted. It was my mother.

"Holy hell!" My father said, coming up beside my mom. That broke me. My father hardly ever cursed. Lilith dropped down deep. The sizzling sphere of protection sputtered and collapsed around my ankles. Teréza pulled away from me and broke my grip on her hair.

I turned to explain myself to Sebastian and my folks, and Teréza tackled me. My head smacked against the flagstone floor. For a dead girl, Teréza fell on me like a sack of bricks. The air rushed out of my lungs. Her hands went to my face, fingernails clawing and grasping blindly.

I called on Lilith's strength and gave Teréza a twisting shove. She flew up into the air and then fell on to the floor with a wet, hard thump. She groaned but lay still.

Sebastian was at my side in that preternatural way he had.

His hand pressed my shoulder where the blade cut me. "Are you all right?" he asked. He spared a glance at Teréza but stayed at my side.

My father stood in the door and shook his head. My mother tut-tutted. I heard her mutter something about not having raised me to catfight.

Out of the corner of my eye, I saw Teréza pull herself up and grab the scythe from where it had fallen. Our gaze met for a second before I yelled, "Watch out!"

I cringed, expecting to die. My peripheral vision caught a sense of movement, but my eyes stayed glued to Teréza. I thought I saw my father pick something up, but I couldn't be sure, as my eyes watched the blade descending toward my head. I started muttering a spell, but I didn't think I'd be able to complete it in time.

I looked up to see Teréza's head whammed to the side, as a two-foot-tall, metal milk can caromed off her head. Her eyes rolled up, and she crumpled to the floor.

I looked around to try to figure out what happened. My dad gave me the thumbs-up. He wiped his hands on his jeans, and I surmised he'd been the one to toss the can.

My mom looked a little green around the gills yet a bit proud of my dad's prowess. "Is she dead?"

"Technically, she's been dead a long time," Sebastian said drily. To me, he added, inspecting the puffy explosion of down feathers at my shoulder, "Your coat took the brunt of the attack. But there is a little blood somewhere." Lower, in my ear, he whispered huskily, "I can smell it."

Great. My vampire boyfriend was getting all blood horny in front of the parents.

I gave him the "down, boy" squinty glare, and jerked my head in the direction of my folks.

My dad was standing over Teréza and peering down into her face. "I think I dented her head."

"Not likely," Sebastian said. "She's really, really, really hard to keep down."

"So I've noticed," Dad said, tentatively poking Teréza's coat with his toe. "She could need medical attention. Or a cemetery."

"I've tried both." Sebastian sighed.

My dad chuckled. My mother sidled closer to us. She shined her penlight into my face. "You put on quite the show," she said. "Was that . . . ?" She paused momentarily and whispered, "Magic? I mean, should I be reconsidering Lutheranism?"

"It's not typical," I admitted. "I had a kind of magical accident."

"Happy accident," Sebastian said. When I gave him a look, he explained. "Given the sorts of things we attract, you'd be dead six times over by now."

"Speaking of dead," my dad said, "what should we do with her?"

My mother shined her penlight around the dusty edges of the barn. A couple of mice scurried away into darker corners. "Does this place have a storm shelter?"

"Of course," Sebastian said, pointed to a spot on the floor none of the rest of us could see in the gloom. "Right over there."

"What this barn needs is electricity," Dad said. He put his hands on his hips and looked around in that way men had when they were thinking about fixing something. "Run a line in from the house."

"It's not worth it," Sebastian said. "I really only use this place as a potting shed."

"You could put in grow lights," I said.

"You've got a lot of space here," my mother agreed.

Teréza groaned.

Sebastian stood up and walked into the darkness, stepping over Teréza. I could barely see him in the gloom, but he kicked around the dusty floor.

"What'cha looking for, son?" my dad asked.

"The root cellar," he said. Kneeling down, Sebastian grasped at something. I stood up to get a closer look. My mom shined her tiny flashlight in Sebastian's direction.

"The ground is going to be frozen," my dad said. "You're going to need a lever. . . ."

Dirt and frozen bits of straw flew everywhere as Sebastian yanked the door open.

"Or you could just do that," my dad said, sounding a little surprised at Sebastian's dramatic show of strength.

"Help me drag her over," Sebastian said to my dad.

"You must work out at the gym a lot," Dad said, adjusting his seed cap.

"He has the strength of ten men," I said drily. "I told you already, he's a vampire."

"Yeah," my dad said gruffly, like he still wasn't sure he believed any of this yet. "Huh. Does that make you dead, too?" He asked Sebastian. "I don't know if my daughter should be marrying a dead guy. Hell, I'm not sure it's legal to marry someone who's already dead."

"You had to bring up the vampire thing again," Sebastian said as he grabbed Teréza's arms. My dad took hold of her feet. Mom and I followed along like some grim procession. I picked up one of the fallen shovels in case we had to whack her on the head again. My mom gave me a concerned glance that seemed to imply I was being a bit bloodthirsty. She wasn't the one whose favorite parka had just been ravaged by a scythe, however.

"Don't vampires shrivel in sunlight?" my dad asked Sebastian.

"Some do. I don't," Sebastian shot me an angry look.

I shrugged an apology. Somehow he managed to bring up occult matters, and my parents rolled with it. The second I did, my dad got all up in arms. How was I supposed to predict that?

"Your magic is pretty impressive," my mom said to me.

"Oh, well, that's mostly Lilith," I said, feeling a little embarrassed. I didn't know why, but talking about magic with my mom felt a little like talking about sex.

"Don't be so modest," Sebastian admonished, as he and my dad negotiated down the creaky wooden stairs. My dad, of course, couldn't see nearly as well. My mom tried to give them as much light as she could, but the flashlight was weak. "Garnet is a very powerful witch in her own right."

"You are? Why don't we know anything about this?" My mom had that same vaguely hurt tone in her voice as when she talked about the dress. Oh God.

"How about garlic? Do you like garlic?" my dad said.

"Watch the last step," Sebastian said. "It felt a little loose to me."

"Dad, we met at an Italian restaurant. You know he can stand garlic," I said.

"That's good," Dad said with a grunt as they reached the bottom of the cellar. "I couldn't deal with a son-in-law who didn't eat garlic. Where the hell does that whole garlic thing come from anyway? It never made any sense to me."

"It's a natural blood thinner," Sebastian said. "Besides, in some countries it's considered a cure-all."

Mom and I peered down into the root cellar. Even from where we stood I could smell the dankness. Mom's flashlight revealed rows of shelves containing dusty, ancient canned beans and pickles. Something that looked like an old slide projector sat in a corner. "Look at this place," I said. "You should be using this."

"We *are* running out of room for my canning in the basement," Sebastian said, glancing around.

Sebastian was an herbalist, but he had a small vegetable garden, as well. We made salsa, tomato sauce, pickles, and anything else we could think of every fall.

"You can? How marvelous!" My mother was thrilled. I could understand her enthusiasm in a way. Canning was a dying art. It was becoming harder and harder for Sebastian and me to find our supplies at the grocery store.

When they set Teréza down on the floor, she stirred. Her foot twitched. I gripped my shovel. My father stumbled back, nearly tripping over a rusty washtub. "Uh," he said trying to gain his composure a little, "we should get out of here before she wakes up."

I had to agree with Dad, but, "What are we going to tell Mátyás? He's just going to let her out, and then she's really going to be pissed with all of us." I gave Sebastian a meaningful look as he came up the dusty staircase. After all, he'd kissed her only last night, and now he was helping toss her into a storm cellar.

Mom shone her light on Teréza's pale face. "She looks like a child."

"She was twenty-three when she died," Sebastian said. Even though I couldn't see his face clearly in the dark, I could hear the pain in his voice. He gave a little sad laugh. "In those days, she was considered an old maid."

Sebastian lifted the storm door. He paused with it halfway open.

Maybe I'm insensitive, or perhaps I was still a little hurt about the whole kiss in the woods, so I said, "Yet you let her get pregnant with your baby, and you never married her?"

"Garnet!" my mother hissed.

Sebastian let the door drop with a bang. "We should find a crowbar or something to lock the door."

"Are you really that cold, or are you just trying to put me off the scent?" I asked.

He grabbed the shovel from my hands, wrenching it from my grasp. "This will work," he snarled.

I gasped. I was surprised by his violence.

"Don't you treat my daughter like that, you bully," my mom said.

Sebastian kneeled down. He jammed the wooden handle of the shovel through the latch on the cellar door. It wasn't a perfect fit, but he pulled at the door, and it only opened an inch or so.

I stared at him. My hands stung a bit from the force he had used to pull the shovel from me. I wiped them on my jeans.

When Sebastian stood up, Mom got in his face. "Did you hear me? You owe Garnet an apology, young man."

I smelled cinnamon toast and butter. "Ma'am," Sebastian said. "You need to back off."

"You need to answer her questions," my dad said. He stepped in, even as my mother moved back a pace from Sebastian's fierce look. "Are you even planning to marry our daughter? Or are you going to run out on her like you did the last one?"

Sebastian glared at me. His glamour smelled very alluring, like fresh bread on a lazy Sunday morning. Part of me was ready to just drop the whole thing and grab a midnight snack. But the magic couldn't quite overpower the way my heart pounded in my chest, waiting to see what Sebastian would do. Also, I was fairly awestruck at the way my parents rushed to my defense. I would have thought my mother would have admonished me about my manners a long time ago.

"Garnet and I need to discuss our wedding plans, sir," Sebastian said to my dad. "There have been a number of complications."

"Are you talking about the dress?" My mother asked, "Because Garnet will wear her grandmother's."

"Or is there something else?" Dad pressed.

Sebastian's lips were tight. I'm sure he was expecting me to blurt out the fact that I'd caught him and Teréza in the woods.

"Uh, Mom, Dad," I said. "Can you guys let us talk about this?" When my dad continued to stare up into Sebastian's hard face, I cleared my throat. "Alone?"

My mom got the hint. "Sure, honey. Come on, Glen."

I could tell my dad didn't want to back down, but my mother had invoked the Christian name. In our family, you knew how deep in trouble you were by how much of your name got used. God help you if you got called by first, middle, *and* last.

Even so, my dad let me call the situation. "Are you sure, Garnet?"

"Yeah, Dad, please. Sebastian and I need to work this out privately."

"All right," he agreed grudgingly. "Come on, Estelle."

My dad protectively glared at Sebastian the entire time he headed out the door, so much so he nearly tripped over one of the fallen rakes. My mother grabbed his elbow and then tucked her arm into his.

"Are you feeling sorry for Teréza now?" Sebastian asked as soon as my folks were out of earshot. "When exactly did this compassion develop? I thought you figured her for a crazy Gypsy zombie."

"Vampire," I added. When Sebastian cocked his head to the side curiously, I repeated the litany, "Crazy zombie vampire. Oh, and witch."

He chuckled a little at that, but the tension hadn't entirely broken.

"Look," I said. "I'm cold, and it stinks like a dead skunk in here. Can we go inside and talk in front of the fire? Besides, all that glamour you sprayed around made me hungry."

"No," he said. "I'm not ready to go inside yet. We need to talk about Teréza. I need to explain."

I glanced over at the cellar door. My eyes had adjusted somewhat, but I couldn't quite make out the details. For all I could tell, she might be peeping out at us right now. "She might hear us," I said.

"That would be fine with me. I never got a chance to explain myself to her, either."

I rubbed my hands against my arms, bringing down a shower of feathers from the slash in my coat. Now that the excitement had died down, I could feel the chill on my ears. I'd really rather be inside for this. "So," I said with a sigh. "Why didn't you marry her?"

"I was selfish."

That derailed me. I wasn't expecting that answer. "What do you mean?"

"How does the saying go these days? I just wasn't that *into* her. Besides," he said, and the hardness in his voice since I first brought this subject up shattered a little, "I had other children before. None of them lived past infancy. I thought it was part of my curse."

Poor Sebastian. I reached a hand out to comfort him, but he turned away before I could touch him. I wished more than ever that I could see his face. "I'm sorry," I said.

"I held off the marriage because I didn't want to be saddled with a woman I didn't really love for a child that wouldn't live. Then she got sick. Out of a misplaced sense of duty, I had to act."

"Wait, so you're saying that you turned Teréza when she was pregnant?"

"I didn't know what else to do, Garnet." Sebastian said, with a glance over his shoulder. Turning away again, he added, "I thought at least I could save her. In my mind, the baby was doomed from the start. But this way, her family wouldn't have to mourn two deaths."

"But . . ." My head was really spinning now. "She did die."

"Yes," Sebastian said. "And, the baby grew inside her. When he was born, I took Mátyás back to his people. I—" I could hear the tears now. "I wasn't able to take care of him. That whole experience—watching, waiting—it was horrible. It broke me. And Mátyás needed a wet nurse. He needed someone who could love him properly. The whole thing was such a disaster."

"Oh, Sebastian," I said, because I didn't know what else to say. I went over to him and grabbed him into a hug, even though his back was still to me. I could feel him go stiff and rigid at first. I squeezed tighter. Finally, he turned around and let me give him a real hug. "I'm sorry," I said. "I had no idea."

Sebastian's arms curled around my shoulders. Silently, we clung to each other for a long moment. He rested his chin on the top of my head, and I snuggled deeper into his chest. I hated to bring it up, but I had one last question for Sebastian.

"So is that why you kissed Teréza? Because of all this?"

Sebastian tried to pull away, but I tightened my grip on him with a little help from Lilith.

"I understand you two have history," I said, still muffled in the leather of his coat. "What I want to know is: Do you have a future with her?"

I pulled back a little and studied Sebastian's face in the half-light. His gaze was turned inward, his expression a study of indifference. He answered quietly but firmly, "Teréza will always be my son's mother."

"That's an awfully careful answer," I pointed out. "I'm not asking if you love her, because I know you're still entangled with her, out of duty or whatever. When I saw you . . ." It was my turn to feel hurt. I pushed through it. It was important for me to tell him how I felt about this. If not, it would always nag me. "You were like two sides of the same coin, like you were meant to be together. I mean, she's a vampire too, now. That's got to be like a second chance for you to make things right."

Sebastian shook his head, but he said, "I'll admit the thought crossed my mind, so I kissed her to see if there was anything there. But my experience after her death—I'm serious, Garnet—it broke something in me." He glanced at the cellar door. "It broke her too, though. She's not the woman I tried to save. Not anymore. Not after everything. And I'm no longer the man who tried to save her."

I could feel him resisting being held by me. It seemed he was uncomfortable being this close to me while admitting his shameful past. But, for me, it was important to keep touching him, if only to let him know that I still loved him no matter what. "Won't it always gnaw at you? I know you, Sebastian, you're a decent soul. Won't you always wonder if you could have fixed things?"

"Some things are beyond fixing," he said. "But, like I said, that's what I was testing out when I kissed her. I wanted . . ." Finally, he couldn't take it and broke free of my embrace.

Though I could have used Lilith to keep him close, I let him go. "All I've ever wanted was to make it right. But the two of them, they're delusional when they talk about us as one big happy family." It took me a second to realize he must mean Mátyás as well. "That was never us. I never wanted any of it."

I don't quite know why, maybe I was just caught up in the moment in Teréza's story, but I continued to be devil's advocate. "Why not? Why couldn't you be one big, happy vampire family?" I had to admit the moment it was out of my mouth I got visions of *The Addams Family*. I couldn't suppress a little vaguely hysterical giggle, as I added, "A family who drinks blood together stays together!"

"Exactly," Sebastian muttered. He'd turned his back to me again, and stood staring out the window. "Do I smell marijuana?"

The second after he said it, I caught the heavy, sweet, grassy scent of pot. I rolled my eyes. "My folks are probably puffing on a joint somewhere."

Sebastian looked at me for confirmation, like he didn't quite believe what I'd just said.

"Did I neglect to mention that my parents are potheads?"

"Yes, somehow you never brought that up," Sebastian said with a small twist of a smile.

I shrugged. "It's true. They're Mr. and Mrs. Cheech and Chong."

"How hilarious."

"I'm glad you think so," I said a little petulantly. "Try growing up with that."

Sebastian grunted noncommittally. Then, turning all the

way around to face me again, he said, "I want you to under-stand that Teréza and I will never be. There is no future for her and me. I've spent too many years trying to bury my past, literally. I don't want her in my life, not like that. I want you."

"Good answer," I said, striding over to take his hand into mine. "Come on," I said. "I'm frozen solid."

"Does that mean I get an opportunity to try to warm you up?"

The lascivious purr in his voice brought heat to my cheeks. "Warm? Honey, you always get me hot," I teased.

Sebastian and I had just snuggled into a warm spot near the roaring fire and started the kiss-and-make-up pro-cess when my parents stumbled in, giggling like teenagers.

"Oopsie, didn't mean to interrupt," said my mother in that singsong voice she always had when she was high.

"Looks like you two worked things out," my dad said with a sloppy grin. Then he got a faraway look in his eye. "Al-though I don't know how you could have. There's a dead girl in the root cellar."

This set my mother giggling. She was stepping out of her boots somewhat clumsily, with her hand on the wall to steady herself. "That sounds like a horror novel," she said. "*Dead Girl in the Cellar.*"

"Yeah, like, *The People Under the Stairs*," my dad added. "Didn't we see that one?"

Sebastian stood up with a sigh. "I'll go put on coffee."

"That only works with alcohol," I muttered. Sebastian gave me a what-else-can-I-do shrug, and headed for the kitchen.

"It was *Tarantula* at the drive-in," my mother said. She'd managed to get out of her boots and was now working on her coat.

"No, no, *Snakes on a Plane*," my dad countered.

Closing my eyes, I laid my head on the back of the couch. They'd be at this all night. Barney, who was snoozing on the leather chair near the fire, lifted her nose from where it was buried in a fluffy gray tail and meowed. I opened my eyes a crack, and the moment of eye contact was all the encouragement she needed. She bounded over and settled in my lap with a happy purring chirp. I scratched her behind the ears.

Benjamin picked up a stack of books and dropped them on the floor.

My mother squeaked.

My dad, who still hadn't taken off his boots or his parka, looked around with half-lidded eyes and said, "Is this place haunted?"

The lamp next to couch flicked off and on.

"Whoa," my dad said. "The house just talked to me."

"Settle down, Benjamin," Sebastian shouted from the kitchen. I could smell French roast percolating. "Glen and Estelle are just a little tipsy. They're not a threat."

The kitchen door swung open and then slammed shut as if someone had just left the room in a huff. It seemed Benjamin and I had the same opinion of my parents when they were high.

My mother slumped down on the couch kitty-corner to me. "Honey," she asked, "who's Benjamin?"

"The house ghost."

"See, Glen," my mother said to my father, who hadn't

moved from where he stood by the door. "They have a house guest."

"Besides that snarky teenager? This house is crowded."

I had to agree.

I didn't bother correcting my mother. When she was stoned she heard exactly what she wanted, no matter how many times you explained otherwise.

"Dad, you should take your coat off, stay awhile," I said. I really wanted to send them back to their hotel, but one of us would have to drive them, given the state they were in.

My dad looked down at his clothes, like he was surprised to find himself still wearing his coat. "Oh, yeah."

"This house has a great aura, don't you think?" My mother asked dreamily. "Sebastian's energy is so calming."

The only time my parents acted like hippy boomers was when they were high. Otherwise, their default personalities were Norwegian farmers. Even though I'd seen the transformation several times before, it always took me a minute to catch up to speed. Plus I was a little cranky with them for interrupting my make-out session. "People have auras. Places have energy."

My mother nodded sagely, as though I had just given her the answer to life, the universe, and everything. "People have auras, like angels have nimbuses. Like, wow, man."

My mother just said, ". . . like, wow, man." Could this night be over yet? I nestled deeper into the comforter, wishing Sebastian would come out of hiding.

As if in answer to my prayers, Sebastian swept into the room holding a silver platter with chips, Oreo cookies, and a couple of homemade blueberry flaxseed muffins left over from breakfast. As he placed the tray on the end table, Sebastian gave me a wink as if to remind me he'd lived through the 1960s too.

"Munchies!" My dad smiled happily, reaching for the muffins. My mother grabbed the chips and cradled them in her lap. Barney hopped off to investigate the possibilities of something a cat might find edible.

Sebastian reclaimed his spot next to me and put an arm around my shoulder. For what seemed like interminable minutes, no one spoke. Oblivious, my parents snacked greedily. I stared at them like I had so many times when I was growing up, wishing they were more like normal people. Sebastian stroked my hair, but that made things worse. I was embarrassed that he had to witness this. I looked over at Sebastian, but he just observed the spectacle with an amused smile playing on his lips.

"I still don't think it's legal to marry someone who is already dead," my dad said after polishing off a second muffin.

"I'm not dead," Sebastian said. "Undead. It's an important distinction."

"Yeah, but nobody knows about vampires, right?" My dad leaned on his elbows. He loved a good political debate. "It's not like there's laws about this sort of thing. Isn't it considered fraud?"

Barney rubbed against Dad's legs, and he reached down and gave her a rub across the back.

"Only if Garnet didn't know," Sebastian said. "If we're going to get into legal technicalities, when I marry Garnet, I'll be a bigamist."

"I told you he was married to that woman in the cellar,"

my mother said. She looked asleep with her head back against the couch, but her hand kept methodically putting chips in her mouth.

"No, I never married Teréza," Sebastian said. "But Garnet is really two people in one."

"Far out," my mother said.

"How's that?" asked my dad.

Barney jumped up onto the space on the couch between my parents. Daintily, she placed her two front paws on my mother's thigh and stuck her head in the bag of chips.

"Lilith," I said. I mean, what the hell, it wasn't like they'd really remember this conversation in the morning. "I share my body with the Queen of Hell."

"That's freaky," my mother said, putting her hand down and finding a cat's back. As if forgetting the chip she'd been reaching for, Mom started petting Barney. Barney, meanwhile, was no doubt licking the cheese flavoring off each chip.

"I hope she's paying rent," my dad said with a shake of his head. He leaned back on the couch and threw an arm around my mom. "There're too damn many lodgers in this place as it is."

That reminded me. "What are we going to do about Mátyás?"

"I left a message on his voice mail," Sebastian said.

"Saying what, exactly? 'Hello, son, we've imprisoned your mom; don't let her out, love Dad'?"

My mother chuckled, and my dad gave a little derisive snort.

"No, I lied," Sebastian said. "I told him that I needed

some space tonight because I was working things out with Teréza. I suggested it would be a good night to stay over at Izzy's."

"Well, it's not entirely false. You *are* working things out," my mother said. "Just not pleasantly."

"Do you think he'll believe you?" I asked, ignoring my mother's comment. My dad, meanwhile, had started to snore.

Sebastian lifted his hand off the back of the couch in a kind of shrug. "I don't know, but the boy *is* desperate for Teréza and me to reconnect."

Leaning over, I snagged an Oreo cookie. "Did I tell you that Jane canceled?" I asked Sebastian. "I guess the flights are booked because of the holidays."

"Jane?" My mother perked up, "Jane Yorgleson from Central High?"

I nodded around a mouthful of crumbed cookie. "I guess it's Jane Rathmussen now, but yeah. She got my astral invite."

"You mean the dream?" my mother asked.

"What dream?" asked Sebastian.

Meanwhile, Barney snagged a large triangular chip in her teeth and marched off with it proudly, like she'd caught a fat mouse. She quickly escaped to the privacy of underneath the table. My father snorted himself awake and then resettled.

"It was the clearest dream I've ever had," my mother explained. "It was like a TV ad. There was a picture of Garnet in a white dress and a man I now recognize as you in a black tuxedo. A voice-over told me how to get in contact with Garnet if I wanted to attend her wedding. At the end there was like this screen with the wedding date and a phone number. I think I dreamed it more than once."

"You sent out an astral commercial for our wedding?"

"I didn't know how else to contact my old friends. I mean, some of them thought I was dead."

Sebastian scrubbed his face with his hands. "No wonder Parrish is back. You put a filter on this, of course, so it would only go to your friends, right?"

"Uh . . ." I had, hadn't I? I couldn't quite remember. I'd gotten kind of caught up in the moment.

"We wouldn't want the Vatican to get the message that we're alive and well, would we?"

My mother, finding her bag empty of cat, started munching on chips again. "Why not? Does this have something to do with your being Catholic?"

"More the fact of my being a witch, Mom. There's a group of paramilitary witch hunters called the Order of Eustace that may or may not be officially aligned with the Vatican," I said, polishing off my cookie. I eyed another one but decided against it. "Who are very anti-witch. To the point of murder."

" 'May or may not'?" Sebastian broke in. "Are you kidding me? Most of the Order's members are ordained priests and nuns." We'd had this argument many times before. Ironically, it was Sebastian, the Catholic, who tended to be certain that the Vatican funded the Order. "Of course they're under the Vatican's aegis."

"Just because they're priests doesn't mean they're not part of a rogue organization. We don't have any proof the Vatican approves."

"Except that Mátyás claims his friends in the Order arranged for the pope to perform an exorcism."

My mother snorted in disbelief. "I find that hard to believe. Exorcists are specialists. I think we'd have heard if this pope was an exorcist. CNN would have uncovered information like that."

"Like how there are vampires and zombies running around," my dad piped up. His eyes were still closed, but he must have been listening in.

"Oh." My mother chewed another handful of chips, considering. "Yeah, why is it we haven't noticed all this sort of stuff before?" She looked at Sebastian quizzically. "You don't really seem to be hiding who you are. Not that you need to, mind you. I mean, I'm sure you're a perfectly nice vampire and everything. And so good-looking. My, such broad shoulders and trim waist. I love your arms. I noticed when your sleeves are rolled up you've got lovely muscles."

I was afraid she might go on, so I interrupted. "Mom," I said reproachfully, "stop."

"I understand your concern, Mrs. Lacey," Sebastian said, ignoring all the weird flirting from my mom. "You don't have to worry. I don't usually go around broadcasting my vampirism."

"And I don't usually blurt out the whole vampire thing either," I said. When Sebastian shot me an "are you sure about that?" glance, I returned with a "let me finish" glare. "See, the thing is, I, well, I guess I just wanted you to love him for all that he is—like I do."

Sebastian gave me a curious sort of smile-grimace, like he wasn't sure if he should take my saccharine comments seriously. I jabbed him in the ribs.

"Because I do," I said.

"Aw, honey, that's sweet," my mother said. "Of course, we like him."

"I don't," my dad said, sitting up and opening his eyes. "Not only is he dead, which can't be good, but if he's a vampire, that means he drinks blood. Our daughter's blood."

"It's not like that," Sebastian said, sitting up a little straighter as well.

"Actually, he mostly feeds on other people," I explained quickly. "They're called suppliers or donors or . . . well, mostly we call them ghouls."

That little bit of information killed conversation completely. My parents stared at us with a combination of incredulity and disgust.

Barney, having noisily crunched up her stolen treasure, hopped up on to the arm of the couch near my mother, clearly ready for another one.

Sebastian shot me a way-to-blow-it glance and stood up. "I think the coffee is done," he announced.

"So what is this," my mother asked, "swinging or something?"

I got up and went over to adjust the logs on the fire. I didn't know how to explain our blood donor arrangements with my parents; I hardly knew how to deal with the complexity of it all myself. I jabbed at the logs with the poker. Sparks flew and quickly faded to ash on the stone hearth. "When did your generation get so conservative?" I asked. "I mean, weren't you guys the ones who became swingers? It's not like Sebastian is out cruising for people to bite. He's got a regular list of willing volunteers who have all been vetted by some kind of supplier's guild. I don't really ask, but I know he's faithful to me. That's all that matters, right?"

"If you say so, honey," my mother said.

"What was wrong with Brett Cunningham, anyway?" My father asked.

"Brett?" I said. "I dated him for two months senior year."

"At least he was human," my father said.

"Sebastian is human too," I said. "He's just . . . altered." Wow, what a ringing endorsement. Even though I knew he had super hearing, I was glad Sebastian had retreated to the kitchen.

"I liked that Daniel Parrish fellow," my mother said. "He only came over to the place once, late at night, but he was a real gentleman. Didn't you date him in Minneapolis for a long time?"

I couldn't quite contain a laugh. "Mom, Parrish is a vampire too."

"Christ, how many of them are there?" my dad asked. "Brett Cunningham was nice."

He was also a horny jock who did things with me I was certain my dad wouldn't approve of.

Sebastian came out with two coffee mugs. "Anyone else want a cuppa?"

"Oh," my mother smiled, " 'Cuppa,' how British." Barney took advantage of my mother's distraction to stick her paw tentatively inside the chip bag that sat forgotten on my mother's lap.

"I'll take some," I said, reaching for the mug. Maybe caffeine would help stave off the stress headache that was tightening along my shoulders and neck.

Sebastian handed it to me. "There's more in the kitchen."

My dad hauled himself off the couch. "I'll help myself," he said.

"It's getting late," my mother observed. The clock on the mantel read quarter to two in the morning.

Barney's claws snared another chip. She scooped it up in her mouth and ran off with it. This time she disappeared under the couch. If she kept this diet up, I'd no doubt be stepping in regurgitated piles of Doritos in the middle of the night.

"I'll drive you back to the hotel," Sebastian offered. "We can bring your car around in the morning."

"We could crash in your spare bedroom."

"Not a good idea," I said quickly.

Benjamin rattled the china in the kitchen. "Holy shit, the cabinets are haunted," I heard my dad yell.

"Why not? I peeked in there earlier. It's a beautiful room. Your son seems to prefer the couch, and . . ."

"Actually, you could use the sunroom, if you'd like," Sebastian said. "There's a lovely fold-out futon in there. It's a little chilly, but it's beautiful."

I stared at him openmouthed. He was going to offer my parents the sunroom? Sebastian never let *me* into the sunroom. It was off his private sanctum sanctorum, his alchemical workshop. It was the only room in the house he kept locked. I only knew about it because I'd broken into it once with Lilith's help.

"Why couldn't we . . . ?"

I smelled cinnamon and cloves, like pumpkin pie. "Because the guest room belongs to our house ghost. I think you'd be more comfortable in the sunroom."

"Oh, okay," my mom was a pushover when she was high.

My dad came back in with a coffee mug that said Witches Do It By Moonlight.

"Come on, Glen," Mom said. "We're heading to bed."

"But I just got my coffee."

"Let's leave these kids alone for a while."

My dad frowned petulantly at his cup. "But I thought they'd kissed and made up."

"I want to have sex," my mother said.

I spat my coffee back into my cup. "Mom!"

"Oh!" My dad set the cup down on the nearest surface, which happened to be a leather-bound book.

Sebastian scooped it up quickly. "Uh, I hate to rain on your parade, but I need to make up the bed. It will only take a moment, I promise," he said with a broad wink. "So you two will just have to simmer down for a minute."

Sebastian took the stairs two at a time.

That left me huddling under the green comforter again. My dad came over and gave my mother a shoulder rub. He leaned in and whispered something in my mother's ear. I tried not to watch, because I was deeply embarrassed, but it was kind of sweet too. It was nice to know my parents still loved each other. Although I did *not* need to know they were about to have sex.

I tapped my toes and glanced at the ceiling. Did Mátyás feel like this when Sebastian and I went at it? Because of how close they looked in age, I tended to forget that Sebastian was Mátyás's father, like my dad, who was right now kissing the top of my mother's head.

It seemed like forever, but eventually Sebastian came back down. "You're all set. Let me show you upstairs," Sebastian said.

I'd never seen my folks move so fast. Apparently, marijuana made them frisky too.

Despite the coffee, I was awfully drowsy by the time Sebastian returned. I yawned deeply.

"Hey, none of that," Sebastian said. "You promised me some making up."

He sat down on the couch and snuggled up close. I fluffed the blanket to let him under. Our legs entwined. With a smile, I threw my arms around his shoulders and pulled him close. He chuckled low in his throat. Our lips met. Heat raced along my inner thigh. All thoughts of sleeping evaporated.

As his hands roamed the contours of my back and ribs, Sebastian's palms grazed the swell of my breast. My nipples hardened at even the briefest touch. I wanted more, now. I kissed him harder and deeper, encouraging. My fingers twined through his hair.

Lips brushed my earlobe. "Will you still want me like this in a hundred years?"

I grabbed a fistful of his hair. With my free hand, I put his where I wanted it. "Always."

He growled and slid his fingers under my shirt. The contact of skin on skin made me gasp.

The front door opened. I heard the storm door snap back on its hinges. Boots stomped on the welcome rug.

I kept my eyes shut, hoping it was just Benjamin playing tricks on us.

Mátyás cleared his throat.

The groan that escaped my lips hurt somewhere deep inside.

"Oh, a little coitus interruptus?" Mátyás said with a smile.

Letting his hand slip from my breast, Sebastian leaned back with a sigh. "I thought you were staying the night with Izzy."

"I did, Papa," Mátyás said with mock innocence. "It's morning."

I rubbed my face, tiredness washing over my body. Despite the slight remaining ache between my legs, I could use some sleep. "Maybe we *should* go upstairs," I muttered absently.

"Are you sure you wouldn't rather go out to the barn?" Mátyás asked, inspecting his fingernails. "Seems there's a really nice root cellar there."

Sebastian stood up. The blanket fell away from his legs, and his hands balled into fists at his side. He was ready for a fight.

Mátyás, meanwhile, leaned casually against the door, crossing his arms in front of his chest. His black hair fell across his forehead, shadowing his eyes.

At times like this I noticed how alike they could be. They stood completely differently, but my mother was right; they appeared nearly the same age. Their hair was the same midnight black, although Mátyás's was short to Sebastian's long. About the same height, Sebastian had a bit more bulk, but they had the same body type.

When they were mad, their eyes narrowed in exactly the same way.

"We had to put her in the cellar. She was trying to kill me. Again."

I heard a squeal from upstairs.

Mátyás glanced at the ceiling. "Benjamin's sounding awfully feminine."

"Uh," Sebastian glanced at me.

"It's my mom," I said.

"What is she doing, exactly?" Mátyás asked.

Sebastian and I looked at each other and then gave him the what-do-you-think eyebrow waggle.

He frowned. "In your bedroom?"

"The sunroom," I said.

"My, my," Mátyás clucked. "The house *is* crowded. The barn too."

Benjamin or the wind rattled the window sash.

"You haven't let her out, have you?" Sebastian asked.

Mátyás flipped his hair back, like he was bored. "Let my mother out? Now, why would I free my mother from being entombed in the dank earth? That's not my style."

Of course that's exactly what he'd been doing most of his life.

Sebastian ground his teeth. If he were a cartoon character, smoke would have been curling from his ears.

I stood beside him and put my hand around his fist. He

looked down at our hands, and I felt him consciously relax. Sebastian took a deep breath and switched tactics. "She'll be safer in the cellar," Sebastian said. "The sun will be up soon."

"Safer? Oh, you were just thinking of her well-being when you blocked the door with the shovel. How kind," Mátyás sniffed.

"Actually, we were trying to keep her from tearing my throat out," I said. It wasn't like I didn't already have scratches on my face from where she'd tried to claw me the first time we met.

"She must have been hungry," Mátyás observed. "Good thing I brought her someone to eat."

"Someone?" I repeated.

"You left someone alone with her in the state she's in? She'll kill them," Sebastian said, horrified. He shook off my hand and headed for the door. Mátyás shifted out of the way. Sebastian didn't even bother putting on a coat as he headed out into the wind and snow.

Mátyás smiled as he shut the door behind Sebastian, and that's when I knew Sebastian had reacted just the way Mátyás had planned.

"It's nice to see Papa rush to her side," Mátyás said. Pushing off the wall with a stocking foot, he headed for the kitchen.

"Is there even a donor out there?" I asked.

Mátyás swung the door open. "Do you want eggs? I'm making breakfast."

I walked away without answering. I started putting on my jacket, which hung by the front door. When I had one boot on, Sebastian opened the door.

"Where the hell is she?" he stomped through to the kitchen, going right past where I knelt by the door. "There's no one in the barn."

"What?" Mátyás's voice had none of his usual smarmy self-righteousness.

"You stupid boy. She's gone."

"We have to find her."

I was halfway to the kitchen, when I heard the back door slam. "Sebastian?" I called. I expected to see Sebastian sitting dejectedly at the kitchen table or pacing back and forth in front of the door. But the room was empty. Barney padded after me, looked around, and sat down in front of her food bowl. "Sebastian?"

Walking over to the door, I pulled aside the curtain to try to catch sight of them. The barn stood like a shadow in the breaking dawn. Snow fell in thick sheets. I opened the door. The snow flew in. My shout was muffled by the storm. "Sebastian?"

Barney mewed pitifully.

"They left without me," I told her.

She licked her whiskers and looked at her bowl.

"I can't believe they left without me." Shutting the door, I poured some kibbles into her bowl. She started crunching wetly. I petted her head, even though she rippled her back in clear indication that she would like to be left on her own with her breakfast.

Even my cat didn't want me.

Yawning, I sat back on my heels. I rubbed my eyes. They felt scratchy and sore. I hadn't slept at all, and I had an afternoon shift at the store tomorrow, no, today. I should go after

Sebastian and Mátyás. My eyelids closed for a moment, and I nearly fell over.

I pulled myself upright, determined to at least pass out in bed for a couple of hours. Halfway up the stairs, I heard what sounded like a cow lowing. Then I remembered my parents were having noisy sex on the second floor. Turning around, I flopped down on the couch. I pulled the comforter over my head. "I can't believe they left without me," I muttered. I was angry and hurt but too damned exhausted to do anything about it. Barney hopped up to settle on my shoulder just as my eyes closed.

Mátyás was waiting for me in my dreams.

He was sitting in the seat next to Orlando Bloom on the number six city bus. Meanwhile, I was in a full Princess Diana wedding dress, stuck in the standing room only crowd with my hand on the overhead bar. I was desperately late for a fitting or the wedding or a high school class I forgot to take, but as soon as I saw Mátyás sitting there in that black trench coat, I knew it was all a dream.

Mátyás is the boogeyman.

His people have some kind of fancy name for him that translates into "moon thief" or something like that. All I know is if you get that creepy feeling that someone is watching you in your dreams, it's probably Mátyás.

I sat down next to him. Orlando, sadly, disappeared with little more than an I'll-see-you-in-another-dream wave. The bus became a park bench in the Como Zoo's Conservatory in Saint Paul. It was a favorite hangout of mine when I lived in

the Twin Cities, because no matter what the temperature outside, inside the Conservatory it was always eighty degrees
and steamy.

Water dripped from palm fronds. Condensation covered
the plate-glass ceilings. The place smelled of warm dirt and
green growing things. I tucked a bit of the dress under my
legs and lifted the veil to peer at Mátyás. "I didn't think you
could come into dreams unless you were sleeping too."

"Unconscious works too."

I nodded. Then a few seconds later I caught his meaning.
I stood up and started pacing around the bronze fountain of
a woman pouring water from an amphora. "Unconscious! As
in knocked out! Oh my God, are you okay? Is Sebastian
okay?"

I almost fretted myself awake, but Mátyás put his hands
on my shoulders and gently pushed me back onto the bench.
I felt myself settling deeper into sleep. "I never saw you stand
up," I told him. "How did you . . . ?"

"Dream logic," Mátyás said. "It's kind of cool; once you
get the hang of it, you can do almost anything."

"Are you okay?" I asked him. "I mean, where are you? Are
you lying in a ditch somewhere? Will you get hypothermia?"

"I don't actually know," he said. "We followed my mother's
magic trail across the cornfield."

Suddenly, the scene shifted, and we were standing out in
the snow-covered field behind Sebastian's house. The nubs of
tough, sheared cornstalks stood in orderly rows. Blowing
snow made it difficult to see, but Sebastian raced ahead of us
at superhuman speed.

Somehow, we could nearly keep up. I'd never run so fast

in real life. It was kind of invigorating, the supple way my muscles felt as I athletically bounded across the ground.

"Is this how it feels when you run?" I asked Mátyás.

"Only in dreams," he said with a wry smile. "In real life, I'm a lot more chuffed. My side aches, and I sweat. I can nearly keep up with him, but it's a lot of work."

I was a little disappointed because with each of Mátyás's words, I got the same sensations. Running was no longer easy. By the time we came to where Teréza and Sebastian stood together, we were nearly bent over with exhaustion.

Teréza was angry. Her fangs had dropped, and her eyes flashed with barely contained fury. As we recovered, we could hear her yelling over the wind, "You betrayed me."

Not good.

"I don't know what you did to her in the barn," Mátyás said to me, "But she wasn't happy about it. She thinks that Papa was complicit and that he was too cowardly to face her alone, so he sent his errand dog."

"Actually," I said, watching Teréza's lips move silently as Mátyás gave his voice-over recollection of the conversation, "I think the word she used was 'bitch.'"

"Believe it or not, I was being nice," Mátyás said.

"That's hard to believe," I said. "Now I know I'm dreaming."

"Ha-ha."

"So what happened next?" I asked.

"They started to fight," Mátyás explained just as Teréza pushed Sebastian. I could see Sebastian straining not to hurt her, but Teréza wasn't holding anything back. She bit him in the arm like a shark closing in on a kill. Blood flew . . . and then everything went black.

"Wait," I said, standing in an unearthly darkness. "You're missing something. What happened? Did you faint?"

"I suppose I could have," Mátyás said, "But it's not like I've never seen a vampire bite someone. I think . . . I'm not sure, but I think something explosive happened when Mother bit Papa, something neither of them was expecting."

"Something magical," I said. Lightning flashed in the darkness. "Because Sebastian's blood isn't normal vampire blood, it's magic. And partly Lilith since, well, since that night you and your Vatican pals tried to kill us."

Mátyás gave me a raised eyebrow as if to remind me that he could have told the Vatican what he'd seen that night but didn't.

"Right," I said. "Have I ever thanked you for not, you know, telling them we weren't dead?"

"How do you know I didn't?"

I pursed my lips. "No one has come after us since. Besides, I know you have your problems with Sebastian, but you still—"

"If it is something magical," Mátyás cut me off sharply, "it could have affected mother too. The sun will be up very soon."

"I need to find you," I said out loud, as I pulled myself awake. I'd fallen asleep the second my face hit the pillow. I hadn't even bothered to take off the one boot I'd gotten on.

Stumbling from lack of sleep to the coatrack, I pulled on the other boot clumsily. I grabbed my coat. I jammed my hat on my head and pulled on my mittens. If Mátyás's vision of the weather outside was right, there was a serious storm raging out there. I pulled open the front door to near whiteout conditions.

Great. My fiancé, his lover, and their son were all caught out in a blizzard. And the sun was about to rise.

A good farm girl knows that the dumbest thing you can do in a blizzard is go anywhere. Even walking a short distance like from the house to the barn can result in disaster. People have gotten lost in the blinding conditions of a blizzard and frozen to death before anyone found them.

Good farm girls, however, didn't harbor the Goddess Lilith. I stepped outside and put my back against the door, even though the porch provided a bit of shelter. The wind whistled through the railings. Huge drifts of snow covered the area where the front steps should be. I closed my eyes and tried to calm my beating heart. Luckily, as tired as I was, it was fairly easy to fall into a trance. The hard part was actually staying on my feet and staying conscious.

That gave me an idea. Though I'd never tried to contact Mátyás on the astral plane, I wondered if I could reach out to his dream self while in a meditative state. Mátyás's bogeyman persona was a bit scarier than the real-life version. His face was often shadowed, and he always wore a long trench coat the color of a raven's wings. I imagined him appearing out of the whiteness, striding with that certainty and presence he seemed to only have in dreams.

"You rang?" he asked.

"The weather has gotten worse," I told him. "I need your help to . . . uh, find you."

"Aren't you asleep?"

"Not entirely," I said. "I'm in a trance."

"Sleepwalking," he said.

I was hardly going to argue semantics with the bogeyman when Sebastian and company were lost in this storm. "You could be right," I said. "Does it matter as long as I'm mobile?"

He laughed at that, showing off crooked, sharp teeth. "No, I suppose it doesn't. Just make sure you stay upright."

"That's the goal," I said. I gestured for him to get going with a "Lead on, Macduff" half bow.

He stepped out into the whiteness, and suddenly we were at the scene of the fight. "You fell asleep," he said.

"What? Uh," I roused myself from where I'd slumped down against the door. "Crap, I wonder if I'm too tired for this?"

Mátyás reappeared. "We don't have much time. I can feel myself fading."

"Fading?" I asked. "But you're already out cold."

"I think cold is the problem," Mátyás said grimly. "Unlike my parents, I'm not impervious to cold. I'm freezing to death."

That woke me up, or, rather, kept me from falling further asleep. For added strength, I called on Lilith. Her fire raced across my skin, warming me and rousing my magical senses.

Interestingly, with Lilith's added vision, Mátyás's image

softened. He appeared less demonlike, though he glowed with a pulsating purple aura so dark it almost seemed black. I got the sense that Lilith considered him a kindred spirit. Given that she was Queen of Hell, I wasn't sure that comparison actually flattered Mátyás.

"Well," said Mátyás with a look that swept me from head to toe, "Look at you."

I had no idea what he saw, but I didn't appreciate being gawked at by my fiancé's son, no matter how old he might really be. "Keep your eyes on the prize, kiddo."

"Yes, ma'am," Mátyás said with a mock salute and a click of his heels.

This time, when we stepped off the porch, the first thing that happened was that I sank into snow up to my knees. Apparently, I missed the step entirely. Not that it mattered much in the drifts. I pushed through some that were hip high, only to stumble into patches only ankle deep.

Mátyás led the way, sometimes disappearing as the cold momentarily jolted me out of my trance every so often. He was always there, waiting patiently when I returned, though his face was growing frightfully pale. "Hang on," I told him. "I'm going as fast as I can."

Although what I was going do with them when I found them, I had no idea. Then, I remembered: Mátyás had left without his coat. I could at least cover him with mine, and maybe, if I could rouse Sebastian or Teréza, they could help me carry him back. But without him to guide us, would we be able to find the farm?

At last we reached the spot where the fight had taken place. I knew we'd arrived because, in the trance state, Mátyás indicated the spot with a freeze-frame of the last thing he saw: Teréza's teeth sinking into Sebastian's arm.

"I need to go," Mátyás said weakly. "I need to sleep."

"No," I told him, reaching out the way he had in my dream. "You need to stay with me. Stay separate, if you have to. Then, if your body dies . . . Well, maybe we can find a way to reconnect you."

"Are you serious? What if you can't?"

"At least part of you would be alive," I said.

"Wandering around in people's dreams for all eternity? Sounds like hell. I think I'd rather die."

"Don't die," I said. I wanted to tell him how fond I'd grown of him and how much he meant to me, but I was worried that if I got all sentimental, he'd shut down on me again, like he had when I'd tried to remind him that he still loved his father. So instead, I said the one thing I knew would piss him off so much he'd refuse to die. "It would ruin my wedding."

He growled in a nightmarish way, and his image sharpened.

"Hold on to that thought," I said, shaking myself awake.

I could hardly see them. Someone's arm—I thought it might be Mátyás's by the pale, almost bluish tint to it—stuck up out of the snow. When the fingers curled painfully slowly to give me the finger, I knew it must be.

Frantically, I began to dig. Even as I pulled snow off his body, I wondered if I should let it blanket him. Was it worse to be exposed to the wind? Despite my doubts, I couldn't stop digging. I had him uncovered in a matter of minutes.

The snow had stopped coming down quite so hard. Though

it still fell in furious sheets, I could now clearly make out a second, funny-shaped pile of snow that probably contained Teréza and Sebastian.

I shimmied out of my coat and tossed it over Mátyás. I rubbed at his exposed skin to try to warm it. The vampires, I knew, would be safe under the snow. Teréza might even be mostly protected from the sun. However, despite the snow, the sky had begun to lighten. Dawn had arrived.

After what seemed like a lot of rubbing, I pulled Mátyás upright and hugged him close to me. Lilith turned up the heat of my body until my nerves felt almost painfully scorched. Steam rose around us in huge puffs as the snow hit my over-heated skin and turned to steam.

Mátyás stirred.

"Oh thank the Goddess, you're alive," I said. Tears came to my eyes. I didn't realize just how grateful I'd be at this moment. I think I even kissed his cheek and pulled him closer.

"Uh, I'm being mauled by my future stepmother."

Now I wept in earnest. Mátyás hated the idea of my marriage to Sebastian; I never thought I'd hear him acknowledge it, not even in a wisecrack. "I love you," I said.

"Stop," he said, pushing away from me. Even so, I saw him smile as he said, "You're going to make me sick, and I don't think my body can take that kind of strain."

"We need to get you to shelter," I said. "You're not out of the woods yet."

"But what about them?" He pointed to the place where I thought Sebastian and Teréza were buried.

"The snow is only going to get thicker. They'll be safe until nightfall."

"That's twelve hours from now!"

I pointed to the sky, which had definitely brightened. "If we dig them out, are you sure Teréza can handle that?"

He stared at the sky for a long time. Finally, he should his head. "She can't even tolerate an overcast day. The torpor takes her the second the sun is up, visible or not."

"So she's already asleep."

"Aren't you worried about Papa?"

"Of course I am, but he's a thousand-year-old vampire. Besides, he'd kill me if anything happened to you."

Somehow, Mátyás and I made our way back to the house. I stoked up the fire and got Mátyás blankets. "Get out of those wet clothes," I told him. "I'm going to run you a bath."

I ran into my mom in the shower. She was wrapped in a towel and putting on mascara in the mirror. "Oh, sorry, honey," she said with an embarrassed smile. "Did we wake you?"

"No," I said, wondering how she failed to notice my soaking-wet clothes. "Mátyás got lost in the storm without a proper coat," I said. "What's the right temperature to make this bath if he has hypothermia?"

"Oh, God!" Mom shouted, dropping her tube of makeup. "Are you serious?"

I nodded.

"Glen Lacey!" she shouted. "Get in here! We need some help."

My dad came rushing in wearing only blue and white striped boxers. Large curls of gray frizzled hair stood out on his slightly pudgy chest. It was more of Dad than I really needed to see.

"What's going on?"

"Mátyás is downstairs," I explained. "He might be suffering hypothermia. I know I'm not supposed to make him a hot bath, but how warm *should* I make it?"

"Room temperature to start with," my dad said authoritatively. "Hell, I'd think anything just short of cold is going to be a shock."

"Could you start it for me? I'll go get him."

Back downstairs, Mátyás had stripped off his clothes. They were steaming on the stone tiles in front of the fireplace. He huddled, shivering fiercely, nearly on top of the fire.

"I can't seem to get warm," he said pitifully.

"We're going to get you into a bath. It'll help. Hopefully, you didn't get any frostbite. I don't think it was cold enough, but you were out there a long time."

I helped Mátyás negotiate the stairs. In the bathroom, I let my father deal with getting him into the tub. Coping with my dad's chest hair had been weird enough; the last thing I wanted was to see Mátyás buck naked. Even so, I managed to glimpse a tramp stamp tattoo before I scurried out the door.

"Good-looking kid," my mother said appreciatively when we were in the hallway.

"Mom," I protested. "He's going to be my stepson."

"Just saying," she said. "You and Sebastian would make lovely children too."

I pinched the bridge of my nose between my fingers. My head started to hurt.

"Oh, I forgot to tell you that while you were out cavorting at the bar last night, a package arrived. I think it's that other dress."

"You mean my dress—the one I ordered—actually came?" I couldn't keep the excitement out my voice, but my mother gave me a look like I'd wounded her to the core.

"Yes." She sniffed. "And your grandmother's arrived at the hotel yesterday, so it's ready to be fitted. I brought it along. I thought I could do the work."

The pounding of my head increased. Great. Now I had to deal with the dress crises while snowed in with my mother. Plus, I had to call William's SCA lady and cancel the dress she was making or I'd have an embarrassment of riches. "Oh. Wonderful."

The radio predicted eighteen more inches before the storm system moved on. My mom and I sipped coffee and listened to the listings of school closings, neither of us quite ready to deal with the whole dress thing. I called William at home and told him not to bother trying to get in to open up the store. It sounded like the whole city was shut down.

My dad made bacon and eggs. In the living room, Mátyás was asleep on the couch with Barney curled up near his head. When I last checked on them, they both snored softly.

I got up and went to the kitchen window. The snow fell much slower now, but it still came down in constant, thick flakes. The sky was muted, but I chewed on my lip at the reflection of light on the whiteness. I knew Sebastian would be all right, but I found myself worrying about Teréza. I'd

promised Mátyás that snow would be enough cover to protect her.

"You're worried about him," my mother said.

"Yeah," I admitted, although, strangely, it was Teréza I
was thinking about right now.

"He's a smart man. He'd have found shelter," my dad said.
"He's probably trying to get back right now. You still like
your eggs sunny-side up?"

"Uh-huh," I said absently. "I'll be right back."

I snuck quietly and quickly past Mátyás and Barney and
headed upstairs to the bedroom. I got it in my head that I
should try to do another protection spell. Maybe I could vi-
sualize a shield between Teréza and the sun. If nothing else, I
figured it couldn't hurt.

In the closet, I kept a cardboard banker's box full of magical supplies. I had a number of votive candles in every color
of the rainbow. There was a ceramic cup and a magical, cer-
emonial knife. Incense of every flavor, ribbons, scissors, and a
box of matches were included among little things to repre-
sent the directional elements: a clamshell for west and water,
a polished snowflake obsidian for north and earth, a goose
feather for air and east, an ornate incense burner for fire and
south, and a small silver statue of the Nile Goddess for spirit
and here.

I sat down cross-legged on the area rug. Pulling out five
candles, I laid four of them around me at the cardinal points.
The last one I put in the center in front of my crossed ankles.
I lit them one by one, starting in the east. As I struck each
match and lit a candle, I imagined a protective circle around
myself.

Though Lilith's power would strengthen my magic, I let her continue to slumber. She wasn't a protective Goddess. She destroyed. Though she was the mother of demons, and Teréza might qualify as one of Lilith's brood, the truth was, I didn't trust her. So often when Lilith got involved in my spell work, things went awry.

Once all the candles were lit and the circle imagined, I closed my eyes. I envisioned Teréza and Sebastian under the snow. As a kid, I'd spent some time in snow forts, which were little more than holes dug in the piles at the side of the road. I remembered the sensation of the ice under my snow pants and the hot/cold feeling of sweat on a cold day. The smell was wet. On sunny days, brightness would penetrate deeply. It wouldn't be the same for them, however.

At least today, the light was muted. Parrish had told me that, unlike in Hollywood, the quality of light didn't matter to a vampire. Rainy days were still *days* to them. Any light could kill.

What they needed was a shield, something opaque. The first image that popped into my head was of Athena with her shield with the head of the Gorgon, Medusa, affixed to it. So I'd found a goddess; now I just had to convince her to help Teréza.

I'd had no problem calling down Lilith the night my coven was attacked. But that had been a desperate cry for help. I just sent out an SOS, no fancy spells, nothing. That was part of why Lilith and I were stuck together forever. If I contacted another Goddess, I had to be careful on so many levels. The last thing I needed was another piggy-backer.

But I didn't really know how to call down a Goddess on purpose.

So I meditated. I tried to reconnect to that moment on the night I'd called Lilith into me. Fear had torn open my consciousness. As worried as I was for Teréza, I couldn't quite conjure that kind of need.

I hummed. I fidgeted. I watched the candle flames flicker. I was still tired, and I found myself drifting off to the gentle sounds of my parents moving around downstairs.

The moment my chin hit my chest, I saw her. She was a vision, but not quite in the way I might have first imagined. Tall and stocky, she had muscles like Madonna on steroids. Thick, black curls spilled from a bronze, crested helmet. She wore a Roman skirt like Russell Crowe in *Gladiator* and had black hair on her legs and under her arms almost as thick as his. She carried a ginormous pointed spear and the shield, though she kept her shield arm turned away from me. A hoot owl sat on her broad shoulder.

"Uh," I said, when presented with this glorious image of the Goddess. "Hi?"

She nodded as though she understood me, but at the same time gave me a glare that implied that her time was precious, and I'd better get to the point, or I might be on the receiving end of one.

"I have these friends, see," I said, at the same time projecting a mental image of Sebastian and Teréza as I imagined they must be huddled under the snow. "They . . . well, really, she needs to be protected from the light or she will die."

At the pronoun "she," Athena's attention sharpened, as

though the Goddess was more interested in helping a fellow female.

"Anyway, you've got that awesome shield," I indicated the arm she had turned away from me. I swore I could see the twist of a snake's head, and I heard the whisper of a thousand hisses. "Would you help me, please?"

She nodded but didn't instantly disappear. I got the distinct impression I'd forgotten something important. I'd remembered "please." Did I need to add "thank you"?

Then it occurred to me that most cultures offered something to their deities, a sacrifice to pay for services rendered. Lilith had taken what she'd wanted: lodging in my body. I didn't exactly have a goat handy to slaughter, and, anyway, that didn't jibe with modern Wicca or my personal belief system, being a vegetarian and all. Somehow I didn't think plunging a knife into a kohlrabi would be the same. But I also wasn't sure that's the kind of thing that tripped Athena's trigger. So what would this mountainous butch Goddess want?

I gave up trying to guess. "Tell me what you require of me."

That brought a smile to her lips, and I realized at that moment she could be beautiful as well as terrible. I got the impression of one thing: worship. She wanted a devotee.

"As long as you don't require me to be a virgin, I'm down with that," I said.

She frowned a little before she disappeared, but I got the sensation that a deal had been struck.

"Thank you," I whispered, just to be safe.

I guess I was officially a priestess of Athena. Now I just hoped that Lilith was okay with it.

Rubbing my face, I stretched my arms until my shoulder blades popped. The room smelled of melted wax. One of the candles had dribbled onto the hardwood floor. After carefully and deliberately undoing the circle I'd cast in reverse order, I set the other candles on the dresser to cool. I scraped at the wax on the floor with my fingernail, but it was still too warm to do much more than smear around. I gave up and left it to harden.

Though the smell of breakfast that lingered in the air made my stomach growl, the bed looked even more inviting. I crawled under the blankets, praying that Mátyás would stay the hell out of my dreams this time.

I woke up to the sensation of being watched. My mother stood over me with a soft expression. "Oh," she said, as if she hadn't woken me, "you're up. Good. We can try on the dress."

My mother had placed the box from the dress shop containing the one I'd bought at the foot of the bed. Next to the box, she'd lain out the white beaded . . . thing.

I sat up. "Mom," I said as gently as I could. I raked my fingers through my spikes of black hair. "It's so old-fashioned."

She patted my hair, as though trying to smooth it down and tame it. "I know, honey. But it's the dress I wore. And your grandmother. Just see if it fits, okay?"

Well, there wasn't any harm in that, was there? I mean,

given my luck so far with this whole wedding thing there'd be no time for a fitting, anyway. I gave her a smile. "Okay."

She brightened. The crease that had been steadily deepening between her brows smoothed out. "Thank you, honey."

I stared at myself for a long time in the mirror that hung on the closet door, not quite knowing what to say to my mother's hopeful expression. The dress actually fit pretty well, which gave me some trepidation. What daughter wants to know they have their mother's body?

But the high neck and heavily beaded waist made me look . . . old, and a little like the Madwoman of Chaillot. I hadn't really combed my hair since my mom woke me, and part of it wadded flatly against the side of my head in the shape of a pillow. Unruly spikes stood up in back, and something really bad had happened to some of the "product" I put in days ago. My mascara had been smeared by sleep and snow.

More than that, the dress was just not me. I mean, okay, it did sparkle nicely when I waved my hips from side to side, and it made a satisfying swishing sound with each twirl. It had a bit of retro chic, almost Vera Wang-ish. But, it was just so lacy and beaded and heavy and stiff. I felt a little like I'd been jammed into a princess straitjacket, and that was not the sensation I wanted while getting married. The whole ceremony was a bit too much like a binding spell, anyway, without feeling constricted and constrained by a dress that represented all the things about old-fashioned marriages I found wholly un-liberating, if you know what I mean. I did not want to be Ward Cleaver's bride. Of course, with my hair like this, I looked more like the bride of Frankenstein.

"Well?" My mother finally broke down and asked nervously. "I mean, we'll do *something* with your hair, right? Though you could wear the veil. I did."

"Veils aren't very fashionable anymore, Mom," I said.

"Oh, I know. It was my generation that started all that brouhaha about removing the 'obey' clause from the vows and stripping out all the stuff that made women feel like property, but . . . well, it's kind of pretty, honey, and it would hide a lot of sins."

Nice one, Mom. "I'm not wearing a veil."

"There's still time to find you a nice tiara. I really think you need something to tie the whole thing together, you know? Maybe something with pearls to match the dress."

"I'm not wearing this dress," I said before I meant to. My mother's mouth gaped open like I'd just punched her in the stomach. "I mean, it's lovely, but . . . but . . ."

My mother pulled her lips together tightly. "I understand," she said curtly. "It's too old-fashioned. You need something different, I suppose."

"I'm glad you understand, Mom," I said, even though I knew she didn't.

After the whole dress "discussion," my mother and I hardly spoke a word to each other over brunch. My dad cooked up an awesome casserole thing and the crispiest hash browns I'd had in years. I made appreciative noises all through the meal, but my mother stayed frosty and brooding. Eventually, after a couple of more attempts at benign, safe conversation gambits, I gave up and went back upstairs for a nap.

I started awake to the sound of Pete Seeger singing "We Shall Overcome" at Carnegie Hall. It was an album I'd heard a thousand times as a kid, and for a moment I thought I'd woken up in Finlayson, Minnesota, at my parents' farm. A glance at the clock told me it was about time to get up anyway. It was closing in on the dinner hour.

I threw my feet over the edge of the bed and shook the cobwebs from my brain. I'd slept hard. I had vague memories of restless dreams involving two angry Goddesses arguing over who had the most control over me, while being buried alive in an avalanche of snow. Well, I thought with a snort, at least I wouldn't need to pay a psychologist to interpret my subconscious.

After tucking my toes into my fluffy pink slippers, I shuffled over to the closet. I paused before my overwhelming array of choices in attire. I blinked at the racks of sweaters, blouses, skirts, leggings, jeans, T-shirts, and one slinky black evening dress way in the back that I'd bought for Sebastian's birthday last year. I couldn't decide. So I did what most Midwesterners did in situations like this; I looked outside.

Frost laced the window almost completely, with thick ice on the interior corners where the condensation had settled. Beyond the glass, everything was white. The fading sun sparkled blue and yellow like diamond dust on the newly fallen snow. Only a few, scattered flakes drifted from the sky.

I grabbed the thick, black sweater I wore on snuggling-around-the-house days. It weighed at least two pounds on its own, with extra-long sleeves and a long body that covered my butt. After pulling a cheery pair of red and white polka-dot underwear out of the dresser, I grabbed my "fat jeans" from where they lay crumpled at the bottom of the closet. My dad's cooking was hard to resist, and I felt a little bloated and puffy. Taking my treasures, I headed for the bathroom and a long shower.

Hot blasts of water soaked my skin. I almost started to relax and forget about dresses and worry about Sebastian and Teréza, when I felt a cool breeze as someone pulled aside the shower curtain. I quickly covered my breasts and turned toward the wall to shield myself. "Not funny, Mátyás!" I shouted.

I cowered in the corner, waiting for a response. There was only silence. I peered over my shoulder cautiously. The plastic hung pulled to the side as if held open by an invisible hand.

"Benjamin?" I asked tentatively. "Are you—?" I almost said "spying on me," but I didn't want to piss off the creepy Peeping Tom ghost. "What are you doing?"

Not like it wasn't obvious: Benjamin was watching me, admiring me . . . ogling me.

"Okay," I said, my mind filling with all the times I'd wandered around the house naked, not to mention all the times Sebastian and I had sex. "We need to talk."

With the shower still running, I let myself drift into a

semiconscious state. When I focused my astral sight, Benjamin appeared. Rail-thin, he was dressed in a simple white button-down shirt and black trousers. Inside hollow sockets, his eyes glinted darkly. Dark hair was shaved close to his scalp in a style I might have pegged to be from the thirties or forties, but it could have been any era, really.

Benjamin looked surprised and, I was pleased to notice, a bit taken aback to see me. "It's my job, you know," he said, a little defensively. "To keep you safe."

"You do a good job of that," I said. It was true, after all. I could always count on Benjamin watching my back during a fight, especially a magical one. Now how to get him to stop, well, watching the rest of me?

"It's not like that," he said, a little offended. "I keep to myself most of the time."

Except at night, in bed, I thought.

His eyes flashed darkly. "You need protecting."

"You can read my mind?" I asked, too startled by the revelation to really notice the snarling curl of his lip or how his face became skeletal when he was angry.

Sidetracked, he shrugged. "I guess."

"I suppose on the astral plane thoughts are closer to words than in reality."

"What are you talking about? This is real," Benjamin said. His eyes narrowed, sharp as obsidian.

Did Benjamin not know he was dead?

He snarled again, showing chipped, rotting teeth. The scent of decay jolted me out of my trance. I blinked. Benjamin had disappeared, leaving only a lingering smell of rot. The water had grown cold. Down the hall, I heard a door slam.

Crap, I thought. I shouldn't try to talk to anyone today. I twisted the faucet to turn off the water and stepped out onto the mat. Especially not in the astral plane where I can't shield my thoughts. At least in the here and now, I had a prayer of surviving a conversation by just keeping my mouth shut.

By the time I'd finished and gotten dressed, Pete had ended his concert, and Bob Dylan had taken the stage. My folks looked up a little guiltily from the pile of vinyl records they sorted through on the floor of the living room.

"Mátyás said it was all right," my mother said. "You don't think Sebastian would mind, do you?"

Sebastian had a lot of antiques, but he never treated them that way. He didn't believe in putting away "the good china," for instance. If he bought it, he wanted to use it. "I'm sure it'd be fine," I said. "I guess you guys have similar taste in music, eh?"

Apparently willing to let go of our dress argument for the sake of music, my mother excitedly showed me Joan Baez, Janis Joplin, and a number of other bands from her generation that I was supposed to be impressed that Sebastian owned. Frankly, I was just grateful that his musical taste continued to evolve. I wasn't a huge fan of country western, which was his current favorite, but I'd learned to appreciate it from him.

When it seemed appropriate to interrupt Mom's gushing over Sebastian's albums, I asked, "Where is Mátyás, by the way?"

"He's gone out to look for Sebastian and that crazy woman," my father said.

"We told him not to go out. He's really not in any condition yet, but he said something strange about a mutant healing factor. Do you know what that means?"

It meant he was the son of a vampire, but I shrugged it off. I headed for the door, snatching up my coat. If Mátyás had gone after them, who knew what he'd do with Teréza. "It's not even dark yet," I said. "What is he thinking?"

My guess was that he was thinking he'd get the jump on me. Mátyás didn't want me around when Teréza woke up, probably so he could spirit her away somewhere again.

I fumed as I pulled on my mittens. There had to be a solution to Teréza and all the problems she posed. I'd tried to get Parrish interested in taking care of her, but that had failed pretty spectacularly. Yet every time I tried the direct approach and confronted her, we both ended up bruised and battered with neither one the clear victor.

"Don't you have a snowsuit or something warmer?" My mother clucked.

"It's real deep out there," my dad said. "I almost had a heart attack shoveling out your driveway."

"You shouldn't have done that, Dad," I said. The drive was nearly eighty feet long. Besides, Sebastian had a snowblower in the barn.

"Well, I needed to get outside a bit," he said.

I nodded and stood there silently for a moment. I needed to get going, but I felt like there was something else I was supposed to say. Why was it always impossible to do quick good-byes to Minnesotans? "Well, thanks, anyway. Okay, I have to go."

"Okay, good-bye," my dad said.

"Bundle up, honey," my mother added.

I dutifully wrapped my scarf tighter around my neck and waved as I headed out the door. As it swung shut, I heard my mother say, "We'll pray for you and Sebastian and his, uh, friend."

That gave me pause. I stood on the porch for a moment and stared at the door. My mother was a devout enough Lutheran, but she wasn't usually given to bouts of praying for me or anyone I knew. Sure, when I was a kid, the family went to church most Sundays, and I dragged myself to Bible study in the summer. But church was kind of the *social* thing to do in a small town like Finlayson.

Seeing me throw magic around must have really bothered her. I resolved to sit down with Mom and have a heart-to-heart about Wicca. I didn't want her to be scared of magic . . . or me, for that matter.

Turning, I headed down the steps that my father had somehow shoveled into perfect rectangles.

Well, at least with the deep snowfall, it would be a fairly simple matter to track Mátyás. A snaky, waist-high trail cut through the yard toward the cornfield. Thanks to Mátyás's struggles before me, I was able to set a good pace. The clouds had moved on, and hardly any wind blew. The sun hung low on the horizon, casting long, purple blue shadows on the white blanket covering everything. Wetness soaked into my jeans, and I wished I had taken the time to put on my snowsuit like my mother suggested. I hate when she's right about things like that.

Before long, I could see Mátyás. He stood at the spot where Teréza and Sebastian were buried. He hadn't noticed me yet.

Instead, he seemed lost in thought, staring at the snowpack. Though he was still several feet away, due to the stillness of the air, I heard him talking softly to someone.

"I know you're scared, *miri dye*. Be patient; the sun is setting."

Sebastian told me that Mátyás used to sit beside Teréza when she was dead. He'd lay her out in a bed, hold her cold, stiff hand, and tell her things like you might to someone in a coma.

Mátyás looked up then, as though checking the progress of the sun, and caught sight of me.

"Goddamn it," he said and crouched a bit in a kind of fight-or-flight stance. He glanced around like he wished he had a weapon. Finding nothing, he stood resolutely in front of the two humps in the snow.

"I come in peace," I said with a little laugh at Mátyás's overreaction. "Seriously."

A glint of gold caught my eye in the sunset light, and, for a second, I thought I could see the edges of a giant shield lying over them.

"Peace? Don't be absurd. I trusted you," he said. "But you didn't tell me how you viciously attacked my mother in the barn. That's why she ran away when I opened the door. She's afraid for her life."

"How did you find out about that?" I asked, and then instantly realized it was the wrong thing to say.

"She's reliving it in her dreams," he said, pointing at the ground. "Do you realize how close they both are to going into torpor?"

Vampires called the deathlike sleep they went into when

buried torpor. You need blood to wake a vampire in torpor, a lot of it. "I guess that leaves you and me as volunteer donors, eh?" I said. "I take dibs on Sebastian."

"You're not coming near either of them until you promise never to attack my mother again."

"Fine, as long as you can guarantee that she won't come after me."

Mátyás said nothing, and his breath came out in short puffs. We seemed to be at an impasse.

"That's what I figured," I said. "But I don't really want to hurt her, Mátyás. I just want—" My cell phone rang. Ricky Martin serenaded me again. I fished it out of my pocket to check caller ID. The Unitarian minister? Great Goddess, was she canceling too? I had to know. I held up a finger to Mátyás.

"Are you kidding me?" he said.

I ignored him and answered. "Yes?" I asked wearily, expecting the worst, like maybe she was calling from the hospital because she'd been hit by a bus. Instead, she said she was just checking in. I breathed a sigh of relief and started to thank her profusely for not being yet another foul-up in my wedding from hell. Before I could speak, she said she just wanted to say one more thing: remember the rehearsal is all set for tomorrow evening.

"Tomorrow?"

That's what she had on her schedule. She cheerfully read me the date and time.

"But the wedding isn't for another week."

She hemmed and hawed and made a lot flipping through her calendar noises. Oh, yes, there was the wedding on the twenty-first, that was all booked, but it seemed the church was packed with holiday events until then. We'd simply have to do the rehearsal early. Unless I wanted to skip it?

"No," I said emphatically. The way this wedding was going, I needed all the practice walking down the aisle I could get. "It'll be fine. I'll let everyone know."

I hung up the phone. The sun set with a deep, amber color. The chill in the air made the colors that much more vibrant. Mátyás and I watched as the last sliver of light sank slowly below the horizon.

He started to dig. I knelt beside Mátyás, shoulder to shoulder, and began pawing at the thick, heavy snow.

As cold wetness seeped into my calves, I remembered a time last summer when Mátyás and I silently, methodically unearthed Sebastian from a cemetery. My fingers in my mittens were getting chilled, but at least I wouldn't have blisters this time.

This time, I though ruefully. I wondered how many times this scene would repeat itself. Would marriage put a stop to the supernatural insanity in our lives? Somehow I doubted it, especially given the fact we could hardly *get* married without someone throwing a curse on us.

"Are you all right?" Mátyás asked. "You're mumbling to yourself."

"Sorry," I said, just as I uncovered a pale hand. Sebastian, it seemed, had already started to dig himself out. His arm stuck straight up, and his fingers, slowly, painfully twitched.

"That's Father," Mátyás said with a touch of pride. "Nothing keeps him down long."

Once his whole hand was revealed, I kissed Sebastian's

ice-cold palm. His fingers curled around my face, and I knew he was going to be okay. Tears threatened to cloud my vision.

"I can't find Mama!" Mátyás shouted. After we'd exposed Sebastian's hand, he'd renewed his own excavation with vigor. Now he was frantic.

I saw the problem instantly. Teréza, in fact, was already exposed. He couldn't see her, however, because of Athena's shield, which protected her from discovery.

"Hold on a minute. I can fix it," I said to Mátyás, but he didn't hear me. He kept scrabbling at the snow. So I closed my eyes briefly to reconnect to a meditative state. I was still tired enough that it took less than a half a minute to get there. Once in the trance, I imagined Athena standing over Teréza's body and said, "I thank you and release you."

With a Romanesque salute, she disappeared.

"Mother!" Mátyás cried out. "Oh God, you're okay!"

"You protected her." Sebastian's voice was scratched and gravelly. While I'd been discharging the spell, he'd pulled himself upright. "Does Mátyás know?"

Mátyás had pulled Teréza into his arms and hugged her tightly. I shook my head.

"Are you going to tell him?"

I didn't want to wreck Mátyás's moment by making it all about me. "You need blood," I reminded Sebastian. He didn't look very good. Snow streaked his hair, which hung in wet, limp strands in front of his face. He'd grown gaunt with the effort of keeping himself from freezing. His clothes, which looked ridiculously inappropriate for the weather, clung wetly to his frame.

"If we're distracted, he'll take her away and hide her again," he said tiredly.

"Let him," I said.

Sebastian stood behind me and put a hand on my shoulder. I could hear the frown in his voice as he said, "It's not a good idea. This has to end."

"We can't kill her. How does that joke about men go? You can't live with 'em and you can't kill 'em."

"So, what do we do?"

I covered his hand with mine. "Do you think Teréza will ever stop trying to kill us?"

We watched as Teréza began to revive. Her hands twitched as they combed through Mátyás's hair, like a blind woman seeking something. Mátyás was already rolling up his sleeve.

Sebastian leaned in close to my ear, his breath warm on my skin. "When I talked to her in the woods, I came to realize she was gone to me. Being dead for so long has changed her irrevocably."

"So your little kiss was a kiss good-bye?"

He nipped my earlobe. His fangs stabbed like a needle. "Don't be so cheeky."

Teréza hissed hungrily before her fangs plunged into Mátyás's bare arm.

Sebastian growled against the flesh of my neck. Except, if he bit me there, he'd surely hit an artery and I'd bleed out in no time flat.

"We need to go somewhere," I said. I could take my coat off, but I wasn't sure that Sebastian could bite through my thick sweater. Getting naked in subzero temperatures and then "giving blood" didn't really seem like a winning combination to me.

"We can't leave them to their own devices," Sebastian murmured, as he licked the spot on my ear where he'd bitten it. "She will never back down. We must finish this."

Despite the growing dark, cold, and awkwardness of standing in front of Teréza slurping on Mátyás's arm, I moaned. Sebastian's tongue lightly followed the contours of my earlobe. A hot spike of delight throbbed between my legs. "I can't. Not here."

"I don't know if I can wait," Sebastian whispered. His teeth nicked my ear again. "I'm weak."

He'd never get enough from that tiny pinprick. I turned around and kissed him hard on the mouth. We usually avoided tongues when his fangs had dropped because they were sharp enough to sever flesh to the bone. So it didn't take much before our mouths filled with blood.

I started to gag, but his arms pulled me tightly to him. Somehow his hands, still ice-cold, found their way under my coat and sweater. My skin raised in gooseflesh. My nipples stiffened as his fingers found the swell of my breasts.

All the while, Mátyás was two feet away.

I shivered. Sebastian's hands began to warm as he expertly stoked my passion.

Then, as a complete mood killer, I heard Mátyás moan. It was more of a weak, protesting kind of sound, but still. Meanwhile, Teréza made sucking sounds.

I pulled my lips from Sebastian. "Okay, this is just too weird."

Sebastian looked dazed. His eyes were completely dilated, and my blood was on his lips. "Just a little more," he said.

I shook my head. "I'm all for father-son bonding, but this—"

Sebastian plunged his teeth into my neck before I had a chance to finish my sentence. My first panicked thought was: I'm going to die. But even though I'd underestimated how hungry Sebastian was, he apparently still had enough sense and willpower to aim for the muscles of the lower part of my neck. Even so, I wasn't used to being nabbed like this. All I could do was look over his shoulder and hold on tight.

His teeth—all of them—broke my skin. Involuntarily, I gasped. Lilith began to ripple along my nerves. I could feel her strength digging my fingernails deep into Sebastian's back.

But, after the initial bite, the violence of the experience mutated into something much, much more sexy. Sebastian's tongue probed and tasted tentatively. Meanwhile, his hands stayed busy, keeping me distracted by fondling and stroking my ribs, breasts, and stomach.

Lilith relaxed slightly, but I could sense her wariness just under the surface. For my part, I still felt strangely paralyzed and could only watch the growing darkness. Stars had begun to appear. I felt a little dreamy, like the pain belonged to someone else. I thought, maybe, I could let go and float up into the sky.

"You're killing her, Papa," Mátyás said drily. "Not that it matters to me, but you were planning on marrying this particular chew toy."

Somewhere, far away, I heard Teréza hiss. Then, without

further warning, Sebastian and I were pulled apart. Teréza grabbed my arm. The copper tang of blood on her breath as well as her cloying scent of decay choked me. "Mine," she said, her fangs bared.

That was all the excuse Lilith needed. I felt my body go all Jackie Chan. I pulled away from her and raised my foot to slam it squarely into her solar plexus. She flew backward into the snow.

"No, child, *mine*," I said with Lilith's voice. I crouched, ready for action. My fists were raised slightly in front of me.

"Such a lovely moment," Mátyás said to his father as he helped Teréza to her feet. "You must feel like the faerie princess the knights fight over."

"Shut up," Sebastian said quietly. Then, looking at me, he added, "Anyway, there's no contest. I've already made my choice."

"Like a raindrop in the ocean," Teréza said. She had a steadying hand on Mátyás's shoulder. Though, given how pale Mátyás's face looked, I wasn't sure who was supporting whom. "Choices are ripples."

We all stood silently in the snow for a moment, as though absorbing Teréza's words of wisdom.

Finally, I said, "Did that make sense?"

"You'll return to true, Von Traum," Teréza said. "You always do."

"Not this time," he said. "I've carried your burden long enough. I've buried and reburied you a thousand times. But you're free of death now. Go with my blessings."

"You think you can dismiss her so easily?" Mátyás said with a snarl.

"If only," I muttered to myself. The moon was coming up on the horizon. My cheeks felt frozen solid. My ear tip began to throb where Sebastian had nibbled at it.

"I'm doing more than dismissing her," Sebastian said. Despite the dark, when I looked up into his face, I thought I could see a faint golden glow around the circle of his pupils. "I'm breaking the blood bond."

Moving with superspeed, Sebastian snatched a fistful of Teréza's hair. She screeched with indignation. Returning to a position some distance from her, their eyes locked.

"What? What are you doing?" Mátyás shouted. "No! You can't!"

"I have to," Sebastian said sadly. "Besides," he added, looking at me, "she has another Sire. I'm absolutely sure of that now. Maybe it won't kill her."

"Maybe?" Mátyás repeated. "Don't."

He dropped his fangs and bit deeply into his other palm. Blood and hair mixed and, to my surprise, began to smolder. Mátyás had said that when Teréza had bitten Sebastian, there'd been a flash. Perhaps their bond, being mostly made of volatile magic, was literally explosive.

Teréza screamed as if pierced by an unseen arrow. She clutched at her heart and fell to her knees. After shooting Sebastian a withering glance, Mátyás sank into the snow beside her and threw his arms around her shoulders.

Sebastian started muttering something in Latin . . . or German . . . or Greek. Honestly, I had no idea, but it sounded impressive. Though I didn't know what the words meant, I could tell the sounds repeated. He was saying the same thing over and over, like a chant or a spell.

"You can't do this," Mátyás begged. "Are you trying to kill her?"

I glanced up at Sebastian. His face was stern and resolute as he continued to repeat the phrases.

"Are you sure this is a good idea?" I asked quietly. Teréza didn't seem to be faring very well. Her skin had started to shrivel.

"Mother, oh God, no," Mátyás shouted. He stood up, his hands balled into fists. He launched himself at Sebastian. "Stop! I won't let you kill her!"

I, stupidly, stepped in between them.

We all went over into the snow like a football skirmish. I heard Sebastian grunt underneath me when we hit the ground at full force, but he went on with his spell otherwise uninterrupted. Mátyás tried to get his arms around his father's throat. I mostly just tried to untangle myself. Sebastian continued to drone out the magical words. I could hear Teréza whimpering.

"Maybe you *should* stop," I said to Sebastian, once I'd freed myself from the various body parts I'd been wedged between. I was on my hands and knees. Sebastian held Mátyás's wrists at arm's length. Teréza had curled into a fetal position and appeared to be smoldering.

After the illicit kiss in the woods, I knew Sebastian needed to prove his love for me. But I didn't want him to kill Teréza to do it. The fact that he'd even consider tying to break the bond seemed like proof enough to me. Besides, Mátyás would never forgive Sebastian if he killed Teréza.

And Teréza did not look healthy.

"Stop!" I shouted, but no one listened. Mátyás continued

to grapple with his dad, and Sebastian continued to repeat his measured phrase. I knew that if I called up Lilith, that would be the end of everything. She'd see all of them as a threat and, instead of a wedding, I'd be attending a funeral. Several of them.

Things were getting desperate, so I called out to Athena again. This time, however, I took little time to prepare. I simply asked for help.

Suddenly, I felt a presence. Looking over at Teréza, I saw Athena standing over her once again. Athena wore full battle armor, including a feather-crested helmet like the one Brad Pitt wore in *Troy*. She held a spear and a short sword in her muscular hands.

The Goddess looked at me and then put up her shield. I caught only the merest glimpse of bronze and serpentine hair before I remembered to look away.

Thunder clapped overhead. The sound made everyone jump. I looked down at Sebastian and Mátyás, who had frozen in place. For a second, I thought maybe the Medusa's head had turned them to stone, but then Sebastian blinked. "Is it over?" he asked.

Daring a peek in Teréza's direction, I saw that the Goddess had gone.

Teréza lay still—deathly still.

Ninth Aspect: Occultation

"She's dead," Mátyás said, peering into Teréza's wide-open eyes.

"She's in torpor," Sebastian said, putting fingers on her wrist as though checking for a pulse. Given that Parrish didn't have a heartbeat, I wondered if Sebastian really sensed something or simply did the gesture to reassure Mátyás.

"She's probably cold," I said. I stood some distance away, shivering in earnest. I'd been out in the cold far too long. My toes had lost all feeling some time ago. "Let's bring her back to the house. My folks are probably worried sick."

At the thought of them, I stared in the direction of the house. I felt kind of surprised they never came out after us. Maybe we hadn't been outside as long as it felt like.

I glanced back to see Sebastian and Mátyás looking at me like I'd suggested something preposterous.

"What?" I asked. "We could all use a cup of hot chocolate. I'm freezing."

"You would invite Teréza in?" Mátyás said, incredulous.

"Why not?" I said. "I mean, I know she's a vampire. . . ."

"Now she's a vampire of someone else's blood," Sebastian reminded me.

"Oh, right," I said. "Still, we can't leave her out here. She'll freeze to death, and so will I."

"If she's not already dead," Mátyás said.

"She's not dead," I said, feeling quite certain of it. I didn't know exactly what Athena had done when she raised her shield between Teréza and Sebastian, but I was sure it didn't kill her. Athena had sworn to protect Teréza. So had I. "I wouldn't let that happen," I said.

"Garnet did protect Teréza earlier from the sun," Sebastian said, still frowning into Teréza's glassy-eyed stare.

"She did?" Mátyás said.

"I felt it," Sebastian confirmed.

"It's true," I said. "Now, can we all make nice before I get frostbite on my toes?"

Mátyás gaped at me. Then, as if deciding something, Mátyás looked down at his mother. "Fine," he said. "We'll take her home with us."

After standing at the threshold for a moment to allow us to officially invite Teréza inside, Sebastian carried her upstairs to the guest room. The guest room had belonged to

Vivian, the late wife of our house ghost, Benjamin. Benjamin had probably axe-murdered her in there. He wouldn't let Sebastian redecorate it and got very violent when any living human slept in the bed. We thought Teréza might be safe, however, being dead and all. Sebastian would have a talk with Benjamin, though, just to be sure.

The second they were headed upstairs, I tossed my clothes and boots into a heap by the front door and settled in as close as possible to the fire. My parents must have tended it, because it was blazing. The light scent of oak smoke mingled with the smells of butter-sautéed mushrooms, garlic, and onion. The odor of baking spinach and ricotta cheese pried me away from the fire to peep curiously in the kitchen.

My mother sat at the table reading the *New York Times*. My dad washed the dishes in the sink. Something bubbled in the oven.

Folding the paper down slightly, my mother peered at me. "Hello, honey," she said. "Your father and I were making a late din—oh my God, what happened to you?"

Abandoning the paper on the table, my mother rushed over and cradled my face in her hands. "You're so cold," she said. Taking me by the elbow, she propelled me back out into the living room toward the fireplace.

Before I could say, "It's nothing, I'm fine, Mom," I found myself wrapped in the down comforter and deposited in front of the fire. My mother clucked her tongue and inspected the bite mark on my shoulder.

"The heck," my dad, who had followed us into the living room, said. "Did you get bitten by a timber wolf or something?"

"No, just Papa," Mátyás said from where he'd thrown himself on the couch.

Upstairs, something crashed to the floor.

"Oh, look at your arm, dear," my mother said, pulling up Mátyás's torn and bloody sleeve to examine his wound. She shook her head. "I'll get a warm washcloth for this. Do you have any antibacterial cream or anything?"

"It's all in the medicine cabinet," I said, starting to get up. My father put out a hand.

"I'll get it. You tell your mother what happened." As my father headed upstairs, the lights flickered. He paused for a moment and leaned down toward us. "You know, I think this house is haunted."

"It is," Mátyás and I said in unison.

Mátyás caught my eye and then said, "Jinx! Buy me a Coke."

"What are you talking about?" I asked him.

"You're not supposed to talk again until he says your name, honey," my mother explained absently, from where she still fussed over Mátyás. I could see her fingers trying to smooth out the ragged edges of his shirt, like they were itching for a sewing kit. "Didn't you kids do that in school?"

"I'm not doing that," I said with a little smile. "He'd never let me talk again."

"Too true," Mátyás said with a touch of snark, but the fight was out of his voice. We were back to our usual pleasant exchange of harmless barbs.

Doors slammed upstairs. I heard my father swear, and then Sebastian followed suit, only his was in another language. Lights flickered throughout the house.

"If it's not a ghost," my mother said, "you've got really bad wiring."

"It's a ghost," I reassured her.

Mátyás pulled the patchwork quilt from where it hung on the back of the couch. Since my mother still scrutinized his one hand, he did it rather awkwardly with his other hand. But he still managed to fluff it around his legs and feet. "I don't think Papa is winning this argument with Benjamin, however," Mátyás said.

As if in response, we heard the sound of books falling to the floor. Sebastian yelled, "Stay out of my room!" I could only imagine the mayhem Benjamin must be causing in the sunroom, which doubled as Sebastian's occult library. "Fine, you win!"

Mátyás and I shared a look. My mother glanced up the stairs. "What's going on up there? Glen? Are you trespassing?"

My dad came loping down the stairs. In his hand he had a Tupperware container I recognized as holding all our bandages and antibiotic salves. "Jesus Christ, Estelle, there's a supernatural battle going on upstairs."

Standing up and holding out her hand for the container, my mother shook her head. "What are you going on about?"

"You remember those floating lights in *Poltergeist*? It's like that, except real. And here in this house." My dad sounded genuinely freaked out.

"Benjamin is mostly harmless," I was quick to add. I wiggled my stocking toes closer to the fire.

"Except when someone messes with Vivian's room," Mátyás said.

"Who's Vivian? Who's Benjamin?" my dad asked. "How many people do you have living here, anyway?"

"Vivian's dead, and so is Benjamin. I told you about him," I said, but they swore they didn't remember, so I explained the whole axe-murder thing to them. Mátyás interjected a few points, mostly designed to help make it a good ghost story. Just as we were wrapping things up, Sebastian came downstairs, and the oven timer dinged.

"Who's up for spinach gateaux?" My father announced. Then to me, he asked, "You are still an herbivore, aren't you?"

I nodded. Even though my stomach growled in anticipation, I tried to catch Sebastian's eye. He briefly met my glance but looked away. I held back while the others made their way to the kitchen so I could walk beside him. "Are you okay?" I asked.

He continued to avoid looking at me when he said, "Teréza is sleeping in our bed." Sebastian cringed like he anticipated a bad reaction. When I didn't say anything, he added, "It's temporary. Benjamin decided to be stubborn. Well, I'm sure you heard."

I nodded, not trusting myself to say anything yet.

"I promise she'll go into the sunroom after dinner," he continued. "I would've put her there right away, but it's not well-heated, and, frankly, if she wakes up, I didn't want her to have that much access to all my alchemical work and magic books."

Everyone had gone into the kitchen but us.

His eyes searched mine with a hint of desperation. "You're mad, aren't you?"

"A little," I admitted. "That's *our* bed."

"I know. Goddamn Benjamin, anyway."

A cold, unnatural breeze tickled the back of my neck. I turned instinctively, sensing a presence behind me. I saw nothing, of course. "Don't damn him, okay? He's grumpy enough."

Sebastian snarled a little. "I'll fix this after dinner."

My stomach rumbled, reminding me I hadn't eaten all day. "I know we invited her in, but my dad's right. This is a full house as it is. She can't stay."

"I know. I know," Sebastian said with a worried glance toward the top of the stairs. "I don't like her being here any more than you do."

The savory smells coming from the kitchen made my mouth water. I was really ready to go in and eat, but I paused with my hand on the swinging door. "Do you think she'll wake up soon?"

Sebastian frowned. "I'd be surprised. Breaking the blood bond seemed to really suck the life out of her. Honestly, for a moment there, I started to believe that it really was going to kill her."

"It—" I started to tell him that it nearly had, but my mother interrupted by pulling the door open to stare curiously at us.

"We're about to say grace. Come sit down."

Grace? Sebastian and I glanced at each other and then followed my mother in. "We need to talk about this later," I whispered.

My father had laid out a great-looking spread. The spinach cake, which seemed to be spinach and mushroom—stuffed crepes, sat steaming in a glass pan in the center of the table.

There were fresh, homemade popovers in a basket, and tall, cold glasses of milk set out at everyone's spot. Mátyás sat at the head of the table nearest the back door. He looked a little incongruous among the white china and linen napkins my mother had set out. His hair was still wet and mussed from our adventures. It hung limply in front of his eyes, which twinkled above a twisted, sarcastic smile.

"Come say grace," Mátyás echoed. "Really, let's have a little happy family, shall we?"

"Mátyás," Sebastian growled warningly. "Behave."

"Oh, yes, of course, Papa, I wouldn't dream of anything else. How is Mom? Resting?"

"She's fine," Sebastian said rigidly.

My father cleared his throat. My mother hovered at our elbows. "Now, Sebastian, you sit over here by me, and Garnet, have a seat over there," my mom pointed to a three-legged milking stool that usually sat in the corner.

Great. I got the kid's seat.

"Sorry, honey," my mom said, no doubt noticing my look. "It was all I could find at short notice."

"It's fine. Really," I said, avoiding Mátyás's deepening smirk.

Once everyone was seated, my dad bowed his head. Sebastian, Mátyás, and I all shared an "are you going to?" glance. Sebastian shrugged and joined in. That left Mátyás and me staring at each other. My mother, who was sitting next to me, gave me a little poke with her elbow. So I laced my fingers and dutifully dropped my eyes. In his usual quick, barely devotional way, my father sped through, "Come, Lord Jesus, be our guest, and let this food for us be blessed. Amen."

Everyone said "Amen" in chorus but me. I muttered, "Blessed Be," the traditional Wiccan closing. My mom gave me a sharp look, but I wasn't going to be cowed. Wicca was my religion; I had a Goddess piggybacking in my body to prove it.

My dad started dishing out the crepes. Mom passed the popovers. No one really talked. Instead, there was a lot of clinking of plates and silverware.

With the evening's blackness reflected outside the windows, the small kitchen felt even more snug and close. The overhead light was an antique bowl of frosted glass. The Formica countertops gleamed dully.

I could feel my toes starting to tap nervously. I stuffed crepe in my mouth to keep from blurting out one of my usual inappropriate conversation starters. The food, at least, was delicious. My father was a good cook, and he'd unearthed one of my favorite cookbooks, *The Ovens of Brittany*, which was a restaurant started here in Madison in 1970-something by a group of naturalistic, hippy types who considered themselves "flour children." Now, in the days of organic, shade-grown coffee, their approach seems like nothing special, but it was an early attempt to move away with cooking from cans and frozen foods.

"Yum," I said, figuring that was a pretty safe thing to say.

"Hmmm," Sebastian agreed around a mouthful of popover.

"You're an excellent chef, Mr. Lacey," Mátyás said without managing to sound too sarcastic, although I felt a stab of weirdness. Luckily, I knew it wouldn't last.

"So, your mother is a vampire too?" My mother softly asked Mátyás.

It hadn't.

Mátyás actually looked to me for direction, so I answered for him, "Well, she is now. She used to be mostly dead, remember?"

"Your father and I were trying to figure out how this works. I mean, well, that is, we thought maybe there won't be grandchildren if you married a vampire."

It was Sebastian's turn to choke. He nearly spat up the milk he'd been drinking at that moment.

Mátyás laughed. "Perfect timing, Mrs. Lacey."

My mother ignored Mátyás. "You *are* going to give me grandchildren, aren't you?"

I looked at Sebastian. Sebastian struggled to recover his composure. It wasn't working. If anything, he looked greener around the gills. "Sebastian and I haven't really talked about it."

"If it really is possible, you should." My mother sniffed. My father, meanwhile, intently ate his food without meeting my eye. He obviously wanted no part of this conversation.

Mátyás chuckled to himself as he sopped up the spinach sauce with his popover crust. "Once they're married, you'll always have a stepgrandson," Mátyás said, touching his fingertips to his chest. "You could take me to the park on Sundays."

Okay, this was getting surreal. "Speaking of the wedding," I said, trying to steer the conversation from its disastrous course, "somehow the rehearsal got scheduled for tomorrow night. Can you make it? I think I'd better call everyone first thing tomorrow."

"Well, how did that happen?" My mother tutted. "There certainly seem to be a lot of things going wrong with this wedding."

You could say that again.

"You could cancel the whole thing," my father muttered.

"I second that motion," said Mátyás.

My father looked up, and he and Mátyás seemed to have some kind of strange bonding moment over the fact that neither of them wanted to see me married to Sebastian.

"The wedding is cursed," Sebastian said. "But we're not going to let that stop us, are we, Garnet?"

I smiled. "No, we're not."

Surprisingly, the rest of the evening passed without incident. My parents decided the roads were clear and headed back to their hotel. We even managed to relax a bit in front of the fire. Sebastian read the *Times*, and I caught up on the latest celebrity gossip in *In Touch*. Mátyás intermittently dozed and glared at us from the couch. It was much like old times.

Finally, I yawned one too many times. "I'm headed to bed," I announced and then promptly remembered that someone was sleeping in my bed already. "Oh crap, where are we going to put Teréza?"

After some debate, we decided to set Teréza up on a cot in the basement. The sunroom, Mátyás had pointed out, would be a fine place until morning, when Teréza would be fried. Outside of wedging her into the hall closet, there didn't seem to be another place dark enough. The only drawback to our plan? We were all terrified of that basement.

Basements are generally creepy places and a haven for all sorts of multilegged horrors and dust and mold and general unpleasantness. But Sebastian's basement was the basement of a haunted house. Something down there was wrong. Maybe it was the uneven dirt floors that seemed ripe for buried bodies or the crooked passageways that led to multiple, tiny, odd-shaped rooms, but the whole thing just screamed *Silence of the Lambs*.

The three of us stood in the kitchen staring at the door to the basement. Sebastian had a folding cot under his arm. I carried sheets, and Mátyás had a comforter and pillows. We each looked warily at the other, as if daring someone to touch the doorknob. No one moved.

"I don't know if this is such a good idea," I said. "I still say she'd be happier out in the barn's cellar."

"She might be safer too," Sebastian murmured.

We'd all had strange things happen to us when we'd ventured down to do the laundry. Mostly, I'd felt a malevolent presence watching me. It made my skin crawl, although Lilith rather liked it. She was, after all, Mother of Demons. Even so, I hated walking through the cold spots. All the hostility emanating from the basement made my shoulders hunch every time I went near it. In fact, I could feel them rising even now.

"Shouldn't she be in the house?" Mátyás asked Sebastian. "I mean, wouldn't you feel better knowing she was here?"

"I don't know," he said, his lip curled at the basement door. "I wouldn't sleep down there. Not if my life depended on it."

"Me neither," I agreed.

"Yeah, I wouldn't either," Mátyás said. "Okay, let's haul her out to the barn's cellar. But no locks."

"Are you kidding? What if she makes another break for it?" Sebastian said.

"She doesn't have anywhere else to go," Mátyás said. "Besides, you saw her. She's in no condition to do anyone any damage. You sure set her back. I'm wondering if she'll even wake up from this."

"Of course she will," I said reassuringly. "Teréza is strong."

Mátyás sneered at me. "Don't talk. It's your fault she's like this."

I was about to deny it, but then I remembered Athena and how she'd raised her shield between Sebastian and Teréza. Had Mátyás sensed that? "I've never wanted her hurt," I said truthfully. Gone, yes, but not hurt.

"Let's not waste time arguing. We need to get Teréza somewhere safe before morning."

I took the cot from Sebastian, and he went upstairs and gathered up Teréza in his arms. It was very *Bride of Franken-stein* to watch him move down the steps with her head lolling to the side. I had to agree with Mátyás; she didn't look good. Her face had aged. There were stress lines around her mouth and wrinkles on her forehead. Veins bulged out in her neck. In the way of a vamp in dead sleep, her eyes were open and glassy.

"She's gone into torpor," Mátyás observed with some concern.

"I think it's a healing torpor," Sebastian said, as they waited for me to put on my outside gear. Sebastian studied

Teréza's face for a moment and then nodded his head as if deciding something. "She'll wake up on her own in a matter of days, I'm sure of it."

"And if not?" Mátyás wanted to know.

"Then she needs more sleep," Sebastian said. "The body has a way of regulating these things, even undead ones."

I'd finally struggled into all of my various mittens and hats and such, and we took her out to the barn. We made a comfy nest for her. Mátyás even provided a candle and one of Sebastian's older books, a Bible written in German, and left them by her side. Watching Sebastian tuck the blankets around her shoulders gave me a pang of jealousy, but I reminded myself that he'd willfully broken his blood ties to her.

"Come on," he said to me as he stood up and squared his shoulders. "Let's go to bed."

While Sebastian fussed in the bathroom, I quickly slipped into my sexiest nightie. It was a low-cut, black silk chemise with spaghetti straps and a bit of lace around the bottom. I didn't bother with the matching panties. Then I arranged myself in what I hoped was an alluring, come-hither pose and waited for him to come in.

As I lay there listening to the sound of the faucet running in the other room, I knew I was being a little petty about wanting to have sex with Sebastian right now. Thing was, Teréza had been sleeping in our bed. I needed to claim it as mine again.

The expression on Sebastian's face was priceless. At first,

he didn't seem to notice me. He just tossed his jeans into the laundry hamper. Then, turning, he caught sight of me. He did a classic double take.

I couldn't help but smile when his jaw dropped in surprise, and his eyebrows rose in appreciation. I love being able to do that to him.

"I feel a little underdressed," he said, giving a tip of his head in the direction of his usual cotton pajama pants. He'd chosen a pair I'd bought for him. One of the novelty shops on State Street had them on clearance: dancing elves dotted the fabric.

"Actually, darling," I purred. "You're way *over*dressed for the occasion."

Sebastian gave me a long, slow smile. "Am I? Well, let's see what I can do about that."

He surprised me by walking over to the dresser to where the MP3 player perched. The sound of Duke Ellington's trumpet flicked on. To my curious look he said, "Mood music, plus this way Mátyás can't complain about the noise."

"How considerate," I said.

"Hmmm," he agreed, but instead of coming to bed like I expected, Sebastian swayed his hips slightly to the music and toyed with the drawstring of his pants. "Do you want to take these off me, or shall I?"

Both options excited me, but I felt devilish lying on the soft cushions like a princess. "I'd like to see you do it," I said wickedly.

"As you command," he said, trying to look demure, but I could see the flash of fire in his eyes.

He certainly had the moves. Turning around so that his

back faced me, he slowly and provocatively slid the waistband down an inch. Then he quickly pulled it back up. He glanced over his shoulder as if to say, "Did you like my tease?"

"You're a very bad boy," I said, trying to sound severe. "Didn't I tell you to take those off?"

He let out a laugh. "Oh, that's how it is, eh?"

"Aren't you going to promise to obey me in a couple of days?" I said, teasing.

In a heartbeat, I found myself pressed onto the bed. His hands gripped my wrists and pulled them over my head. "It's usually the woman who agrees to obey," he murmured in my ear.

My back arched instinctively. Where our bodies met, I could tell he'd removed his pants after all. "Yet you did exactly what I asked."

"And now you'll do as I say."

My breath caught on his shoulder as he thrust his hips against mine as if to show how he intended to press the issue. I dutifully spread my legs for him.

"Ah, I hadn't said to do that." He smiled devilishly. "But I like that you anticipated my needs."

Oh, it wasn't just *his* need I was anticipating. My core ached for his touch. No doubt seeing the readiness in my eyes, he pulled himself back a little. Removing one hand, he stroked and teased my instantly hardened nipples. I squirmed desperately under him, and I felt myself getting wetter and wetter as he continued his agonizingly slow exploration of my body. When his hand slid between my legs, I gasped. With deliberate and slow gentleness, Sebastian's fingertip stroked me until I started panting with the sweet torture of it all.

"Please." I moaned.

"Please, what?"

"Please make love to me."

"Your wish is my command," he said, letting my wrists go at last. We sprang together like hungry beasts. I wrapped my legs around him, and he plunged deep inside me. I came the first time in a hot rush; then, as he reached climax, we came again together.

I was a little wobbly legged the next morning, but if Mátyás noticed, he kept his own counsel.

I poured myself a bowl of flax flakes and filled Barney's with kibbles. Glancing at the clock on the wall, I decided to call everyone about the rehearsal as soon as the hour was decent. Mátyás eyed me blearily over his "I heart herbs" coffee mug, but neither of us said anything. The kitchen filled with the sounds of my noisy mastication.

"Papa is still out?"

I nodded. He was upstairs doing that lying-as-he-fell-in-battle thing. "Your mom still in the root cellar?"

"As far as I know," he said, taking a slow sip of coffee.

Barney lightly sank her claws into the leg of my jeans, begging for my leftover milk. I set the bowl on the floor. She happily lapped it up.

Mátyás watched the whole thing with barely contained disgust.

I smiled. It was nice to be back to normal.

Pouring nearly half the pot of coffee into a thermos, I grabbed the keys to Sebastian's junker car from the hook by the back door. Once Barney sat back licking her whiskers, I placed the bowl in the sink.

"Have a nice day." Mátyás sneered, as I bundled up and headed out the door.

"You too," I replied cheerfully, humming "Winter Wonderland" under my breath just to irritate him.

Sebastian borrowed a beater from Jensen's, the car shop he sometimes worked at, for times when the snow got deep. At those times, the fancy car stayed in the driveway under a tarp. Sometimes he moved it into the barn, but with all the excitement with Teréza, he hadn't found the time. In deference to me, this year Sebastian's loaner was a Ford—an automatic, which I could drive.

No one had bothered to unearth the Ford since the blizzard. My father had nicely shoveled the driveway, but the car remained covered in about twenty inches of snow. It took me almost a half hour to brush the snow off and scrape away the ice that had formed on the windows underneath. I worked up a sweat under all my layers of clothes. Finally, I was in the car and on the road headed to work.

Once there, I wasn't sure I should have bothered. The place was dead. Hardly anyone came in, just a slow trickle of customers. Yule/Winter Solstice was usually a busy time; pagans liked to give each other gifts just like everyone else. Maybe people were still digging out from the big storm, or perhaps the cold, gray overcast sky made saner people roll over in bed and pull the covers over their heads. Even William came in late, looking sleepy.

I took the opportunity to catch up on all the things I'd gotten behind on. I placed orders for candles and incense, finished sending out Yuletide greeting cards to all our Wiccan-friendly business contacts, and paid bills. While I felt so efficient, I called everyone involved in the wedding rehearsal to let them know that it had accidentally gotten scheduled for tonight. Most people promised to be there. That finished, I tidied the office. I swept floors, dusted shelves, and even cleaned out the public restroom.

William mostly sat at the register reading. He helped me rearrange the children's area—something I'd been meaning to do for months—and I caught him up on all the various disasters in my life. I even told him about how my high school friend Jane had called to say she probably couldn't make it.

"I'll be your extra bridesmaid," he said. "I've even got a skirt! Well, it's a kilt, but I look awfully fine in it."

"I'll bet you do." I laughed. "But you could wear a tux. Anyway, I thought you were going to be one of Sebastian's groomsmen."

He shrugged. "I'd rather be your bridesmaid."

"Sebastian needs you on his side. He doesn't have a lot of friends around here," I said.

"Are you kidding me? He's got his accountant, the dude from Jensen's, and some mountaineering friend of his flying in from Alaska or Australia or somewhere. He doesn't need me, and I'm one of your best friends." William paused for a moment, uncertain. "Aren't I?"

"Of course you are!"

So it was settled.

I passed the rest of the day organizing, filing, and the like. After we counted up the till and got the nightly deposit ready, I told William I'd see him at the church tonight.

The Unitarian church was an A-frame building in the middle of a densely wooded lot. A vaulted ceiling showed quarter-sawn oak beams, and the wall behind the altar was made entirely of plain glass. Polished hardwood floors and a spectacular view of snow-covered evergreens gave the place a sense of awe without being ostentatious.

My mother, however, saw only folding chairs in lieu of pews and unadorned walls, and said, "Is this the best you could find?"

"Well, the Unitarian church designed by Frank Lloyd Wright was booked."

"What the heck is Unitarian Universalism, anyway?" asked my dad. "It sounds like a cult."

I rolled my eyes. "You're thinking of the Unification Church, with Reverend Moon? These are the Unies, not the Moonies," I said.

"I think it's beautiful," William said, browsing through a pamphlet called *What Is UU?*

Sebastian came in with the minister. She was an athletic, trim woman in her fifties with salt-and-pepper hair and deep laugh lines around her mouth and eyes. She shook everyone's hand with a firm, steely grip. "While we wait for everyone to arrive, why don't we go over the events of the wedding?" she suggested.

As we sat on the folding chairs and reviewed the program and the places we'd stand and the words we'd say, I started to realize I was really going to get married. I reached over and took Sebastian's hand to steady myself. He gave it a reassuring squeeze.

Izzy and Marlena arrived together, and soon after followed Hal from Jensen's and Sebastian's other groomsmen. I knew Walter, his accountant, because I once accidentally mistook him for one of Sebastian's ghouls, but I'd never met Smitty, though his photograph was in our living room. "You're a lot older than I expected," I told him, upon seeing his completely gray hair and weather-beaten, tan face.

"Not everyone ages as well as old Sebastian here," Smitty reminded me.

"Where's Mátyás?" Sebastian asked. "He's supposed to be my best man."

"Don't get your knickers in a knot; I'm here," Mátyás said, coming up beside him. "I was just checking to make sure Mom was, uh, well-fed and taken care of."

"Oh, is there a mother of the groom too?" the minister asked. "She's more than welcome. We have special transport if she's infirm."

"Actually Teréza is Mátyás's mother and Sebastian's . . . uh, ex," I explained.

"Oh!" The minister looked from Mátyás to Sebastian and then back again. "I assumed you were brothers."

"I thought so too," my mother said conspiratorially.

"He's older than he looks," Smitty said. "We used to go mountain climbing in the seventies."

"We should probably get started," I said, trying to derail the whole discussion of the age of my vampire lover.

When everyone was arranged, we noticed the imbalance. Sebastian had more friends than I did. Walter, Smitty, William, and Mátyás made four, while I had only Izzy and Marlena, thanks to Jane's cancellation. William said, "It's fate. I'm meant to be a bridesmaid."

"But, but, but," my mother sputtered, "Who will you walk down the aisle with?"

"Oh, that would be me," Walter volunteered in a grizzled Brooklyn accent. Walter was quite fabulously gay. He was a short, bespectacled man in his late forties with wiry hair going gray and frizzy at the edges. His partner Larry rolled his eyes from his seat in the front row.

Before my mother could open her mouth and say something unintentionally homophobic, I said, "Great, it's settled then. Let's give this a try, shall we?"

My dad and I were instructed to go downstairs. The dressing rooms were in the basement, as well as the office and child care room. It was determined that I'd make a more dramatic entrance coming up the staircase, plus that way no one would see me before the service started. My dad and I huddled in a room off the bottom of the stairs and waited for our cue.

Unexpectedly, Dad took my hands in his. "Are you going to be ready for this?" he asked.

"Sure," I said. "When they start 'Here Comes the Bride,' we'll just—"

"No, hon, I mean this," he said, putting two fingers around where my engagement ring encircled my right ring finger.

"Oh, Daddy," I said, getting a little choked up at the thought of really walking down the aisle with Sebastian. "I don't know. I mean, I love him, but you can't really know how it's all going to go until you live it, right?"

"You've thought everything through?"

"We've been through a surprising amount of stuff, Sebastian and me," I said. "You wouldn't believe half of it, but I think it's made us stronger as a couple. I think—"

There was a loud explosion upstairs that definitely wasn't part of the script.

Tenth Aspect: Semi-Square

❧

I ran upstairs to discover that Vatican witch hunters were crashing my wedding rehearsal. Literally.

The windows in the front that I'd been admiring were completely destroyed. Glass and shattered wood littered the floor. Upturned folding chairs lay scattered everywhere. Ice-cold wind blasted through the gaping hole the witch hunters had smashed.

My dad and I had just reached the top of the stairs when someone burst in through the front doors. I turned to see a black-robed priest duck out of the way. Behind him stood a man holding a longbow, cocked, with an arrow pointed right at my breast.

"Get down," I said to my dad, giving him a shove off to the side.

The archer, however, didn't shoot. He seemed to be scanning for someone else. I had a good idea who, given that the last time we encountered the Order of Eustace, they stuck Sebastian to the wall with an arrow exactly like that one. That time, however, they'd had surprise on their side.

Though I tried to grab at him, the archer pushed past me into the main room. Sebastian was on the opposite end near the broken windows, wrestling with two other hunters who'd apparently come in that way.

The rest of the wedding party seemed to be in hiding, although I wasn't sure how much cover folding chairs actually provided.

I turned back in time to see the archer take aim.

"Sebastian!" I yelled, "behind you!"

Unfortunately, half the wedding party poked their heads up to see why I was yelling. My mother stood up with the fierce look of a lioness protecting her cub. "Get away from my daughter!" was her battle cry, as she started moving toward the archer just as he let his arrow fly.

I screamed. My mother was going to step between Sebastian and the arrow.

Sebastian moved faster than I'd ever seen him go. He vaulted over the witch hunter, trying to block his way and hit the ground running. Reaching out, he caught the arrow in his hand. At least that's what it looked like at first, until my eyes registered the fact that his fist closed around a shaft that had pierced him clean through his palm. A spray of blood spattered my mother's face. The arrow had been that close to hitting her. While still running toward the archer, Sebastian snapped the shaft with his fingers. The barbed point stuck out the back of Sebastian's hand; I could see it as he sprinted past me. The guy who'd kicked the door in for the archer launched at him. Sebastian backhanded their hunter, leaving the point embedded in his cheek.

Now I wasn't the only one screaming.

More hunters streamed in the door. Over his shoulder, he yelled, "Get back. I'll take care of them."

Dazed, I stumbled to a stop and tried to take stock of the situation.

Sebastian's show of strength, however, seemed to have rallied my friends.

Closest to me, a knot of people, which included Smitty, Izzy, Marlena, and a confused and battered-looking black-robed priest, wrestled. Punches flew haphazardly, but Team Wedding Party seemed to be kicking the hunter into submission.

Mátyás and my mother teamed up against another one. Mátyás had the hunter in a stranglehold, while my mother bashed the fellow about the ears with her handbag.

Walter and Larry had tackled a hunter too. Walter sat on the guy's chest pinning his arms under his knees and seemed to be yelling at the man about his lack of manners. Larry had his hands on his hips and occasionally nodded his head in agreement with whatever Walter was saying.

The minister hid behind the altar. She peeped out to check out the scene, let out a gasp of despair and/or horror, and retreated to safety again.

Meanwhile, William stood in the center of the chaos,

talking on his cell phone. He had a finger in his ear to keep out the sounds of the fighting, ducking and dodging whenever various bits of debris flew near him.

"The heck?" my dad shouted, coming to my side. "Are we being attacked by rabid priests?"

I was about to answer my dad, when Lilith growled.

"Whoa," my dad said. "You don't need to be like that. It was an honest question."

Through Lilith's heightened awareness, I picked up the scent of what was bothering her: a Sensitive. When on assignment, the Order always traveled with someone conversant in magic. This Sensitive fought for the Order on the astral plane. He or she broke wards of protection, threw counterspells, and the like. Lilith could sense an impending attack. I had to do something quickly, or the tide of this battle might turn.

"Fine, be like that," my dad muttered as he rolled up his sleeves and waded into the battle. He picked up a nearby bit of smashed wood and held it like a club. Without a moment's hesitation, my dad whacked one of the two guys squaring off against Sebastian on the back of the head.

In the movies, the hunter would have dropped like a stone. Instead, he looked really, really pissed off as he turned around to see what'd hit him.

The image of a black-robed priest bearing down on my dad with murder in his eye brought it all back—the night I walked in on the Order after they'd slaughtered my coven. I'd lost my best friends—no, more than that, my surrogate family—that night. They were dead because I hadn't acted soon enough. I would not let the Order take my family from me again.

No way in hell.

Lilith's power surged through me like an electrical storm. My fists sparked with static. The charge raised the hair all over my body. Spits of lightning snapped with pinpricks of pain out of my pores.

I felt the eyes of the Sensitive focus on me. He'd hidden in the shadows of the coatrack, but, with Lilith's perceptions, his magical aura stuck out like a flare to me. I could see too that he'd been using a spell to try to contain Sebastian and Mátyás's magic.

Well, that just made me madder.

The charge I'd built around me released with a thunderclap.

Flaming coat bits flew everywhere. The rack twisted into a melted heap. The Sensitive collapsed, though my magical senses revealed that he was still alive.

The room, meanwhile, went dead silent.

Every head in the room stopped and stared at me.

"You," I said to the nearest witch hunter, "are not welcome here. Get out."

They got the hint. Though they had the reputation of never backing down from a fight, they ran away. I'd never seen anyone scramble to their feet so fast, much less such an orderly, hasty retreat. They left the Sensitive where he'd fallen and disappeared into the night.

"Dudes, you forgot somebody," Marlena said, noticing the guy I'd zapped.

"He should probably get to the hospital, if I can ever get a damn signal," William said, his phone still pressed to his ear.

"They were probably jamming it," Sebastian said and looked at his ruined palm with a grunt.

"Damn, that was fun," Smitty said with a laugh.

"I think I'm going to faint," said Larry, as Walter put a steadying arm around his shoulders.

"I broke a nail," muttered Izzy. "Goddamn it."

"Are you planning a full assault for the real wedding?" Mátyás asked wryly. "Because we definitely rehearsed that."

"Who's going to pay for the damages?" My mother was worried. "Look at this place."

"Uh, I'm afraid I can't officiate at your wedding," the minister said, coming out from behind the altar on shaky legs. "I no longer have a church."

"Yeah," I said, feeling Lilith's power melting from me. I sat down on the floor, feeling wasted and drained, "Yeah, sorry about that."

"How did they find out about us, anyway?" Mátyás asked.

Normally, I would have accused him of tipping them off. But he seemed genuinely concerned, plus he'd been fighting for his life along with the rest of us.

"The dream," William said.

"The astral wedding invitation," Sebastian agreed with a shake of his head in my general direction.

"Oh, yeah, I had a dream about the wedding," said Marlena. "It was the weirdest damn thing."

"We all had it," Izzy said.

"Apparently, Garnet forgot to set a friends-only filter," William said.

I looked out at the shattered remains of the church I was supposed to be getting married in, and I started to cry.

It was never going to happen now, was it? I had no cake, no band, no reception hall, no flowers, no bridesmaids' dresses, no license, and now no minister and no church.

I put my head in my hands and sobbed.

An arm slipped around my shoulder. "Hey," said Sebastian. "It's going to be all right."

I broke. "All right? Are you insane?" I went down the laundry list of everything that had fallen apart one more time. "And now you have to buy a new church for the Unitarians. You can't even say no one's been hurt. They shot you with an arrow. Again."

He tucked a loose lock behind his ear. Glass fell out of his hair.

"Actually," he said, cradling his bloody palm in his lap. "It could have been a lot worse. They usually carry machine guns."

Unbidden memories of my coven came into my mind. They'd been gunned down, unarmed, in their own home.

Sensing my tension, Sebastian pulled me closer against him.

"Yeah," William said absently. "Why no guns?"

Mátyás lifted a hand toward the stone altar. "I'm surprised they brought the longbow in. This is a church. It's an old tradition of respect not to bring weapons into God's house."

"Does God live in a Unitarian church?" Walter asked.

"If you were a true believer, would you take the risk?" Mátyás asked.

"They shot Sebastian," William pointed out.

"In their mind, he's the devil incarnate," Mátyás said. "Like I said, they probably bought an indulgence or something for that one."

I pinched the bridge of my nose. Tears threatened to spill again. I took in a ragged breath. "I can't even believe this conversation. Why can't we have one normal minute?"

Sebastian squeezed me even closer. He looked out over the assembled crowd. I followed his gaze. Everyone had begun to form groups. Larry and Walter were righting chairs. William had found a broom and was sweeping up bits of broken glass. Smitty seemed to be regaling Izzy and Marlena with embellished tales of former glory. My mom and the Unitarian minister were in some kind of tight knot of negotiation near the shattered coatrack.

"You know, darling," Sebastian said. "This is kind of normal for us."

"What do you mean?"

"I mean—" He waved his injured hand in the direction of the wreckage and our friends, and then he laughed softly. "I hope you're not expecting a settled life with me."

I had to laugh too, although another sob caught in my throat. "Oh, Sebastian," I said, laying my head against his shoulder. "I never defeated the curse. Teréza won."

Sebastian kissed the top of my head softly. "Not by a long shot," he whispered. "We're still together."

I pulled my head up to look him in the eye. "We are, aren't we?"

He flashed me a soft smile. "To me, that's what's important."

I kissed him, full on the mouth. "You're right," I said once I pulled away. "That is all that matters."

As we were sitting there, my mother came up to me. Unexpectedly, she came down beside me and gave me a big, giant hug. I could feel her arms shaking a little, and I wrapped mine around her and squeezed as tightly as I had when I was four. Into my ear, she said, "You should wear whatever makes you happy. I'm just glad you're okay."

"I love you too, Mom," I said.

The police showed up a few minutes later. While the minister talked to the two uniforms, Izzy and I organized people to help board up the broken windows.

The officer who took my statement seemed pretty unconvinced, despite having heard the story six times already. He had curly black hair cut almost military short, and his face had a lot of rough edges like he'd been a professional boxer in his younger days. "So you didn't see these, uh, priests come crashing through the windows?"

I'd seen the one come through the doors, but not the first assault. I shook my head. "I was downstairs with my dad."

"Uh-huh," he said and raised his eyebrows like I just told him that I liked to snort marshmallows up my nose.

Eventually, after dutifully writing it all down, they left.

The minister thanked us for helping clean things up, but she told us she still had to call the insurance company and things like that. As we left, I apologized profusely, and Sebastian quietly made arrangements for a "donation" to help cover the costs.

The wedding party stood around outside in the cold, dark night, wondering what to do.

So I invited everyone back to the farm, and we picked up takeout on the way. Someone, it might have been Smitty, raided a liquor store and bought enough wine and beer for everyone.

We had an impromptu post-rehearsal dinner, casual-style.

Chinese noodles and beer can cure a lot of ills, as can silly stories told by a man with an Australian accent. It didn't take long before the house rang with laughter. Even Benjamin didn't complain about all the company for once. Barney came out and had her pick of laps. After soliciting scratches from nearly everyone present, she chose my dad to snooze on, of course. He'd had one beer and fallen asleep in the armchair closest to the fireplace.

Sebastian disappeared upstairs to change out of his bloody shirt. I followed after to check up on him. Someone hooted, like we were off to do some hanky-panky. Much laughter and good-natured teasing ensued.

Upstairs, I found him struggling with his clothes.

"I lost blood," Sebastian noted, as I helped him out of his jacket. The shaft had made an ugly hole in his hand, but I could tell it was already healing. Still, I thought it could use some Bacitracin or something. Given how fast Sebastian recovered, I worried that infection could set in even as the wound closed.

"You can have some of mine," I offered when I came back from the bathroom with the salve. "Blood, I mean."

Sebastian sat on the bed. He smiled at me a bit wickedly.

"I thought you assured your friends your intentions were honorable."

"They are," I said, handing him the tube of disinfectant. "The entire wedding party is downstairs. We can't have sex."

He squeezed out a handful of goo and slapped it over the puncture haphazardly, like it was suntan lotion or something. "Why not? It'd be naughty."

I blushed a little as I helped smear some on the back of his hand. "Very, and kind of rude. They're expecting us back."

"At least let me nibble somewhere fun," Sebastian insisted, putting his hands on my waist and leaning up to nuzzle my breasts.

Pleasure instantly stiffened my nipples. I playfully pushed him away. "Sebastian," I complained, though not too hard.

He slid his hands under my sweater. "C'mon," he said. "Let's make this fun."

Well, he had a point. He had to bite me somewhere, so it might as well be somewhere pleasurable. I pulled my sweater over my head. "Okay," I said. "But make it quick."

His legs straddled me as I stood next to the bed. Pulling me close, his teeth nipped at the lacy edges of my bra.

I was just getting into it when I heard the screams from the living room.

I rushed down the stairs, pulling my sweater over my head as I went. Teréza stood in the middle of the room. My friends had formed a loose, wary circle around her.

"I'd really been hoping for torpor," I muttered.

"Me too," Sebastian agreed, flexing his wounded hand.

Teréza looked up at Sebastian imploringly. Her eyes seemed

brighter than usual, less clouded by insanity or whatever it was that kept her constantly leaping for my throat. Curious, I tapped into my magical vision. Even without going deep into a trance, I could discern the edges of Athena's shield. My protection spell still guarded her.

"I'm cold," she said with a tremor in her voice. She glanced wildly at the faces of the people around her. "Sebastian? Where am I?"

Everyone looked at Sebastian. How do you tell someone she's been dead for a hundred and fifty years?

"Come sit by the fire," he said. Coming down the stairs, he steered her toward a nearby chair.

"Yeah, have the blanket," William offered the afghan he'd wrapped around his shoulders like a shawl.

"I'll put the kettle on," Smitty offered, heading to the kitchen.

"Isn't that the crazy lady from the restaurant?" my dad said, waking up with a start. Barney jumped from his lap with a hiss. She bolted up the stairs. Her claws clattered on the hardwood. Izzy, Marlena, and my mother huddled together on the opposite side of the room and whispered to each other. Larry and Walter watched from the couch with eyes like dinner plates. Sebastian deposited Teréza in the overstuffed chair. William draped the blanket over Teréza's knees. She smiled at him kindly and pulled it up over her arms. Sebastian knelt beside her but looked at me when he said, "The sleep has done you some good."

I nodded, considering. Maybe given time for the healing factor to do its magic, Teréza could become more stable, less bloodthirsty. Perhaps she needed a little Sleeping Beauty time, vampire style.

Mátyás came to crouch beside his mother. "*Miri dye*, do you recognize me?"

"Of course, my darling boy." She laughed, taking his face in her hands. She kissed his cheek. "Oh, Mátyás! You're so hot."

He wrapped her hands in his and looked her in the eye. "No, Mama, you're cold."

"Isn't she dead?" William wondered out loud.

"Shhh," my mother said. "That's rude."

"What's he saying?" Teréza asked, searching Sebastian's face wildly.

"You've been asleep," Sebastian explained. Then he started speaking in another language, Romany, I'd hazard to guess. Teréza looked very pale.

Smitty came out of the kitchen with a steaming cup of tea with milk. He leaned against the stair banister and glanced up at me. He whispered, "What are they speaking? Russian?"

I shrugged. "What I want to know is what he's saying to her."

Teréza stood up. "You did this to me!" she shrieked. "How am I supposed to live? Like vermin?"

"Doesn't look like it's going well," Smitty observed.

"Vermin?" Sebastian repeated quietly, as he stood up. He said a few more words in their shared language, and I didn't need a translator to hear the hurt in his tone.

This wasn't going well. I signaled to William, who came

hurrying over to me. I leaned over the railing, "Do you have a way to contact Parrish?"

"Why would I . . . ?" He looked uncomfortable, like I'd busted him on a secret.

"Come on, William, just fork it over," I said. "I think we need another vampire perspective."

He gave me a look that said we'd talk about this later. Pulling out his cell, he retreated to the kitchen.

Smitty and I checked in on the action. Teréza's eyes narrowed. Sebastian looked angry too. I thought Mátyás might cry. Everyone else held their breath.

"That's my cue," Smitty said, sauntering over with the cup of tea. He offered it to Teréza. "Tea?"

Her lips parted a little, and I thought she might accept with a smile. Then I saw the hint of fang.

Even as I yelled, "Look out!" to Smitty, I dropped my consciousness into my meditative state. If the protection spell I wove earlier still clung to Teréza, maybe I could strengthen it. Ideally, I'd have my whole coven here, and we'd fashion a charm or amulet or something for Teréza to wear to keep the magic close by, but I'd have to make do with what I had.

I could hear pandemonium breaking out. Opening my eyes a crack, I could see Smitty trying to pull his arm away from where Teréza had latched on with her teeth. The teacup and saucer had shattered onto the floor. Sebastian and Mátyás were trying to grab Teréza from Smitty, while everyone else shouted helpful remarks like, "Oh my God!" and "Holy shit!"

I needed to hurry if I was going to be any help. It was tempting to call up Lilith to strengthen my spell, but the protection of Teréza was something I'd negotiated with another

Goddess. I conjured the image of Athena again. Her bronze war helmet shielded her face, except for jet black eyes that glinted like obsidian. Well-muscled arms hefted a sharp-tipped spear. A burnished breastplate hid her feminine features, as did the knee-length toga and leather belt. She held her shield at her side, and snakes curled and twisted at the edges. I heard a hiss and rattle anytime she moved it. Her otherworldly eyes stared into mine for what seemed an eternity; then, without warning, she quickly turned and tossed the spear directly into Teréza's heart.

Teréza's eyes went wide. She looked at me and where the image of Athena stood in my mind's eye. Releasing Smitty's bloodied arm from her teeth, Teréza grasped at her heart. Her eyes rolled up into her head, and she fainted.

Smitty grabbed at his arm, which was spurting blood, and swore up a storm. Larry grabbed a handkerchief from his pocket and pressed it against the wound with a lot of fussing. Sebastian and Mátyás crouched over Teréza, checking for her pulse. Athena stood at the bottom of the stairs and glared at me with inhuman eyes. I gave her a salute, and she faded away, her eyes never leaving mine. I wondered how I'd look as a modern-day Athenian priestess.

William came out of the kitchen and looked at a bloody Smitty sitting between Larry and Walter, the smashed porcelain, and me waving at the air. "What'd I miss?"

Sebastian looked up at me. "She's asleep."

"She just fell asleep? What is she, narcoleptic?" My father asked, rubbing his own eyes.

"It's like someone cast a spell on her," Mátyás said, looking up at me accusingly.

Sebastian picked her up off the floor and carried her over to the couch. My dad got out of the way.

"Who would cast a spell on her?" Izzy asked, then followed Mátyás's gaze to where I still stood on the stairway in my stocking feet. "Oh."

I came down slowly. I noticed Sebastian didn't look at me. His jaw twitched, as he smoothed a strand of Teréza's hair from her face. "I know what it looks like," I said.

"Looks like you saved my life," Smitty said.

"And sabotaged my mother," Mátyás muttered.

"It was a protection spell," I explained. "I didn't know she'd pass out. I guess sleep is the best thing for her."

"She does seem peaceful enough," Sebastian said, taking the blanket off the floor and arranging it over her. His eyes skimmed mine before returning to her. "Is Lilith protecting her, then?"

"No," I said. "Athena."

Everyone looked at me then.

"What?"

"You've got two Goddesses now?" William asked. "Man, I leave the room for ten minutes, and I miss everything."

"Is she going to be all right?" Mátyás asked Sebastian.

"I think so. Torpor does seem to do her good. Maybe she needs to heal the damage from being dead."

"Torpor?" Marlena asked. "What's that?"

Izzy leaned in to explain in quiet tones.

Mátyás continued to glower in my general direction.

"You people live the strangest life," Smitty said a bit drunkenly.

The doorbell rang. Since I was standing closest, I opened the door. Parrish stood on the porch. He smiled at me. "Hello, love. You called?"

"Hey," I said. "Come on in."

Sebastian was suddenly at my side. "What's he doing there?"

"I thought, well, Teréza needs a minder. She may sleep a while, but when she wakes up, well . . . someone has to teach her the ways."

"Him? For all I know, he turned her," Sebastian said.

"He didn't," I said. "Remember the burn? It's not like anyone with a blood bond is going to let that happen."

Sebastian's fists clenched at his side.

Parrish glanced around Sebastian's shoulder at the room full of people all watching us. "Are you having a party?"

"A private one," Sebastian growled.

"My wedding rehearsal party," I said. "Come on in."

"Ta," he said. With an imaginary tip of the hat, he pushed past Sebastian.

"We need his help," I whispered to Sebastian. "Oh, and I might have promised him a retainer if he helps with Teréza."

"What?" Sebastian snapped.

"Let's talk about it later," I suggested, giving my chin a jerk in the direction of the room full of people.

Sebastian shook his head in disbelief but let it drop for now.

I made introductions all around. Parrish perched on the end of the couch with a bottle Smitty offered him. He looked down at Teréza. "Sleeping Beauty, eh?"

"A monster in disguise," Smitty said holding up his arm. Teeth marks broke his skin. "She bit me. Like a bloody vampire, she is."

Parrish shot a knowing look at Sebastian and Mátyás. "Yeah, you've got to watch out for those vampires, don't you?"

"You should clean that, man," William said. "The human mouth is filthy."

"I'll just pour some alcohol on it," Smitty joked.

My mother, ever sensitive to awkward social situations, sighed. "I can't believe there really are vampires, can you? And it turns out witchcraft works too. I pray and pray, but does God answer me? No. My daughter over there says 'Boo,' and she has Goddesses at her command."

Izzy patted my mom's knee.

"There are zombies, too," Marlena said. "My sister dated a guy at UW for two weeks before she found out he was, like, totally reanimated."

"No werewolves, though," William said. "I guess the whole shape-shifting thing violates the law of conservation of mass or something."

"And there's fairies," Larry said with an exaggerated limp wrist. "I know a whole contingent of them."

"Honey, you've dated every fairy in Wisconsin," Walter teased.

Everyone laughed, the tension broken. The wine flowed freely after that. Mátyás and Izzy snuggled on the couch. My dad went back to sleep. And, miracle of miracles, Parrish, Mátyás, and Sebastian passed the evening without trying to kill each other. Sometime after midnight, we ushered people out the door. Parrish stayed on at my insistence. We all stood around the couch, staring down at Teréza's inert body.

"Can she stay with you?" I asked. "Thing is, she needs protection from the sun."

Parrish looked at Sebastian. "She does?"

Sebastian nodded.

"She does," Mátyás said.

"Well, well," Parrish said. "So another vampire claimed your wife, did he?"

I gave him a punch in the arm. "Parrish, please. Think of it as a wedding gift to me?"

That seemed to soften him. He scrutinized Teréza. "It wouldn't be such a terrible burden to look after such a beautiful woman."

Sebastian snarled, and, though I shouldn't have, I felt a pang of jealousy.

I had to admit Teréza had cleaned up pretty well. When she was in torpor, we'd given her a bath, washed and combed her hair. I loaned her some clothes that didn't fit very well, as I was a little more substantial, shall we say, around the hips. She almost looked like a normal person, except for that crazed, lost look she perpetually had in her eyes.

"That's my mother you're talking about," Mátyás said.

"She's still a beautiful woman," Parrish said. "It's no shame."

"If you lay a hand on her," Mátyás threatened. "I'll haunt your every dream."

Parrish glanced at me as if looking for a translation.

"He's the bogeyman; he will," I explained. "And Sebastian and I will hunt you down."

"I see," he said, giving each of us a look in turn. "I should hope to be so well-loved."

I reached for Parrish's hand and held it. "I called you because I trust you."

"And I came because I love you," Parrish said. Then he looked at Sebastian. "Despite everything." Returning his gaze to me, he added, "I should go. If I'm going to get her to a safe, dark place, I need to leave now."

I nodded. "Thank you."

"You owe me," Parrish said, scooping Teréza gently into his arms.

I nodded. "I do. A lot."

As the door closed, Sebastian said, "I don't like being beholden to him."

"I know. But I don't know any other vampires, do you?"

We all stared at each other for a moment, then Mátyás and Sebastian both shook their heads. "Not in the area," admitted Sebastian.

"Come on," I said to Sebastian. "Let's go to bed."

Each night over the next week, Parrish stopped by to give us a report on Teréza's prognosis. He'd show up an hour after dusk. I'd hear the rattling motor of the loaner car Sebastian arranged for him roaring into the drive. According to Parrish, Teréza mostly slept in torpor, but if she stirred, he provided nourishment. I didn't ask for details. It satisfied me to hear that the road to recovery seemed long enough that she'd be out for the wedding. But Mátyás and Parrish sat heads together in the kitchen most nights conferring for at least an hour.

Sometimes I heard laughter. They seemed to be becoming friends.

Meanwhile, Sebastian often found work to do at the other end of the house when Parrish showed, although occasionally they'd have awkward moments if he happened to open the door.

I went to work during the days and had stress dreams about the wedding at night. There were no churches available on Solstice or any other night this close to Christmas. I couldn't find a decent replacement band. Thanks to the holiday season, the bakery still hadn't hired a new cake maker. We did, at least, manage to file our application for a license, and I heard from Jane that she could make the wedding after all.

If there would even be one.

Two days before Solstice, Sebastian found me sobbing in the bathroom.

"We don't have a church," I told him, when he put his arms around me and asked me what was the matter.

"We don't need one," Sebastian said. "I've got room here."

A spark of hope stopped the flow of tears momentarily. "But we don't have anyone to officiate," I said.

"Someone in the coven can do a simple handfast," he said. "We've got time to plan that."

Suddenly, I knew what to do.

Eleventh Aspect:
Sesqui-Quadrate

On Winter Solstice, Wiccans traditionally light a bonfire when the sun goes down and tend it until dawn. It's representational magic; on the longest, darkest night of the year, we keep the light alive.

Seemed to me like a good metaphor for a marriage.

Plus, once I let go of an idea of what my marriage was supposed to be, everything fell into place.

Turns out, William had one of those ministry degrees you can buy from the back of a matchbook. It was a simple matter to rent a tent for the backyard. Not a lot of call for those in the winter, especially when we agreed we'd set it up ourselves. It took some doing to shovel a spot, but everyone pitched in. The Unitarian minister even let us borrow a few folding chairs. Sebastian and I made a fire pit from bricks in the barn and set a huge pile of firewood nearby. I baked and frosted cupcakes to stand in for the wedding cake. My mother did the alterations to make my grandmother's dress fit, and it looked gorgeous. Plus it was way warmer than that tea-length thing I'd bought myself. White looked better than silver in the snow, anyway.

To top off the outfit, I'd rush-ordered an absolutely fabulous ankle-length white coat with feather trim that made me look like the Winter Queen.

I found a hairstylist willing to work with my wreck of a haircut, a fluffy white hat, and pearl beads. Then I spent the day being pampered in ways I didn't even know I needed: manicures, pedicures, facials, and makeup. Izzy, Marlena, Jane, and Mom came along for it all. We had a blast being girly and giggly for an entire day.

The night before, the coven did a spell to make sure the weather cooperated. At first, I thought maybe we were still cursed. But, as the day progressed, the clouds cleared. By nightfall, it had even warmed up at little—for a day in late December, at any rate.

When we got back to the farm, it looked like the circus had moved in. The tent was big and white. Sebastian had strung up every Christmas light he could buy and had made a path to the tent. My bridesmaids helped me get dressed upstairs in the bedroom. The house smelled of my father's cooking.

I looked at myself in the full-length mirror. The pearled dress looked a little strange when combined with the crazy coat, hat, white gloves, and boots, but I thought it would do.

"You look great, girl," Izzy said.

"So do you," I said.

We all had matching hats and mittens, but otherwise I told them to wear whatever would keep them warm and make them happy. Lady Candice had knitted the mittens, despite the fact that I'd had to cancel the dress. Izzy had a retro-cut, bright red coat and white go-go boots, like a hip, black Mary Tyler Moore. Marlena wore a puffy white parka over a gorgeous ice blue, silk kimono that hugged her curves. Jane, who in the intervening years since we were friends in high school had come out as a lesbian, looked resplendent in a tux and tie to match the groomsmen. My mother would probably have a heart attack when she saw my motley crew sauntering down the aisle, but I thought we made an awesome-looking bunch.

I couldn't believe it was finally happening.

A knock on the door startled me. William poked his head in. "The sun is going down. Are you ready to start the fire?"

My dad met me at the bottom of the stairs. He looked handsome in his tux. He'd even brushed out his ponytail for the occasion. "Wow, that's quite a look," he said of my feathers and pearls.

"I know. But you know what? It doesn't matter what I'm wearing," I said. "It's all about who I'm with."

"No, honey," he said. "That's not it. I think you look amazing."

"Thanks, Dad," I said, giving him a peck on the cheek.

"Argh," Izzy teased. "Don't muss up the makeup!"

My dad escorted me outside. The groomsmen met their counterparts at the door of the tent. Walter protested his disappointment at not getting to take William down the aisle, although he was satisfied that Jane made a fairly good substitution.

The polka band began playing "The Wedding March." I'd asked people to bring any instruments they might play, so friends joined in on guitar, drums, cymbals, and even flute. Sebastian waited at the far end of the tent, which we'd left open to the air. He smiled when he saw me. My heart leaped.

William stood in front of the makeshift fire pit in a tuxedo-kilt. He held two unlit torches. Behind him, the groomsmen had prepared the fire, Boy Scout–style, with layers of twigs and paper.

Once in front of the fire, Sebastian and I joined hands. Looking up into those chestnut eyes, the world faded away. This *was* the only thing that mattered.

William said something really poetic about love and how it's like the sun's light on a cold day, but I barely heard it. I only remember trying not to set my heirloom dress on fire once the torches were lit and Sebastian and I used them to start the bonfire. They must have had lighter fluid on the woodpile, because it went up easily. Both Sebastian and I had to jump back with a laugh to avoid being singed. Then William wound a silk ribbon around my wrist and then around Sebastian's for the traditional handfast. Sebastian produced rings from his pocket: a garnet surrounded by diamonds for me, and a simple garnet embedded in gold for him.

I told him I'd love him forever in front of all my friends and family, and I meant it.

When he said the same to me, I cried.

The tent flap at the back parted, letting in a blast of cold air. I looked up and saw Teréza's pale face. She had a white-knuckle grip on Parrish's arm. I held my breath. I could feel Sebastian's muscles tighten. Mátyás said something that sounded like an epithet in another language. William stumbled over his words and stuttered to a halt.

People started to turn to see what we were all staring at. But Parrish simply nodded an encouraging acknowledgment and steered Teréza toward seats in the back.

We let go of our collective breath. William finished by saying the traditional phrase: "I now pronounce you husband and wife."

Sebastian and I kissed. My mother sobbed. Somehow, it was perfect.

At some point, the license got signed and the party got under way. We drank home-brewed mead that Griffin brought. We handed out cupcakes, and my father kept a steady stream of appetizers rolling out from the kitchen. We cleared away the chairs and danced. The polka band played "Roll Out the Barrel," and an Austrian waltz for Sebastian. My other friends made an impromptu drum circle, and someone brought bagpipes.

I was twirling to something with a Mediterranean beat when Parrish cut in. "May I have this dance?" he asked. I looked over at Sebastian. Teréza stood in front of him, offering her own hand. Sebastian and I shared a look that said, "Why not?"

"Of course," I said to Parrish.

He twirled me into his arms. Out of the corner of my eye, I could see Sebastian tenderly take Teréza. She was clear-eyed but wobbly on her feet. "Is she okay?" I asked Parrish.

He looked over my head at where she and Sebastian waltzed slowly, despite the more frenzied beat. "She'll sleep for a week after this, but she didn't want to miss it."

"Is she angry, do you think?"

Parrish glanced down at me. "Sad," he said. "Like me."

"Oh, Parrish. Daniel," I said, using his Christian name. "You know I'll always—"

Putting a finger to my lip, he stopped me. "I know. I'll always love you too. But . . ." He took a deep breath. I held mine. I'd never heard a "but" from Parrish before. "But I'd like my ring back."

"The wedding ring," I said, remembering the one I kept in the bottom of my jewelry box. I frowned a little. I treasured that gift from him, but I could understand it. He had just seen me pledge my life to someone else. "Of course you can have it."

He smiled sadly, his gaze straying to Teréza again. "I thought I'd never have need of it again, but I think perhaps someday I might."

When he twirled me around, I caught sight of Teréza, who glanced at Parrish and smiled. "Parrish," I said, giving him a little nudge in the ribs as a tease. "Are you falling for Teréza?" Then I scanned the room to make sure that Izzy and Mátyás weren't nearby. "Don't let Mátyás find out."

"Oh, I think he knows." Parrish smiled.

"Do I say congratulations?" I asked.

"Not yet," Parrish said. "I must woo my lady when she's fully functional. That may not be for decades yet."

"Decades? You're going to wait that long?"

"I pledged myself to be her guardian, did I not?"

I stared at him with a strange mixture of pride, jealousy, and desire. "I do love you," I said. "You're the most loyal man I've ever met."

"And to think I was but a robber on the king's highway."

"You're so much more than that, Daniel Parrish," I said.

He gave me a crooked smile. "Don't tell anyone else. You'll ruin my reputation."

With a kiss, he left me. Teréza had begun to weaken, and he quickly helped Sebastian get her to a seat. When Sebastian and I reunited, I told him about my conversation with Parrish. Sebastian nodded. "I said good-bye too," he told me. "I think my heart would be broken if this wasn't my wedding day to you."

I gave him a deep, loving kiss. "I understand," I said. "I love you too."

I drifted back toward where Sebastian was being congratulated by my aunt Irma and uncle Chet, who'd driven up from Arizona in their trailer. They had a house in a small town in central Wisconsin, but they wintered in the sunny South as snowbirds. As I looped my arm around Sebastian, Chet was inviting him to come out cow tipping sometime.

Now I knew my family had accepted Sebastian. They were going to haze him with the old cow tipping ruse. I was just about to leap to Sebastian's rescue, when he smiled knowingly and said, "Sure, and while we're out, maybe we could hunt a few snipe."

We all laughed. Even though it was nothing like I'd planned, it was the most perfect day of my life.